G

It happened fast.

One moment Nathanial Barrington was riding beside his old West Point friend Johnny Davidson, listening to Johnny's tale of romantic woe. The next, he saw an arrow sticking out of Johnny's chest.

A second later, Johnny was forgotten. Bedlam had descended upon the detatchment of dragoons. Gunshots volleyed around them, arrows zipped through the air, there were screams of pain and the whinnies of horses. Nathanial saw men hit all around him, and then it felt as if a sledgehammer smacked him on the shoulder. Nearly knocked off his horse, he managed to hold on to the pommel. Blood poured down his left arm, the ground was littered with soldiers, and he nearly panicked, but then his long frontier experience took over.

He was an officer. His job was to get what was left of his command out of this devilish death trap. But never had he faced a job as hard as this . . . as he sensed that all the Apache wars of the past were nothing compared to the one to come. . . .

SAVAGE FRONTIER

THE APACHE WARS TRILOGY BY FRANK BURLESON

☐ **DESERT HAWKS.** This enthralling first novel in *The Apache Wars* trilogy captures the drama and real history of a struggle in which no side wanted to surrender ... in a series alive with all the excitement and adventure of brave men and women—white and Native American—who decided the future of America. (180895—$4.50)

☐ **WAR EAGLES.** First Lieutenant Nathanial Barrington was about to undergo his first test as a professional soldier following orders he distrusted in an undeclared war—as well as his test as a man when he met the Apache woman warrior Jocita in a night lit by passion that would yield to a day of dark decision. (180909—$4.50)

☐ **SAVAGE FRONTIER.** First Lieutenant Nathanial Barrington was already a battle-scarred veteran of the Apache Wars, but nothing in his fighting life as a soldier prepared him for the violence sweeping over the southwest in the greatest test the U.S. Army ever faced, and the hardest choice Barrington ever had to make. (180917—$4.99)

*Prices slightly higher in Canada

SAVAGE FRONTIER

Volume Three of
The Apache Wars Saga

by

Frank Burleson

A SIGNET BOOK

SIGNET
Published by the Penguin Group
Penguin Books USA Inc., 375 Hudson Street,
New York, New York 10014, U.S.A.
Penguin Books Ltd, 27 Wrights Lane,
London W8 5TZ, England
Penguin Books Australia Ltd, Ringwood,
Victoria, Australia
Penguin Books Canada Ltd, 10 Alcorn Avenue,
Toronto, Ontario, Canada M4V 3B2
Penguin Books (N.Z.) Ltd, 182–190 Wairau Road,
Auckland 10, New Zealand

Penguin Books Ltd, Registered Offices:
Harmondsworth, Middlesex, England

First published by Signet, an imprint of Dutton Signet,
a division of Penguin Books USA Inc.

First Printing, September, 1995
10   9   8   7   6   5   4   3   2   1

To Diana

Chapter One

On March 30, 1854, two columns of U.S. Dragoons rode through the Embudo Mountains southeast of Taos, New Mexico Territory. They were pursuing hostile Jicarilla Apaches about a day and a half ahead. The Jicarillas refused to negotiate a peace treaty, so the dragoons had to force them back to the bargaining table.

Two Pueblo scouts rode in advance, following Apache tracks. No flank guards could be posted due to the narrow trail, but Jicarillas preferred guerilla war against isolated ranches or solitary stagecoaches, not sixty heavily armed dragoons. Nonetheless, the men and officers ceaselessly scanned ridges, notches, and ravines. Like a dusty, sweaty family of war brothers, they advanced deeper into the Jicarilla homeland.

New Mexico Territory was far from Washington, D.C., so the dragoons had been permitted a certain leeway in uniform. Some wore brown corduroy trousers, and a few favored red shirts with flowing sleeves, but all sported wide-brimmed vaquero hats, all armed with .54 caliber U.S. Percussion Rifles, model 1841, .44 caliber Colt Dragoon with eight-inch barrels, heavy enough to crack an opponent's skull, and a variety of long-bladed knives.

At the head of the detachment rode two lieutenants in regulation blue tunics, vaquero hats slanted low over their eyes, with brass buttons and gold shoulder straps, but tan canvas trousers. Both sat erectly in their saddles, elbows in, rocking with the motion of their steeds.

Lieutenant Johnny Davidson, thirty-one years old, had long dark sideburns, while Lieutenant Nathanial Barrington, also thirty-one, grew a short blond beard. From South Carolina, Lieutenant Davidson recently had been posted to New Mexico, while Lieutenant Barrington, a New Yorker, had been there since 1848. They'd been classmates at West Point, and now fate had thrown them together on a lazy pursuit near Cieneguilla.

Johnny was a few inches shorter than Nathanial, with a long lantern jaw covered with stubble. He looked embarrassed, as he said, out of the silence of the summer afternoon, "I lied to you last night, Nathanial."

Nathanial had been studying the high ground, in case the head of an Apache should appear. "About what?"

"I said I'd transferred to Fort Union because I was tired of office duty back east. Well, that's not the real reason." Johnny paused and cleared his throat. "There was a woman, and I guess I was ashamed to admit it."

"Was she pregnant?"

"No, it wasn't that." Johnny appeared ill at ease as a gust of wind snapped the First Dragoon guidon nearby. "I asked her to marry me, she turned me down, and South Carolina wasn't big enough for both of us, so I put in for New Mexico Territory. I shouldn't have lied to you, old friend, but I felt humiliated after being cast off by the lady. Does that sound strange?"

"I was engaged to get married once," replied Nathanial. "I went off to Mexico, and when I returned, the lady in question had become betrothed to another gentleman."

"I hoped someday she'd see things my way. Evidently Miss Jennifer Butler is waiting for her great love to come along, but she may have to wait forever."

Nathanial grinned. "If it's any comfort, there's not a man alive who hasn't been turned down by a woman, and there isn't a woman who hasn't been turned down by a man."

Nathanial noticed movement on a ledge, and just as he was reaching for his brass spyglass, bedlam descended upon the detachment of dragoons. Gunshots vollied around them, arrows zipped through the air, there were screams of pain and whinnies of horses. Nathanial was shocked to see an arrow sticking out of the chest of Lieutenant Johnny Davidson!

Nathanial reached for his friend too late, as Johnny sagged out of the saddle. Men were hit in all directions, evidently they were surrounded by a huge number of hostiles, and then it felt as if a sledgehammer smacked Nathanial on the shoulder. Nearly knocked off his horse, he managed to hold on to the pommel. Blood poured down his left arm, the ground was littered with soldiers, and he nearly panicked, but then his long frontier experience took over.

"Sergeant Houlihan!" shouted Nathanial.

"Sergeant Houlihan is down!" cried the anguished voice of Private Pell.

Death rained upon the beleaguered detachment as Nathanial made his decision. "Forward!" he screamed, kicking spurs into the withers of his horse. "Follow me!"

Nathanial's left arm was out of action, so he took the reins in his teeth, drew his Colt Dragoon, and looked behind him. About half the detachment followed at a gallop, while the rest had been casualties of the bushwhack.

Wind whistled about Nathanial's ears as his horse gathered speed. In violent pain, he watched an arrow pass the nose of his horse, then a bullet slipped through the crown of his hat. Apache sharpshooters wanted to kill the bluecoat war chief, but he was determined to stay alive.

His plan was to put Apaches behind him, but then he noticed a new obstacle straight ahead. Jicarillas had rolled boulders onto their path, and were opening fire from behind its safety. Nathanial heard hoofbeats behind him, gunshots in front of him, as arrows streaked through the air all around him.

We'll have to fight back the way we came, he decided. He pulled the reins of his horse, who also was anxious to get away. "Go back!" yelled Nathanial to the remaining men, his mouth full of reins. "Get the hell out of here!"

His horse turned, and Nathanial saw most survivors wounded, mouths agape, eyes glazed with horror. They barely could hear him, and they'd have to ride through the hottest part of the ambuscade again. Nathanial wished he weren't wearing gold shoulder straps, but it was too late to take them off. He wondered where all the Apaches had come from as he urged his horse to greater velocity.

That half-crazed creature raced toward ground strewn with dead soldiers, Nathanial's old friend Johnny Davidson among them. Nathanial fired his pistol at puffs of smoke in the crags as the air buzzed with bullets and arrows; he could hear Apaches shrieking taunts from above.

Behind him galloped the remnants of the detachment, and straight ahead lay Lieutenant Johnny Davidson on his back, an arrow in him. Nathanial aimed at a distant Apache head, pulled the trigger, his Colt went *click.*

Time to reload, but he couldn't, due to one unavailable arm. His horse leapt over Johnny Davidson's corpse, but when the animal landed, it didn't bound off again, but instead kept going down, an arrow in its ribs. Nathanial spit out the reins and tried to throw himself free as his horse's knees buckled.

The officer raised his hand to protect himself, rolled over, pitched onto his face. Surviving dragoons rode past him, kicking up clods of dirt, trying to escape Apache death. Nathanial grabbed a gun lying near the hand of a dead corporal, thumbed back the hammer, and fired at a Jicarilla at the mouth of a cave.

The ground was covered with dust and smoke as Nathanial crawled toward his former classmate. The pallor of death was on Johnny Davidson's features as a gold watch chain hung out his shirt pocket. Nathanial tore it away, noticing a spooked riderless horse fleeing toward him.

"Come here, boy!" called Nathanial.

The old war-horse seemed to hear, and had been following orders for three years. Nearly blind with pain, Nathanial struggled to his feet as an arrow bored the ground three inches from his toes. The horse came abreast of him, but didn't look like he was going to stop. Nathanial realized it was do or die, as he leapt into the air.

The horse bucked, Nathanial desperately grabbed reins, and managed to land partially on the saddle. He struggled to right himself, as ahead the others ran for their lives. An arrow passed two feet from Nathanial's nose, then another shaft struck his right thigh.

Nathanial nearly blacked out, but managed to remain in the saddle. Ahead, the dragoons were slowing down. The Apaches had blockaded the rear exit also!

"Forward!" shouted Nathanial. "It's the only way out!"

Nearly all his men were wounded, but fear was wonderfully energizing. Nathanial put the spurs to his new horse and once again took the lead. Boulders had been hastily rolled over the trail ahead, not as formidable a barrier as on the other end, and Nathanial figured they could go right over it.

"Charge!" he hollered, but lost consciousness as the word left his mouth. His face dropped onto the horse's undulating mane, while ahead, Apaches fired from behind their meager barrier. Nathanial came to his senses, struggled to hold on, the barrier loomed closer, and he hoped a good jumping horse was beneath him.

The great beast's muscles were corded, saliva dripped from its lips, and it strained for final bursts of energy. Behind the barricade, Nathanial observed Apaches with red bandannas wrapped around their heads. One aimed an old Spanish blunderbuss at him, and all the West Pointer could do was keep going, although his right leg was aflame with pain and his left arm had gone numb long ago.

But he'd been wounded before, and knew that the race went to the man who held on longest. The blunderbuss, an inaccurate weapon at any range, fired, but the ball flew harmlessly past. Again, Nathanial stuffed salty reins into his mouth, took the Colt .44 in his right hand, and prepared for the jump. His horse raced toward the boulders, then sailed into the sky.

Nathanial dropped toward the Apache, who was holding his blunderbuss like a bat, intending to whack the bluecoat officer out of the saddle. Nearly fainting, Nathanial fired at a range of four feet. A red splotch appeared on the Apache's stomach, then Nathanial's horse hit the ground. Nathanial almost flew over the animal's ears, but managed to right himself. Then he turned and saw the remaining dragoons behind him; another fell before his eyes.

Lieutenant Barrington was tempted to drop from the saddle, but something forced him to hang on. Perhaps it was his wife and son at Fort Union, or the thought of his grandfather who'd fought in the Battle of Trenton, but he wrapped his reins around his good arm, clutched the thick mane of his horse, and summoned his last reserves of energy. The wounded officer and his remaining dragoons descended the mountain defile, praying the Apaches wouldn't follow them.

At Fort Union, a candle burned on the dresser of a tiny bedroom on Officers' Row, as Maria Dolores Barrington put her two children to bed.

Carmen, nearly two years old, was dark like her mother, whereas Zachary Taylor Barrington, aged three, had blond hair like his father. The former Maria Dolores Carbajal, a full-blooded Mexican of good family, had married an Americano officer against the advice of her father, and now her husband had been gone three weeks. It was almost like not being married, and there wasn't much to do on the remote army post.

She never dreamed she'd be married and then abandoned for long periods. Maria Dolores didn't enjoy amateur theatricals, parties, and other nonsense dreamed up by officers' wives to amuse themselves. She was a proud woman, yet had to defer to the colonel's wife. *I never joined the army,* she thought, *but I must live by its rules. At least I've got a roof over my head, two beautiful children, and a husband who's never home.*

Maria Dolores tucked little Carmen into bed, then kissed her forehead. On the other side of the room, young Zachary lay on his back with his hands behind his head, just like his father. "Mother—tell me a story."

"It's time to sleep, Zachary."

"I'm not tired. Please read to me about King Arthur and Sir Lancelot."

If she didn't read to him, he'd keep Carmen awake. "Put on your slippers and come with me."

He rolled out of bed, she helped him with his robe, and it amazed her how similar he was to her husband, a miniature version of the lieutenant of dragoons. Hand in hand they walked to the living room, where she took down Sir Thomas Malory's *Le Morte d'Arthur.* She sat on the sofa, the boy beside her, struggling to comprehend printed words as she read:

"Soon after that King Arthur was come from Rome into England, then all the knights of the Table Round resorted unto the King, and made many jousts and tournaments . . ."

There was a knock upon the door, startling Maria Dolores. She couldn't imagine who it was that time of night, possibly an Apache had infiltrated the camp. She took down the double-barreled shotgun. "Who's there?"

"Corporal Hatfield, ma'am. Got some mail for you."

Maria Dolores recalled a stagecoach arriving earlier that day. She opened the door and a tall, lanky soldier stood in front of her, the letter in hand. "And how are you tonight, young man?" he asked Zachary.

"Fine."

Hatfield was a ten-year army veteran with a broken nose, but to Zachary he looked like Sir Galahad. Maria Dolores closed the door and carried the letter to the parlor.

"Is it from Daddy?" asked Zachary.

"There's no mail to your father." It was addressed to her, written by Miguelito Vasquez, an employee of her father. She assumed it was a routine business manner as she tore open the envelope.

Dear Maria Dolores.
  Your father is very sick. Come quick.

Maria Dolores stared at the message. Her father had been in good health when she'd seen him six months ago.

"What's wrong, Mother?"

"Your grandfather has fallen ill. We must leave on the next stage for Santa Fe."

"But what if Father returns?"

"He'll have to take care of himself till we get back."

"Why can't I wait for him here?"

"Because I need you with me."

Zachary recalled his father telling him, before leaving on his last scout, "Take good care of your mother."

"Yes, ma'am," he said stalwartly, like a miniature knight of the Table Round.

In the moonlight, Nathanial organized his defense amid boulders, cactus, sagebrush, and mesquite trees. Twenty-two dragoons had been killed and thirty-six wounded in the Battle of Embudo Canyon. The survivors were formed in a circle, rifles pointed outward, as Nathanial limped among them. They had twenty rounds each, then Apaches would overrun them. "Let 'em come," said Nathanial bravely. "We'll give 'em a warm welcome indeed."

"I think you'd better zit down, sir," said Corporal Strobeck, who'd been born in Berlin, "before you fall on your face."

Nathanial lowered himself to the ground, his knees like jelly. He wondered how many quarts of blood he'd lost, his wounds bound in rags torn from his uniform. His left arm was unusable, and he feared they'd chop it off when he returned to Fort Union.

His men were bloody, tattered, but ready for Apaches. They'd enlisted for a variety of ignoble and noble reasons, such as receiving three square meals per day. If they were going to die, they preferred to die fighting.

Nathanial barely knew them because they weren't his men. Lieutenant Davidson had been appointed commander of Company B, and Nathanial assigned to supervise his first scout, but now Johnny was dead, stripped and mutilated by savages.

The Apache Wars weren't dinner table conversation for Lieutenant Barrington, because too many friends had been killed. He despised lofty declarations about the nobility of the red man, and possessed deep visceral hatred for them. It wasn't the first time Apaches had tasted his blood and probably wouldn't be the last.

He wondered if Apaches were watching from shadowed purple mountains, planning to wipe him out. Or perhaps they were at their camp, celebrating with whiskey and a war dance.

Nathanial reached into his shirt and pulled out Johnny's watch. The case was gold, carved with floral designs, and on the back:

to Johnny
from Mother and Father

If I ever get out alive, I'll return this watch to Johnny's parents, swore Nathanial. But I don't think I'll get out alive. The damned Apaches will attack at dawn, and that'll be the end.

Two Jicarilla chiefs, Chacon and Lobo, lay on their bellies a short distance away. "We should attack while they are weak," declared Lobo. "I see no reason to wait."

But Chacon was a more deliberative leader. "Lobo," he began patiently, "they will send more armies if we kill them all. We have already shown we are strong, but more would invite disaster."

Lobo smiled bitterly. "They take our land, then promise to pay us, but somehow never do. They are liars and schemers and I think we should kill them all."

"Imagine hordes of bluecoat soldiers coming to the homeland. If we are dead, who will defend our women and children? We must exercise self-discipline, not surrender to our angry desires."

Lobo took a deep breath. "You are so sure of yourself, but I am filled with rage. I wish I could be more like you, my brother. I and my warriors will do as you say."

"Let us send word that we wish to talk. Perhaps the White Eyes will respect us more after today. Otherwise, I shall follow my brother Lobo on the warpath, and my knife will taste *Pindah* blood."

The sun dropped toward the high peaks, casting orange shadows onto bottomless gorges, as victorious Jicarilla warriors withdrew from the field of honor.

Chapter Two

Next morning Maria Dolores climbed into the stage-coach, then her maid passed Carmen to her. Little Zachary crawled aboard without help and sat next to his mother. "I don't want to go," he said in one of his surly moods.

"But your grandfather needs us."

Zachary barely remembered his grandfather, but didn't want to miss his father when he returned. He felt his mother's body warmth through his clothes, as other passengers crowded into the coach. They were all civilian men and one smelled badly. Zachary pinched his nose.

Maria Dolores feared her aging father would be dead before she arrived in Santa Fe, about sixty-five miles to the southwest of Fort Union. *Nathanial will be angry when he finds us gone, but I must go to my father, for I am his only child.*

The maids waved to Maria Dolores and the children as the stagecoach pulled toward the gates. A detachment of dragoons was their escort, and Zachary stared wide-eyed out the window at an officer who came abreast of them. He was Lieutenant Will Marlowe, a friend of his father's.

"Hope your trip will be comfortable, Mrs. Barrington." Lieutenant Marlowe glanced at the unsavory character slouching in the corner. "If there are any problems, just call my name."

"I doubt there'll be any need," she replied, for beneath her serape lurked a loaded Colt Dragoon in a hand-tooled leather holster.

The officer took his position in advance of the stagecoach, then returned salutes from guards at the gate. Zachary smiled, because he loved military customs. When I get big, I'll be a soldier like my father, he swore.

Zachary's father had fallen out of the saddle and was lying on the ground, his eyes showing white. Corporal Strobeck and the other dragoons clustered around.

"Maybe we should tie him down over the saddle," offered Private Adams, of the Boston Adams, a rich man's son who'd joined the army for adventure, but got more than he'd bargained for.

Private Gilhooly of County Cork spat at the ground. "I don't think he's gonna make it. Lost too much blood."

"We can't leave him here," said Corporal Strobeck, who had served a hitch in the Prussian Army. "Help me up vith him."

As they struggled to raise Nathanial to his saddle, his consciousness vaguely returned. "What the hell's going on?" he muttered.

"You fell out of the saddle, sir."

Nathanial remembered riding across the chaparral, but now had a bump on his head. Grunting, they lifted him higher, then Corporal Strobeck tied his waist to the pommel. "That ought to hold you, sir."

I'm not going to survive, Nathanial thought as they led his horse away. He leaned backward, but the rope wouldn't permit him to fall. He figured the buzzards had eaten Johnny Davidson, his bones bleaching in the sun. Each new stab of pain made him hate Apaches more. Someday, in one of these valleys, I'll catch those Apache bastards when they least expect it, he vowed. If I survive, they'll pay for what they've done this day.

Among the People there occasionally rose to prominence a warrior woman, and one of these was Jocita of the Nednai tribe. Lithe, sinewy, she sat in front of her wickiup, watching her two-year-old son stumbling around the fire. "Do not go too close," she warned him. "You will burn yourself."

The stubborn child paid no heed as he continued toward the flames, reaching his hands out. He was built sturdily, deeply tanned like all children of the People, but his hair was a few shades lighter. This was considered a mark of favor from the mountain spirits, but only Jocita, her husband Juh, and one other person whose name she didn't know, comprehended the truth.

Jocita had been first wife of Chief Juh, but she'd never conceived a child with him. So he'd married Ish-keh and two other wives, with whom he had sons. Jocita had assumed she was barren, but then gave herself, in a moment of supreme weakness, to a sunny-haired *Pindah* war chief during a peace council at the Santa Rita Copper Mines three harvests ago. Then she'd become pregnant. Jocita believed her son was exceptional, due to his unusual parentage, and one day he would accomplish great deeds.

Chief Juh had discovered her infidelity, but preferred to avoid disgrace, pretending the child was his. Jocita had refused to sleep with Juh since he'd married Ish-keh, although she noticed that Juh still looked at her in that certain way.

The boy leaned forward and appeared about to fall into the fire, but Jocita didn't move. Then he reached out, placed his fingers in the tantalizing flames, shrieked, fell to the ground and wailed.

His mother rushed to him. "I warned you," she said patiently. "But you wouldn't listen."

She carried her whimpering half-breed son to a mountain stream and plunged his little hands beneath cool rippling waters. "You must listen to your mother," she cajoled him.

She heard approaching hoofbeats as a war party of about fifty warriors drew closer, headed for Mexico. They were led by the popular subchief, Lucero, a tall slender twenty-six-year-old Mimbreno fighter with long black hair and an ocher stripe painted across his nose. Jocita bowed her head and prayed for the success of his mission.

Three suns ago, the *Nakai-yes* Mexicans in the village of Fulgencio had invited the People for free whiskey and food, and some of the People accepted. While the celebration was underway, the Mexicans had opened fire upon the unsuspecting People, massacring them all.

Such catastrophes had been occurring throughout the history of the People, out of lust for whiskey and presents. Jocita would never go near the *Nakai-yes* unless prepared for war. The boy stopped crying as he studied the warriors riding past.

"One day," she whispered into his ear, "you shall go with them."

Lucero's warriors advanced deeper into Mexico, as a half-moon floated across the sky. Stern faces and rigid self-discipline masked the fury of the warriors, for each had lost a relative or friend at Fulgencio. Lucerno's cousin had been killed in the outrage, and the subchief had sworn never to touch whiskey again.

The great chief Mangas Coloradas had not volunteered for the raid. He was growing old, tired, increasingly forgetful. A strong, sagacious warrior was required to replace him. Lucero was being groomed for the highest position among the Mimbrenos.

All the subchiefs and war leaders of Mangas Coloradas's generation, such as Delgadito, Cuchillo Negro, and Ponce, were becoming old. The People were fighting on two fronts, against their longtime enemies, the *Nakai-yes* Mexicans, and now, more tentatively, with the *Pindah-lickoyee* White Eyes. Lucero knew the sad tale of the Jicarillas, who were being driven from their homeland by *Pindah* soldiers. How much longer before the White Eyes set their greedy eyes upon the Mimbreno homeland? wondered Lucero.

The warriors rode down a winding arroyo, beneath a canopy of cottonwood leaves. Creatures of the night watched behind bushes and hedges. Lucero often wished someone else would take Mangas Coloradas's position. For reasons not clear to him, the mountain spirits had elevated him among the

Mimbrenos. He felt unworthy and wished the mantle could be passed on.

Lucero was no power-hungry subchief such as Juh of the Nednai, or a holy man like Nana of his own clan. Lucero enjoyed hunting most of all, and then came his beautiful wife and children. Raiding was an unpleasant necessity, but when Lucero struck, it was like thunder.

Anything could happen in battle, and a war leader could be killed by a stray bullet or arrow. Lucero had purified himself with religious observances, was sprinkled with holy pollen, and wore his Killer of Enemies Bandolier. Pantherlike, Lucero led his warriors out of the arroyo and across a cactus-strewn basin showered with glittering stars.

Chapter Three

A stagecoach rolled down the muddy main street of Santa Fe as vaqueros, soldiers, bullwhackers, and businessmen walked the planked sidewalks. Maria Dolores gazed through the window at her former hometown, worrying about her father.

"Let me see, Mommy," asked Zachary.

She held him to the window. In the eyes of the small boy, Santa Fe was a carnival of colors and characters, gleaming as if jewels were encased in adobe walls.

The dragoons whooped for joy, anticipating the fleshpots of the saloon district. Zachary loved their rough power, because they reminded him of his father. The stagecoach rolled through the gates of Fort Marcy, and the lawyer opposite Maria Dolores said with relief, "Thank God for an uneventful trip."

Everyone grunted and smiled except the strange, sallow man with the bad smell, who hadn't said much throughout the journey. The stagecoach came to a stop in front of the command post headquarters, where a detail of soldiers waited.

Maria Dolores asked them to deposit her luggage in the orderly room, then she put Carmen into her Navajo harness, took Zachary's hand, and together the family headed for the main gate. She looked like an ordinary Mexican mother, and no one would guess she owned a saloon, a hotel, several houses, and large tracts of land, all accumulated during the early years of marriage. She'd left the holdings in the care of her father and gone to Fort Union with her husband, in an effort to save her marriage.

It felt wonderful to be back in Santa Fe, for she missed the town's excitement. The foundation of her fortune had been a small initial investment in the Silver Palace Saloon, and she stood across the street from it, frowning as she noted paint peeling from the facade. She crossed over, entered the main room, and was surprised to see it reasonably clean, the cuspidors polished, the bartender wearing a laundered shirt, just as she'd left it.

It was filled with the usual crowd of drunkards and prostitutes, the latter self-employed, for Maria Dolores wouldn't profit from prostitution, but neither did she prevent the poor creatures from earning their squalid living in her establishment.

All eyes turned to the voluptuous Mexican woman with two children. "That's the lady what owns this damned place," said a soldier sitting at the bar. "Her husband's a lieutenant in the First Dragoons."

Zachary walked alongside his mother, remembering a glorious night long ago at the Silver Palace Saloon. His father had brought him inside and they'd had a serious talk, although Zachary couldn't remember the subject. Then somebody had insulted his father, who proceeded to throw people around and beat them up. Zachary always had a good time with his father, but his mother generally was strict and serious.

Maria Dolores arrived at the office, knocked three times, opened the door. She hoped to see her father behind the desk, but instead Miguelito, the hunchback dwarf, was there, scratching his pen on a ledger. His face lit up when he saw her. "Thank God you are here!" he said, scrambling to his feet.

"Where is my father?"

The dwarf held his hands behind his back and looked at the floor. "We had to bury him, senora."

Maria Dolores felt as if someone had kicked her in the stomach. She sat on the sofa, feeling guilty about her father. "How did he die?"

"In his sleep. He felt no pain, senora."

"Is my house still there?"

"Yes—that is where he lived. I have not dismissed the maids, so you can move right in."

Maria walked home with Carmen on her back and Zachary in hand, but her thoughts were with her strange, remote father, who'd spent most of his life reading books, trying to understand himself and the world. Upon arriving home, she left the children with her maids, then proceeded to the cemetery, where she crossed herself and dropped to her knees before her father's fresh grave.

She felt ashamed about arguing with him, though she'd been right most of the time. Her father had been a dreamer, wanderer, and amateur scholar who never had married after the demise of Maria Dolores's mother over fifteen years ago.

Maria Dolores felt as if she'd lost something, perhaps the opportunity to be a daughter instead of an interruption to her father's endless studies. But her father had died with his deepest secret intact. Only Maria Dolores knew that he had been a *Marrano*, a

Spanish Jew who practiced Christianity publicly, but maintained his ancient heritage in private.

Maria Dolores had discovered she was a full-blooded Jew when she was twenty-one-years old. Her father begged her never to tell anyone, for fear they'd be burned at the stake as in the days of the Inquisition. Not even her husband knew the truth about her Jewish background.

The only prayers she knew were Catholic, and she'd never found any reason to relinquish the religion of her childhood, so she said an Our Father and Hail Mary over her Jewish father's grave, then returned home.

After looking in on her children, Maria Dolores went to her father's private office. She paused at his door, took a deep breath, then opened it. A cloud of dust came toward her, making her cough. She pulled the curtains and saw a desk, chair, bookshelves, and stacks of tomes wherever she looked. They were about geography, history, poetry, religion, morality, the arts, zoology, and every other conceivable subject.

My father was a bookworm, she reflected. He warned me not to marry an army officer and maybe I should've listened to him. She vowed never to disturb her father's room, so it would always be as he left it.

Then she made her way back to the children's playroom, and couldn't help comparing her huge well-appointed home in Santa Fe to her primitive quarters at Fort Union. Thank God I don't have to return right away, she thought. My dear husband will have to get along without me for a while, I'm afraid.

* * *

At Fort Union, a crew of ghostlike dragoons rode limping horses through the main gate as men and officers from across the post gathered to stare. The dragoons were ragged and wounded, and their commanding officer was tied in the saddle, hat low over his half-closed eyes.

Even Brevet Brigadier General John Garland, new commander of the Ninth Department, appeared in front of the headquarters building, an expression of concern on his face. Fifty-nine years old, gray-bearded, he joined other men and officers running toward the survivors.

Nathanial was helped to the ground by soldiers and struggled to come to attention as General Garland approached. "What happened, Lieutenant Barrington?"

"Ambushed by Apaches, sir."

"Take these men to the hospital at once!" Then General Garland held out his hand and steadied Nathanial. "Come with me."

The general placed his arm around Nathanial's shoulders, while a private on the other side held his waist. "We were riding through the mountains near Cieneguilla," explained Nathanial. "I was talking with Lieutenant Davidson, just as I'm talking with you now, and next thing I knew, half the men were down."

In the hospital, Nathanial was undressed by male nurses, then prepared for surgery. Short, baldheaded Dr. Barrow washed his hands in a basin, wiped them on his apron, dropped ether on a rag, and placed it over Nathanial's nose. Nathanial heard the doctor fussing behind him, then everything went black.

The doctor cut into the swollen arm wound. It

didn't take long to find the squashed bullet, and he yanked it out with a pair of pliers. His assistants sopped the blood, he sewed the hole, then covered it with bandages.

He probed for the arrowhead in Nathanial's leg, managed to extract most of it, but a few fragments would remain inside for the rest of the West Pointer's life. The doctor then washed Nathanial's blood off his hands.

The traveler whose body smell had so offended Maria Dolores had been christened Ned Smith, but he hadn't used that name for quite some time. Ahead, a sheriff's deputy sauntered toward him on the planked sidewalk, and the traveler was tempted to cut into the alley, but instead kept going, pretending to be unconcerned.

The deputy paid no attention because the man in the black shirt blended into the sea of humanity that was Santa Fe. As Ned Smith approached the Silver Palace Saloon, he was tempted to have a drink, but didn't want whiskey on his breath during the ordeal that lay ahead.

He came to the church and beyond were the gates of Fort Marcy. He figured the Army was better than prison, or the dance a fellow performs at the end of a noose. The traveler paused in front of the church, raised his head, and appeared to be admiring the architecture, but actually observed a Mexican girl about fourteen years old walking past him, skirts rustling. He suppressed a smile of pleasure. *I've got to be careful.*

He was of average height and build, wearing a vaquero hat and a medium length brown beard to cover his features. If the crowd in San Antone had caught him, they would've torn him to pieces. But he'd been as fast and smart as in Saint Louis and other venues. Ned Smith's favorite pastime was murdering women.

He passed through the gates of Fort Marcy, arrived at the orderly room, and a sergeant with short clipped dark brown hair and mustache sat at the desk. He glanced up and said, "What can I do for you?"

"I'd like to jine the dragoons, sir."

"How old are you?"

"Twenty-eight, sir."

"Your name?"

"Fletcher Doakes, sir."

The sergeant looked him over suspiciously. The applicant looked fairly healthy except for his complexion. "Why do you want to jine the dragoons?"

"I've got no money, sir, and can't find a job. But I was raised on a farm and I know about horses."

Sergeant Berwick looked at Doakes sternly. "It's a hard life—don't make no mistake about it. If you're afraid of fightin' Injuns, the Army ain't no place to be. And it's a five-year enlistment. You think you're up to it?"

"I've always wanted to be a dragoon, sir."

"Sign right here," said Sergeant Berwick, holding out the pen.

Doakes scratched his name in bold sharply defined letters.

"Looks like you've got an edjication," commented Sergeant Berwick.

"I worked as a clerk for a time, sir."

"First of all I'm a *sergeant*, not a *sir*." Sergeant Berwick rubbed his chin thoughtfully. "Just so happens I could use some help in this here office. Sit at that desk over thar and copy this letter. You do it right— you can work for me."

"I was hoping to be a dragoon, sir."

"It's a lot easier here, and you'll get to town more often. Wouldn't you like to go to town every night, Doakes?"

Lucero moved forward on his hands and knees, then raised his head behind a cholla cactus. The village of Fulgencio lay ahead, as the afternoon sun dropped toward the mountains. The workday was over and the church bell pealed. Lucero watched soldiers entering the church while others in the small garrison prepared the evening meal. Everything looked peaceful and no one would guess that the citizens had massacred Apaches only five suns ago.

Lucero glanced to his left and right, where warriors bristled with bows, arrows, lances, rifles, knives, and war clubs. He raised his arm and motioned toward the village.

The surrounding hills basked in spring sunshine when suddenly a contingent of warriors burst from the ground. They headed for the garrison while a second group made for the stable. A dog chained to a back fence started barking, and then an old crone happened to look out her back window. Her eyes bulged with terror, then she screamed, "Apaches!"

Her voice didn't carry far, but the blacksmith heard her. "Apaches!" he yelled, reaching for his rifle.

The most dreaded word imaginable traveled through the village, as men everywhere armed themselves. The warriors reached the outskirts of town, and Lucero was first over the garrison walls, his bow and arrow ready for instant use. He let fly an arrow into the chest of the first soldier he saw, then dropped to one knee, withdrew another arrow, and pierced the belly of a soldier rushing out of the mess hall.

Arrows zipped through the air as Apaches advanced toward the ammunition shed. In his office, the Mexican commandante didn't know whether to hide beneath his desk or rush outside to take command. He decided to do his duty, drew his pistol and opened the door. Apaches were swarming over the parade ground, butchering everyone in their path, and he was about to issue a command when a war club bashed his face.

The army camp was captured as smoke rose from the church steeple. Singing vengeance songs, the Apaches spread throughout the town, killing all the *Nakai-yes*, as the *Nakai-yes* had killed their wives, mothers, and children.

While engaged in this enterprise, an Apache warrior named Chatto happened to look up. It appeared that a large number of distant riders were headed toward Fulgencio. "Look!" he shouted.

The warriors of the People were shocked to see a Mexican cavalry detachment bearing down upon them. Evidently they'd been scouting in the vicinity, heard shots, and now Lucero had a new threat on his hands. "Charge them!" he hollered.

The Mexican cavalry advanced down the incline as the People's warriors rushed on foot to meet them. The soldiers wore shiny helmets and each carried a lance aimed down at the People. Some soldiers were mere boys, and others had received little training.

Swiftly the warriors raced toward them, led by a tall, rangy Apache with long black hair.

The captain of the lancers swung his sword at Lucero's head, but Lucero leapt into the air, grabbed the officer's wrist, and then slammed his war club onto the officer's head. Lucero tore the dead officer out of his saddle, leapt on, wheeled the horse around, and lunged toward the nearest lancer.

The lancer aimed his weapon at Lucero's heart, but Lucero batted it out of the way with his club, then caught the lancer in the face with his back-swing, knocking him out of the saddle. The horse neighed and raised his front hooves in the air as three soldiers crowded around Lucero, trying to skewer him with their lances, but he twisted and spun like a wildcat, his club whistling skillfully through the air. The first lancer felt the side of his skull cave in, while the next had his jaw dislocated. Lucero leapt onto the last lancer and fell to the ground with him.

"This is for my dead cousin," said Lucero as he brought the war club down. Then he jumped to his feet, but it appeared the battle was over. The warriors took several women and children as prisoners, to compensate for the women and children killed in the massacre. They filled a wagon with weapons, ammunition, and other booty, gathered horses and cattle, then torched the village, the desert wind whipping flames into an immense funeral pyre.

The People's warriors sang victory songs as they departed the roaring holocaust. At their head, atop his fleet pinto stallion, rode their long-limbed young leader, waving his war club around his head.

And from that day onward, Lucero became known as Victorio, the victorious one.

Nathanial opened his eyes and was astonished to see an Apache bent over him, hatchet in hand. The West Pointer struggled to block the blow, then went limp, his head rolling to the side.

Dr. Barrow raised the patient's eyelid with his thumb, grunted, then turned to the medical orderly. "If he survives the night, I'd say he has a chance."

"I'm surprised he lasted this long," said the orderly. "I don't know how he made it back from the ambush."

"There are some things medical science can't understand," said Dr. Barrow. "Some men die real easy, and others have tremendous vitality, like this officer. But there's nothing we can do now except make him comfortable. His fate is in the hands of God."

General John Garland stood with his hands behind his back, studying a map of New Mexico, Texas, and northern Mexico nailed to the wall of his office. This was the time of day he appreciated most, late afternoon when his correspondence was signed and on its way to other commands.

General Garland didn't become a general due to connections made in West Point, because he'd never attended that renowned institution. He'd entered the Army as a private during the War of 1812, received a commission due to prowess in battle, had campaigned against the Seminoles, and then distinguished himself in the Mexican War.

As General Garland examined the map, Fort Union was the center of a triangle whose northern point was Jicarilla country, the eastern end was Mescalero territory, and in the west were a conglomeration of tribes known by a variety of names, such as Chiricahuas, Mimbrenos, Mongollons, Tontos, and Coyoteros, among others.

The Jicarillas were being subdued, and soon the Mescaleros would feel the power of the U.S. Army. General Garland knew that Indians were most vulnerable during winter when food was low and snow restricted movements. Perhaps, in December, I'll wage war against the Mescaleros, he thought. I won't provoke them, but sooner or later they'll steal a flock of sheep, or attack a *conducta*.

His most difficult challenge came from the Western Apaches, worst Indians in North America, in his opinion. General Garland intended to campaign against them after he'd finished with the Mescaleros.

Citizens demanded protection from Apache depredations, and the military commander of New Mexico couldn't wait for the Indian agent to transform naked savages into bucolic farmers. General Garland studied the map and scowled, as he was drawn to the logical conclusion. If Apaches persist in harassing American citizens, I may have to exterminate them.

Chapter Four

Nathanial opened his eyes. Simultaneously, two bolts of pain shot through him, one from his arm, the other his leg. He turned and saw Private Pell with a bandage like a turban around his head, out cold. In the other direction lay Private Haines, who evidently had lost an arm. Am I in one piece? wondered Nathanial.

He forced himself to raise his head and count limbs; it appeared everything was in place. "Is somebody on duty?" he asked.

"Yes, sir—what can I do for you?" asked an orderly.

"Has my wife been notified?"

"She left for Santa Fe before you returned, sir. Her father was sick."

"And my children?"

"She took them with her too, sir."

Maria Dolores sat in her father's office behind the Silver Palace Saloon. Through the door, she could hear faint strains of guitar music as she sifted through neat business records, noting that every bill had been paid on time. My father performed his duties conscientiously, she realized.

A tear rolled down Maria Dolores's cheek as someone knocked frantically on the door. "Who is it?"

"Miguelito! There is a fight!"

Maria Dolores opened the door and looked at the hunchback dwarf. "Where is the guard?"

"He has quit and I have not hired anyone to replace him yet."

"And the sheriff?"

"He is out of town."

Maria Dolores adjusted the gun on her hip, hidden beneath her serape. She followed Miguelito down the hall to the main area of the saloon, where everything was deathly still.

Men stood on the bar as others gathered around a Mexican vaquero and an American cowboy facing each other, carrying knives with blades up. The cowboy lunged his steel toward the vaquero's belly, but the vaquero managed to dart out of the way, slicing off a layer of the cowboy's left shoulder as he passed. The cowboy shrieked in pain, then charged again, while the vaquero skillfully danced to the side, ripping the cowboy's face. Bleeding from several wounds, the desperate cowboy was about to make another pass when a full-bodied woman appeared in his vision.

"That is enough!" shouted Maria Dolores. "If you want to kill each other—do it outside!"

"Out of the way, woman," growled the vaquero. "Otherwise you may be hurt by mistake."

"Leave my establishment at once!" ordered Maria Dolores.

"Go to hell," said the cowboy, who was barely able to stand.

She yanked the Colt .44 from beneath her serape,

thumbed back the hammer and aimed at his nose. "I said get out."

"Now just a minute . . ."

She raised the barrel above his head and pulled the trigger. The saloon resounded with the shot, smoke filled the air, and the cowboy thought he'd been shot.

"The next one will be on its mark," she said evenly.

The cowboy backed toward the door, holding his hands in the air, his color a pasty white. The vaquero followed, and he'd become a strange green hue.

"Don't come back," said Maria Dolores as the knife fighters passed through the door.

The madonna of the Silver Palace Saloon thumbed forward the hammer of her Colt, then dropped it into her holster. "Drinks on the house!" she hollered.

In the early morning hours, Victorio was awakened by someone calling his name. "Mangas Coloradas would like to speak with you."

Victorio lay in the arms of Shilay, his wife, who said sleepily, "I wonder what he wants?"

"I'll be back quickly as I can."

When Victorio emerged from his wickiup, the messenger was gone and twinkling stars blanketed the universe. Victorio made his way across the encampment, hearing the occasional snore or sigh. A dog raised his head curiously as the subchief arrived at the wickiup of the great chief Mangas Coloradas.

Light emanated through openings in twigs and leaves that comprised the shelter. Victorio crawled through the entrance on his hands and knees. The chief sat before his fire, a single stripe of ocher painted across his nose and cheeks. "While you have been sleeping," said Mangas Coloradas sonorously, "I have been speaking with the mountain spirits. They said I should tell you about the future of the People. But first we shall smoke together."

Managas Coloradas stuffed his clay ceremonial pipe with a mixture of tobacco and other magical plants gathered by Nana the *di-yin* medicine man. Then he took a metal spoonlike implement, removed a red hot coal from the fire, and dropped it on top. "You first."

Victorio filled his lungs with pungent smoke, then passed the pipe to Mangas Coloradas. After a while, it appeared that mountain spirits were dancing among flames in the firepit. Mangas Coloradas appeared in an exalted state as he raised his hand in the air. "I am growing old," he declared. "The time has come for a young man to lead the people. I consider you foremost among subchiefs, but today I tell you solemnly that you are my chosen successor, and you shall assume command of the Mimbreno warriors following my death."

Victorio bowed. "But there are many warriors more able than I."

"None combines the best qualities as does Victorio. You cannot deny the People."

"But the White Eyes baffle me. I do not know what to do about them."

"Neither do I, for they tell us: 'Stop raiding and become farmers. Otherwise there can be no peace between us.' So some of the People moved where the White Eyes commanded, but the People received no farm animals, no implements, no seeds. The White Eyes act like friends as they sow deceit among us, while their bluecoat soldiers are making

war upon the Jicarilla People. I have signed two treaties with the White Eyes, and twice the White Eyes
have betrayed me. Perhaps Juh of the Nednai is
right. We must fight the White Eyes wherever we
find them, and if they kill us all—so be it."

Next day, Maria Dolores arrived at her office,
eager to get to work. She realized how bored she'd
been at Fort Union, and the proud Mexican woman
didn't like to defer to anybody, as she'd done in the
Army.

There was a knock on the door, then Miguelito appeared. "There is an *hombre* who wants to work as a
guard," he said.

"Is he clean?"

"Sí, senora."

"Send him in."

Miquelito retreated, closing the door behind him.
Maria Dolores returned to land deeds on her desk.
She knew that a transcontinental railroad was being
debated in Washington, and Southern senators were
fighting for a route that would pass through Santa
Fe. I've got to buy all the land I can, she told herself,
because this city could double and even quadruple
in size in the years to come.

America was booming, according to everything she
read. Immigrants from Europe were flocking to its
shores in search of cheap land, gold, and political
freedom. It was exciting to think about, instead of
languishing at Fort Union.

She became aware of a presence in the doorway,
glanced up from a mortgage, and saw a tall, well-
built American cowboy in a loose white cotton shirt,
wearing a gun in a holster, sombrero in hand.

"Your name?" she asked.

"Cole Bannon."

"Have a seat."

His light brown hair was combed neatly, he was close-shaven, and gave the impression of physical strength. She pegged his age at the late thirties as he sat before her desk.

"Tell me about yourself," she said.

"I've worked on ranches, been a cook, traveled here and there, a perfectly useless life, one might say."

She could perceive that he was educated, but had something of the rascal about him. "I should warn you that it's not an easy job. We had a knife fight a few days ago."

He smiled, showing even white teeth. "I was there, and you're a very brave woman, Mrs. Barrington, because what if somebody came up on you from behind?"

"This is not a job for a man who is afraid."

"I never said I was afraid. You can count on me."

She tilted her head to the side. "I think a smart *hombre* like you could do better."

"I have no money left."

"Where do you live?"

He shrugged. "Here and there."

She decided against more questions, although her curiosity was piqued. "You may start tonight," she told him.

Chapter Five

Pain awakened Nathanial in the middle of the night. He lay in his bedroom on Officers' Row, gazing longingly at the dresser. Dr. Barrow had let him return home, where he was cared for by two maids. In the top drawer resided a bottle of laudanum, the opiated medication used to ease suffering.

Nathanial didn't like laudanum, because once he started, he never stopped. He'd managed to give up whiskey three years ago, after Maria Dolores threatened to leave him, but Maria Dolores was gone. *Once I take that first dose of laudanum, it's only a matter of time before I'm constantly drugged.*

Torn ligaments throbbed in his arm and leg while constant around-the-clock pain ground a man to dust. *What's worse?* he wondered. *Being unable to sleep, or being drugged?*

You're older and more mature, he counseled himself. *Isn't it time you developed a small measure of self-discipline?* With a confident half smile, he opened the drawer. Inside, tincture of poppy juice called out to him. He let five drops fall into water, mixed it with a spoon, then gulped the bitter concoction.

He returned to bed and propped up the pillows. It

didn't take long for the sweetness to come on, banishing all care. Gradually his muscles relaxed, his breathing became deeper, pain decreased considerably. Why didn't I do this before? he asked himself.

A bat flew by his window, or was it an Apache on a winged horse? An object glowing on the table caught his eye, Johnny Davidson's gold watch. The numerals were painted deftly, the case vaguely Roman in design; it ticked steadily when Nathanial carried it to his ear.

Johnny Davidson's father and mother would receive a letter from General Garland. *Unfortunately, we were unable to recover the remains of your son.* Nathanial fell back onto his pillow. He couldn't forget those anxious moments in Embudo Canyon.

Dozing on his feather mattress, and for no apparent reason, he recalled the summer of 1851. While on escort duty with the U.S. Boundary Commission, he'd met the great Mimbreno chief Mangas Coloradas and other leading Apache warriors such as Cuchillo Negro, Delgadito, Juh, Geronimo, Lucero, and Nana the medicine man at the Santa Rita Copper Mines.

The summer of 1851 had been the most unusual one of the Apache wars, because both sides had tried to make peace. They'd even moved their camps together, but a few "incidents" had occurred and the Apaches then departed. Relations between the U.S. government and the Apaches had worsened steadily ever since.

There was another reason Nathanial remembered the summer of '51. On one of those lazy hazy nights, he'd made love to an Apache warrior woman on the open desert. Maybe it was mere fantasy, so drunk had he been, but next morning he'd awakened covered with scratches and bites. He didn't know her name and never had seen her again.

I wonder if she ever thinks of me, he mused. Despite the raw, agonizing wounds, he couldn't forget his tawny Apache queen, whose name he didn't even know.

In the afternoon, the great chief Mangas Coloradas was trying to take a nap. He always felt tired, it seemed. Old age is the deadliest foe of all, he told himself, because it can never be defeated.

He heard approaching hoofbeats, then someone climbed down from a horse. "An important message has arrived from Chief Chacon," said Delgadito, another leading Mimbreno subchief.

Mangas Coloradas raised himself and adjusted his headband. His knees creaked as he made his way to the opening of the wickiup. A large gathering of warriors, subchiefs, and women were waiting to hear the message. A Jicarilla warrior stood beside an Appaloosa war pony.

Mangas Coloradas drew himself to his full six feet six inches. "What is the message?"

The warrior stood erectly as he reported. "Chief Chacon wishes to inform Chief Mangas Coloradas that bluecoat soldiers have attacked Jicarilla encampments, killing women and children. He warns you keep your wild young men under control, otherwise the same will happen to you."

A cloud came over Mangas Coloradas's sun-engraved features. "A council will be held first thing in the morning to discuss this matter."

Mangas Coloradas was profoundly disturbed as he

returned to his wickiup. Never before had bluecoat soldiers attacked women and children. We cannot make peace with them because they are dishonest, but neither can we stop them since they are so strong. Sooner or later there will be no place to hide, and then?

It was Saturday night in Santa Fe, and among the crowds strolled a solitary private in a baggy new uniform: the fugitive Ned Smith, now renamed Fletcher Doakes. His regulation blue cap square on his head, he inclined toward the shadows and tried to appear inconspicuous.

The lust was in him, the same craving that had led him to strangle the redhead in San Antone. He hadn't hated her, and her death had been nothing personal. Killing women made him feel alive, whereas usually he was lethargic and sleepy-eyed.

He tended toward low haunts, where victims wouldn't be missed. In Burro Alley, Doakes entered a dark cantina with no name. It was a filthy, grubby room with a bar on the left, tables to the right, filled with Mexican vaqueros, American soldiers, bullwhackers from both nations, half-breed Indians, and low-class whores. It felt like home.

Doakes's mother had been a prostitute, though not of the official variety. She'd been the kept woman of a banker, but also had maintained a series of lucrative paramours on the side. Doakes had no idea who his father was, but he knew how to maneuver prostitutes into dark places. There'd be an outcry if he killed somebody's wife or daughter, and the last thing Doakes wanted was an outcry.

He sipped beer slowly, for he was on a private's

pay. The prostitutes were mostly old, unattractive, with skin diseases disguised cosmetically. All they do is lie, he thought. They deserve to die.

His mother had insisted on school, and a little education had given Doakes big ideas. He was certain he could be a general or a senator if he had the right connections. He felt superior and it rankled to be a mere clerk in the Army.

His mother died when he'd been fourteen, and he'd waited awhile for his father to claim him, but none stepped forward. Since then he'd been roaming America, doing odd jobs, always one step ahead of the law.

Painted prostitutes paraded past the bar, shaking their breasts and buttocks as he watched with amusement. To Doakes, they appeared utterly contemptible. I'd rather be dead than a prostitute, he said to himself.

The cantina was crowded, boisterous, confused. In such surroundings, nobody could prove anything and everyone was an embarrassment. Doakes's tastes ran to the most hideous of the lot, so he selected an elderly chubby prostitute wagging her wide hips as she strolled past. "Lookin' fer a good time, soldier?" She smiled, showing rotted stumps of teeth.

The odor of cheap perfume struck his nostrils, reminding him of the smell of blood. "Don't mind if I do," he replied. "What's your name?"

"Samantha. How about you?"

"Doakes."

"This way, Private Doakes. I'll show you a real good time."

You sure will, thought he, as he followed her across the cantina, then down a corridor, his hat positioned low over his eyes. She opened the door and he stepped inside her tiny room. A narrow bed, rickety chair, and dresser covered with bottles of cosmetics comprised the decor.

"Take your clothes off," she said, a beguiling lilt in her voice.

"You take your clothes off."

"You ain't goin' to do it with yours on, are you?"

"I'm payin', ain't I?"

With a pout, she unfastened hooks at the side of her dress. The garment fell away, revealing a flabby old wench with a wrinkled potbelly. "You got any kids?" he asked.

"Yes," she replied hesitantly. "But I do not want to talk about them."

"I'll bet you don't," he replied. "Lie belly down, because I want to look at your pretty ass."

The whore giggled obligingly, then rolled over. The smile vanished from Doakes's face as he reached into his pocket for the length of cord. Suddenly he came up behind her, and in a practiced movement slipped the cord over her head.

He yanked tightly, preventing sound from her throat. "Your life is in my hands, whore," he whispered into her ear as she writhed in the frenzy of death. He played with her, loosening the cord so she could breathe a bit, then tightening again. He didn't have all night, so he finally gave the cord a final twist.

Panting, he arose from the bed. He looked at his face in the mirror, saw glazed eyes, flushed cheeks, thin lips slightly parted. I am redeemed, he thought happily as he sniffed a bottle of her perfume. Then he took a dress out of the closet, held it before him, and imagined how he'd look as a woman.

He wished he could stay longer, but it was time for Casanova to depart. He glanced at the bed one last time, a rush of pleasure came over him, and he trembled with joy, satiated at last. Hand trembling, he put on his hat, opened the door, then eased into the darkness.

Maria Dolores sat at a back table of the Silver Palace saloon, eating supper alone. There was no reason for her to be in the saloon, she should be with her children, but somehow had found herself working later than usual lately.

At the opposite end of the saloon, her new guard prowled along, thumbs hooked in the pockets of his pants, cigar in his teeth. In spite of herself, Maria Dolores was intrigued by the man of mystery who'd shown up at her office. *Is he running from a wife and five children?*

He appeared a gentleman in cowboy clothes. She wanted to talk with him, purely out of human interest, for Maria Dolores wouldn't dare admit, even to herself, more personal feelings. *It's nice to see people other than army officers once in a while,* she thought as she sliced a tender ribbon of steak. *I wonder what Nathanial is doing without me?*

Maria Dolores knew her husband had a weak character, for once he'd confessed his brief romance with an Apache squaw. She'd never forgiven him, although she'd pretended she had. Maria Dolores and Nathanial had been married over five years and argued fairly steadily. She wanted him to resign his commission, he steadfastly refused.

A shot rang out, startling her. At the bar, a bull-whacker held a smoking gun in his hand. No one lay on the floor, so evidently it was another wild shot at the ceiling which would leak next time it rained. Another expense, thought Maria Dolores with chagrin.

The bartender was a Mexican wearing a white apron. "You'll have to put that *pistolero* away, senor."

"Says who?" asked the bullwhacker, unsteady from high whiskey intake.

"The rules."

"Shove 'em up yer ass."

The barrel of a Colt Dragoon came down on the bullwhacker's head, his legs crumpled and he fell in a heap to the floor. Cole Bannon stood behind him, gun in hand. "Settle down, boys," he said.

Cole grabbed the bullwhacker by the collar and dragged him to the door. Maria Dolores resumed her meal as she thought, Now there's a man who knows what he's about.

Chapter Six

In the season known as Many Leaves, Subchief Victorio and a cohort of Mimbreno warriors rode to Fort Thorn to observe friends who were trying to live like the White Eyes.

They were distressed by what they saw. The peace-loving People had become lazy, flaccid, and disorganized, separated as they were from the holy Lifeway. The ground was muddy around their wicki-ups and the stench of garbage permeated the air. It didn't appear as though chores were getting done.

The clan leader was named Tomaso, and Victorio called him aside for a conference. "Are you happy here?" asked the Victorious One.

Tomaso was forty, potbellied, and always had considered himself a forward-looking warrior. "The White Eyes cannot give us all we need," he said weightily, "but we must live in peace with them anyway."

"Why?" asked Victorio.

"Peace is better than war."

Not always, thought Victorio. "How do you plant food?"

"We set seeds in rows, according to the latest methods of the White Eyes. They know much about these things."

Victorio's face was immobile, but he thought, The White Eyes know how to subjugate weak-minded warriors. "How can you be content dropping seeds into the ground, when you have been a warrior?"

"There is a time for war and a time for peace," replied Tomaso, quoting a missionary. "I have seen too much blood, Victorio. It must end."

Victorio wandered the reservation with his warrior honor guard, observing the new ways. I too hate killing, he reflected, but I'd rather be bathed in blood than live in this dirty place, relying upon the charity of White Eyes.

In Santa Fe, a dusty, creaking stagecoach came to a halt before the Fort Union command post, where a crowd gathered to greet new arrivals. The door was opened by a corporal with a blond mustache, and passengers debarked into the arms of waiting spouses, friends, and lovers.

Last man out was a thickly built officer relying upon his cane. No one was was there to greet him, but that's how Nathanial wanted it. His plan was to locate his wife when she least expected him, so he could see what she was doing, and with whom. If I have to drag her back to Fort Union by the hair, by God, that's what I'll do. How dare she run out on me? Who the hell does she think she is? His anger stoked hotter and he was bursting with laudanum, his Colt Dragoon loaded as he hobbled toward the Silver Palace Saloon.

A few blocks away, Maria Dolores sat in her office. There was a knock on her door, then Cole Bannon entered, hat in hand. "You wanted to see me, Mrs. Barrington."

"Have a seat, Cole. Let's talk, shall we?"

She admired his animal grace as he lowered himself into the chair. He had a certain . . . she didn't know what to call it. Perhaps it was merely the way he wore his clothes.

"I've been thinking about you, Cole," she said. "You have been working for me two months now, and obviously you are a capable man, but I think you are wasting your talents as a guard. How would you like to manage this saloon for me?"

He thought for a few moments. "You're taking me by surprise, Mrs. Barrington."

"You'd be paid double what you are earning now. When could you give me an answer?"

There was another knock on the door, which was opened by agitated Miguelito. "Senora—your husband is here!"

Maria Dolores turned deathly pale.

"Perhaps I'd better be going," replied Cole.

Her heart filled with nameless fear. Shuffling sounds advanced down the hallway, followed by the appearance of her husband, attired in a dusty blue uniform, stumbling with the help of a cane. He took one look at Cole, frowned, then turned toward his wife and said, "Guess what just blew in from Fort Union?"

There were a few moments of silence as she struggled to catch her breath. Then she swallowed hard and said, "I'll speak with you later, Cole."

Cole arose, nearly as tall as Nathanial. Their eyes met, neither liked what he saw. Cole sidestepped toward the door, never turning his back on Nathanial. Finally the husband and wife were alone.

"Have you been hurt?" she asked.

He didn't respond as she kissed him dutifully. Then he asked, "Who was that?"

"He works for me. I think you'd better sit down."

He dropped to a chair as she returned to her desk. They studied each other with barely suppressed anger. "Why haven't you returned to Fort Union?" he asked.

"I have been busy here, I am afraid. My father has died."

"Sorry," he replied, although he barely knew her father. "When did he die?"

"Shortly before I arrived in Santa Fe."

"That's a long time ago. What's going on?"

"You have things to do at Fort Union, while I have nothing."

"Do you call our children nothing?"

"I need other work to occupy my mind, and I am tired of bowing to the wives of your superior officers. Why must I always be the one to make compromises? Why don't you resign your commission and live in Santa Fe like a normal man? Sometimes I think you are married to the Army, not me."

It was the same argument since the early months of their marriage. "How are the children?" he asked.

"They are well but miss their father."

"That's because you left me."

"But you have left me many times to be with the Army. When I received word that my father was ill, you were gone. How did you hurt yourself?"

"Oh, I fell off a horse."

"I hope you have not been drunk while I was away."

"Of course not," he replied as tincture of poppies coursed through his veins.

"You do not look well. Miguelito will take you home in a carriage, and I will join you later."

"What about now?"

"I am busy."

"It appears that your businesses are more important than your husband."

"It appears that the Army is more important than your wife." She headed for the door. "I will find Miguelito."

Nathanial was transported in his wife's carriage to her sumptuous home, where maids prepared his bath, laid out a clean, pressed uniform, and brought him a bottle of whiskey. He began drinking as he undressed and continued as he lay in the hot sudsy water. The more he thought about his wife, the angrier he became.

His mood worsened when she didn't come home for supper. The children were hungry so he sat with them, wondering why she wasn't there. She's getting too big for her britches, he decided. She has no respect for me, otherwise she wouldn't speak to me as she does.

Nathanial recalled the bewitching Spanish princess he'd married, and wondered what had happened to her. I didn't know anything about her and she didn't know anything about me, he realized. We lusted for each other, got ourselves married, and now she's decided that she doesn't want to be in the Army.

"Are you all right, Daddy?" asked little Zachary.

"I'm fine, son, and how are you?"

"I want to go back to Fort Union with you."

"I'll talk with your mother, but now it's time for bed."

He kissed his son and daughter, then maids carried them to their bedrooms. Nathanial limped to the parlor, sat and gazed at expensive furnishings selected by his wife. Where the hell is she?

The alley was dark and gloomy and it smelled like stale urine as Doakes appeared at the end. He looked both ways, hat low over his eyes, then entered, hand near his service revolver. The twin demons of lust and rage were on him, time for another feast.

Every ten feet down the alley, an old faded prostitute could be seen. They were wretches who couldn't get jobs in whorehouses or saloons, and had to sell themselves in the open for the lowest possible price. Sometimes Doakes thought of himself as a fanged beast prowling the gutters of the world. Other times he viewed himself a man of exceptional tastes. We only live once, so what the hell, he told himself.

The prostitutes were undernourished, ragged, ancient, and occasionally scarred. He felt no pity for them because he considered pity an inferior emotion. A real man doesn't follow the artificial rules of the world, he told himself.

About midway into the alley, he found what he was looking for. She was younger than the others, but stood at an odd angle, as she ran the tip of her tongue over her upper lip. "Lookin' fer fun?"

"Sure am," he replied. "Let's go."

"We can do it right here."

"I like a little privacy."

"It'll cost more."

He placed his hand in his pocket and jingled coins that lay beneath the cord. "I rented a room."

She took his arm, and like bride and groom they walked to the back of the alley. After a few steps, he realized she was limping. So that's why she's younger than the others, he realized. She's a cripple. He'd never killed a cripple before and thought it might be fun.

They crossed the backyard and entered another alley, this one deserted. "How about here?" he asked.

"I thought you had a room."

"You're so pretty—I can't wait. Turn around."

She smiled alluringly as she faced the wall. "One of *them*, eh, soldier?"

He reached into his pocket, where his fingers closed around the cord. "Not exactly."

On the reservation, many People were drunk, stumbling about the campsite, with children running wild and dogs barking. Victorio and his warriors watched grim-faced from their fire. "They have become like the White Eyes," commented Geronimo, the twenty-eight-year-old Bedonko warrior and *di-yin* medicine man.

"I have seen the truth with my own eyes," replied Victorio. "The People will destroy themselves if they surrender the holy Lifeway. Tomaso!" he called out. "I want to speak with you."

Tomaso walked with great dignity toward Victorio. Chief of the camp, Tomaso could never hold such a position among People who ran free, but at least he was sober. "What would you like to know?" he asked Victorio.

"Where do your farmers get money for firewater, if they don't have seeds and implements to grow crops."

Tomaso looked away as if he didn't want to respond, and it was as Victorio imagined. Some of them were raiding secretly, and naturally all the People would be blamed.

As if to echo his thoughts, a fight broke out on the far side of the campsite. Tomaso, Victorio, and his warriors gathered around to see two enraged drunken middle-aged warriors trying to slice each other to ribbons.

Victorio watched coldly as they made wild swipes at each other, sometimes drawing blood, but usually missing their marks. They grunted like bears with murderous glints in their eyes as they tried to rip each other. Finally Victorio could tolerate the disgusting display no longer. He glanced at his warriors, they moved in, grabbing fistfuls of flesh and hair, dragging the opponents apart.

"Let me go!" screamed one of them. "I will kill you . . ."

His voice stuck in his throat as he saw Victorio standing before him. Victorio could hold back his rage no longer as he glowered at the two combatants. "The White Eyes hold the People in contempt because of warriors like you!" he declared. "You are sickening, not for the compromises you have made with the White Eyes, but for your inability to control your passions. You are no longer warriors of the People, you are not entitled to our protection, and we are leaving this place right now."

Victorio turned abruptly and walked toward the war ponies. He didn't look back once. Farming on reservations is not the solution for the People, he decided. The future of warriors can be determined only by war.

Maria Dolores sat at her favorite table in the Silver Palace Saloon, slicing a strip of steak. She'd worked late not because she had things to do, but was afraid of facing her husband.

An ugly argument was on the way. Based on past experience, they'd lose their tempers and say things they'd apologize for in the weeks, months, and years to come. He wouldn't give up the Army and she wasn't going back to Fort Union. She wasn't even sure she still loved him.

Surreptitiously she cast a glance at Cole Bannon, new manager of the Silver Palace Saloon, who sat at his favorite table on the other side of the room, having supper and reading a newspaper. There was something remote and untouchable about him. Sometimes she thought she was in love with him in a silly schoolgirlish way. She was married with two small children, but Cole Bannon made her forget inconvenient facts. Maybe I got married too soon, she reflected.

A short cowboy approached Cole Bannon and whispered something into his ear. Cole appeared worried as the messenger receded. What's that all about? wondered Maria Dolores. Cole ate a few more bites of food, looked both ways, then walked across the saloon, headed directly for the boss lady.

She hoped her hair was neat and she hadn't dropped gravy on the white collar of her maroon dress. Most of all, as a decent married lady, she couldn't let him know of her shameful interest. He came to a halt at the edge of the table and sat without an invitation.

Looking both ways, he said, "A prostitute has been found strangled in one of the alleys off the *Calle de la Muralla*. The killer is still out there, and maybe you'd better let me walk you home."

She drew her Colt and lay it on the table. "I can take care of myself."

"This is the second prostitute found strangled within the past month."

She wondered what would happen if she let him walk her home. Should I invite him in for a cup of tea? But her husband was in town, and how could she think such trash? "Thank you for warning me, but I can take care of myself."

He shrugged, about to leave the table when Maria Dolores spotted her frowning husband heading toward her through the crowd. Uh-oh, she thought. Cole Bannon, unmindful of the drama into which he'd dropped, reached his full height as Lieutenant Nathanial Barrington, First Dragoons, arrived at the table.

"Why haven't you come home?" he demanded of his wife.

"I was busy."

Nathanial glanced at Cole. "So I see."

Nathanial wanted to punch Cole through the wall, but Nathanial was a sophisticated New Yorker who abhorred public displays of emotion, if possible.

Maria Dolores also preferred to avoid public scandal. "I shall be home in a half hour," she replied.

Nathanial's face turned purple as he replied in a

barely controlled voice, "You'd damned well better be."

He turned abruptly and limped toward the door, leaning upon his cane. No one paid attention to him in the sea of cardplayers, wastrels, drunkards, and soldiers. Maria Dolores's hand shook as she lay down her fork, her appetite extinguished.

Cole tried to make light of the family disaster. "What's wrong with his leg?"

"He probably fell off a bar stool," said Maria Dolores.

Doakes approached the gate of Fort Marcy as nonchalantly as any soldier returning from a night in town.

"Evenin', Private Doakes," said one of the guards.

"Evenin'," replied Doakes as he shivered with ecstasy. In his mind, he kept reliving the thrilling murder. He crossed the parade ground, recalling the final tightening of the cord, the sweet sensation of her throat snapping in his very hands.

The demons had departed and now he could sleep. Behind the barracks, he washed his hands and face in a basin of water, then dried himself with the common towel. Lord, wash me of my iniquity and cleanse me of my sins.

He entered the darkened barracks, soldiers snoring in long rows. He undressed, crawled into his bunk, and closed his eyes. The night's events crowded his mind and he saw himself as a hero swaggering through the alley, making his selection and seducing her with clever conversation.

He touched himself, as he recalled her thrashing against the wall. Nothing was more exciting for

Fletcher Doakes than to watch someone die. He experienced not a smidgeon of remorse, and indeed smiled contentedly as he lay in his bed of power.

Nathanial waited impatiently in the parlor as his wife opened the front door. Then he rose and stumbled toward the stairs, where he met her on the way to her room. He grabbed her shoulder and stared deeply into her eyes. "You don't think you're fooling me, do you?" he inquired loudly.

"Take your hand off me."

She shrugged him away and climbed the stairs. He grabbed her arm and pulled her back down with him. They faced each other as a gust of wind whistled over the roof. "Let me go," she insisted.

"Have you been unfaithful to me?" he asked.

Her eyes flashed angrily. "I will not dignify that question with an answer."

"I can't understand why a woman would rather be in a saloon than with her children."

"I am sure there is much you do not understand, otherwise you would never have become a soldier."

"What's so superior about selling whiskey to every vagabond and criminal with a few coins in his pocket?"

"In other words, someone like *you*?" she asked haughtily.

If she were a man, he would've smacked her long ago. But since she was a fragile female, and he'd been taught from infancy never under any circumstances to lay his hands on women, he turned her loose. "My duty station is Fort Union. I take it you're not coming back with me?"

"My business is in Santa Fe. I take it you prefer the Army to your family?"

Both knew they were entering dangerous territory, but years of marital discord forced them onward, and neither felt the least bit conciliatory. "I shall return in the morning to say good-bye to the children," he said, "and then I'm off to Fort Union."

"As you wish," she replied.

She turned and climbed the staircase as he watched her ascend to the bedroom where they'd shared happy hours. But he was tired of fighting with her and there was something emasculating about seeing his wife in apparently intimate conversation with a strange man.

To hell with her, replied Nathanial as he headed for the door. I'm not giving in to any damned woman.

Maria Dolores sat on the chair next to her window and gazed at the Jemez Mountains in the distance. She was crying softly, for it appeared her marriage was over. She viewed Nathanial as her jailer, the man who'd made her live at that pesthole, Fort Union.

Now she was in control of her destiny once more, and her husband could visit the children whenever he pleased, which she hoped wasn't often. She didn't need his money, thank God, otherwise she'd be forced to follow him to Fort Union.

She was free, but at the same time felt rejected by her husband, although she'd rejected him equally. We were in love and now can barely speak civilly to each other, she reminded herself. It would be fine with me if I never saw him again.

* * *

Nathanial was so mad, he was ready to tear into the first person he saw. Unfortunately, he could barely move his left arm, while his right leg was stiff as a board. He soon found himself in Santa Fe's saloon district, and across the street sat the Silver Palace Saloon.

He should return to Fort Marcy and take a room in the Bachelor Officers' Quarters. Then, if he was truly intelligent, he'd get on the next stagecoach to Fort Union. But he wasn't intelligent on the night his marriage had come to an end. He didn't want Maria Dolores to think she was pulling the wool over his eyes.

The little voice in his ear told him he was making a mistake, but he didn't listen as he headed for the front door of the Silver Palace Saloon. It opened and three shifty-eyed miners stepped outside, as if someone wanted to steal their gold, but Nathanial shuffled past them, entering his wife's saloon.

Where is the son of a bitch? thought Nathanial as he searched for the man whom he suspected of planking his wife. The new manager of the Silver Palace Saloon was standing at the end of the bar, talking with a prominent Santa Fe lawyer whom Nathanial also knew.

Nathanial stepped into the shadows and examined his adversary carefully. Cole Bannon was no fop in a frilly shirt, but a solid-looking fellow whom women of small intellect might consider attractive.

By God, I'm going to let him have it, decided Nathanial. He navigated behind his cane as he crossed the crowded floor, passing gamblers, newspaper readers, drinkers, and the merry whirl of a chuck-a-luck wheel. "Round and round she goes, and where she stops—nobody knows!" called the croupier.

Cole Bannon glanced up sharply as the vengeful husband approached. "Your wife's gone home, Lieutenant Barrington," he said before Nathanial could open his mouth.

"I want to talk to you, Mr. Fancy Man."

Bannon's lips became a thin line, because a fancy man was a pimp. "What's on your mind?"

Nathanial wanted to draw his gun and shoot his rival's lights out, but then his mind flashed on a gallows, with himself hanging by the neck until dead. "So you're the weasel who's been fooling with my wife."

Bannon's eyes widened. "Lieutenant Barrington, I barely know your wife. I just work here, that's all."

Nathanial leaned closer. "Don't give me that horseshit, Bannon. I know how the game is played."

"I'm playing no game," said Cole, although the accusation was true in a way. "Now I know why your wife is unhappy. With a husband like you, what can we expect?"

Only one response was possible. Nathanial intoned, "My second shall visit you in the morning."

Cole Bannon laughed, as he hooked his thumbs in his belt. "I don't want to kill a crippled army officer, but you come back here after you get healed—I'll give you play."

"You fucking coward!" growled Nathanial as he went for his service revolver.

To his surprise, he saw a Colt Dragoon looking between his eyes. "Settle down, Lieutenant Barrington," said Cole Bannon. "Otherwise somebody's liable to blow your stupid head off."

Nathanial was so humiliated he didn't even care. "Go ahead—I dare you."

"Don't ever dare me," replied Cole Bannon. "You don't appreciate your wife because you're an idiot. Next time I see you, you'd better step lightly."

Cole holstered his gun, the saloon was silent, and all eyes focused on the end of the bar. Cole walked away calmly, showing his back to Nathanial, who realized that he, the West Pointer, had come off second best.

Nathanial headed for the door, and everyone made way for the wobbling shot-up officer. On the sidewalk, he took a deep draft of air, then crossed the street and entered the first cantina. He made his way to the bar and said, "Mescal."

"Sí, senor." The bartender poured a glass, Nathanial raised it to his lips, paused a moment, then tossed it down like a seasoned old drunkard. *My wife's lover nearly killed me a minute ago,* he reflected as the familiar firestorm started up his throat. *It's been one helluva day.*

Chapter Seven

For Maria Dolores, the departure of her husband had been like a blessing from God. Hereafter, I'll live where I please, she told herself one morning as she entered the Silver Palace Saloon.

She spotted Cole Bannon sitting at his customary table, puffing a cigar and reading a newspaper. His eyes were on her as she crossed toward her office, and she knew he desired her as she desired him, but neither had the courage to make the first move.

Then a ruddy-faced red-bearded soldier of medium height advanced into her vision, a big smile on his face. "Howdy, Mrs. Barrington—remember me?"

She stared at her husband's former first sergeant as memories of her life at Fort Union drifted back. "Of course I remember, Sergeant Duffy," she said with a smile. "What brings you to Santa Fe?"

"Stagecoach escort." Sergeant Duffy appeared uncomfortable as he averted his eyes. "I was sorry to hear about you and the lieutenant breakin' up, ma'am."

"It was very sad," she admitted. "But necessary."

"The lieutenant really loved you, Mrs. Barrington. Used to talk about you all the time." Sergeant Duffy removed his hat and scratched his balding skull.

"Wa'al, he's gone back to New York City, but he ain't fully recovered yet."

She raised an eyebrow. "Perhaps he should not fall off bar stools, or whatever happened to him."

Sergeant Duffy looked at her curiously. "He didn't fall off no barstool, Mrs. Barrington. Don't you know what happened? He and about sixty others was ambushed in the Embuda Mountains, and only a handful got out alive."

Back in her office, Maria Dolores pondered what Sergeant Duffy had told her. Naturally Nathanial wouldn't say anything about it, because he was so damned proud. How many times, she wondered, will he be at death's door before he realizes that soldiering is the wrong profession?

At eight o'clock in the evening, she walked home through busy downtown Santa Fe. Love and fury mingled in her heart whenever she thought of her husband. It was dark and fewer pedestrians were about after she left the center of town. She rested her hand on the butt of her gun, as she peered into a shadowy alley. No one aimed a rifle at her, but something moved on the bench to her right. "Good evening, Maria Dolores," said Cole Bannon. "May I tell you a secret, as I walk you home?" He lowered his voice as he drew closer. "What would you say if I told you I was a Texas Ranger?"

"I'd ask why you're working at the Silver Palace Saloon."

"I don't want anybody to know who I am, because I'm looking for that feller I told you about, the one who murdered two prostitutes. He's also killed about five in Texas, as far as I know, maybe more."

"I always figured you were more than a drifter, but you sure know how to run a saloon."

"It's hardly surprising since I've spent so much of my life in them."

"Why is he killing so many prostitutes?"

"He's the strangest critter I ever heard of, but I'm going to catch him one of these days."

They turned onto the street where she lived, a lamp burning in her parlor window. She was tempted to invite him in for a drink, but she was a married lady.

"Thank you for walking me home," she said.

He paused, and it appeared he wanted to say something, but instead turned abruptly and walked away. She examined his square shoulders, narrow waist, the way his cowboy hat slanted forward on his head, gun gleaming evilly on his hip. Experienced in certain pastimes, and feeling lonely now that her husband had abandoned her, she wondered what it was like to make love with such a man.

At the beginning of the season called Heavy with Fruit, the great chief Mangas Coloradas and a selected band of warriors journeyed west to the remote land of the Chiricahua People for a council meeting. A feast was held to commemorate the event, with dancing and the drinking of sacred tizwin. The Mimbreno and Chiricahua leaders gathered around their fire, to discuss ways to cope with the White Eyes.

Mangas Coloradas reported the facts to the Chiricahuas. "The Jicarillas have been brought to their knees," he told the gathering, "and now the Mescaleros are under attack. Next, the bluecoat soldiers will come for us, and then the Chiricahuas. But if we join together, we can stop them."

Many prominent Chiricahua leaders attended the meeting, but greatest of them all was their aging chief, Miguel Narbona. "The Chiricahua homeland is vast," he said, spreading out his arms. "It is seldom that we see the White Eyes. There is no threat that we can envisage."

"Not yet," said Delgadito of the Mimbrenos. "But once we too thought the White Eyes would never disturb us, since there was so much land. Now they are breathing down our necks, with more bluecoat soldiers arriving all the time."

"Nobody will breathe down my neck," said Chief Miguel Narbona. "Bluecoat soldiers die just like Mexican soldiers, when you shoot arrows through their hearts."

Chapter Eight

A stagecoach and its military escort traveled east on the Santa Fe Trail, and in the cab, free from his usual routines, Nathanial Barrington dozed fitfully, headed back to civilization after six years of hard frontier campaigning.

First stop would be South Carolina, to return the gold watch to Johnny's parents, and then he'd continue to Washington, D.C., home of his father. The end of his journey would be his mother's home in New York City. He looked out the window of the stagecoach, trying to distract himself from his failed marriage by remembering family, friends, taverns and oyster cellars in the Empire City.

As he traveled farther east, he noted that formerly barren wilderness had become engraved with intersections, towns, and farms. He found newspapers in remote stagecoach stops, and the issue on every front page was bloody Kansas.

According to press reports, the country was in turmoil over the notorious Kansas-Nebraska Act. Advanced at the beginning of the year by Senator Stephen Douglas of Illinois, chairman of the Senate Territories Committee, it had formed two new territories, Kansas and Nebraska, and mandated that the issue of slavery be settled by votes of territorial residents, instead of the President and Congress.

Senator Douglas called it "popular sovereignty," and it had a certain ring, but he hadn't foreseen that pro and antislavery forces would pour into Kansas, each trying to gain an advantage. The shooting already had begun, Senator Douglas's career had been derailed by the bill, while the President and Congress fought over how to respond to open warfare in the beleaguered new territories.

The most sensational news story concerned a runaway slave named Anthony Burns, who'd stolen a boat in Richmond, landed in Boston, and was captured there by federal marshals on May 24. It so happened that an abolitionist convention was being held in the city, and three thousand federal troops were required to hold back the angry mob. Burns eventually was returned to his owner, who then sold him to a group of abolitionists who set him free. Now Burns was a regular American citizen after it cost the federal government one hundred thousand dollars to return him to his owner.

Farms and forests rolled past Nathanial's window as he read stale news stories. It isn't a foreign power that'll bring us down, but we ourselves, he decided. At the bottom of a page, he read about the emerging Republican Party, formed earlier that year at a schoolhouse in Ripon, Wisconsin. According to the article, former so-called "Conscience" Whigs were filling its ranks, along with Democrats disaffected with the proslavery administration of Franklin Pierce. Republicans were fielding candidates for elections in districts all across the nation, but no prominent leader had yet emerged among them.

At the bottom of page five, Nathanial found a small story about New York City. A new opera hall called the Academy of Music was being constructed near Union Square and scheduled to open that fall. The massive edifice would cost a reported three hundred thirty-five thousand dollars, all contributed by wealthy New Yorkers. The opening night performance would be Vincenzo Bellini's *Norma*.

Nathanial smiled as he recalled his past life as a New Yorker. With every turn, the stagecoach wheels carried him back to the land of music, theater, art galleries, and taverns.

In addition to its other attractions, New York was a magnet for beautiful women from all over the world, and Nathanial thought how wonderful would be the temptations. No matter how pretty they are, I'll never get married again, he swore. Marriage is like war except it's ten times worse.

In late summer, subchiefs and warriors from across the Mimbreno nation gathered in the Pinos Altos Mountains for a conference concerning a request from the White Eyes Indian commissioner, Dr. Michael Steck.

Leader of the convocation was the aging Mangas Coloradas, and at his side sat brave Victorio, with Deladito, Cuchillo Negro, Barbonsito, Cautivo, and Cigarito, among other distinguished warriors.

Delgadito reported the news, standing at the edge of the circle. "I have spoken with Dr. Steck," he said. "He has told me that the Great Father wants peace with the People. He also said that the Great Father has more soldiers than we can count, and they are like sand on the desert. He said we must be farmers, because the road to war is red with blood. He also wants to meet with you, Mangas Coloradas."

Delgadito sat heavily, silence prevailed around the circle, then Mangas Coloradas spoke. "What kind of man was this Steck?"

"He seemed kind, but offered nothing except a threat."

Mangas Coloradas scowled, because it appeared the White Eyes were pressuring him. "I do not want to be a farmer," he declared.

"Nor do I," added Victorio.

Most subchiefs and warriors nodded in agreement, but Cuchillo Negro raised his hand and asked to speak. He was an older warrior, and one of his sons had been killed in a raid on an ammunition convoy. "I do not want to be a farmer," he said, "but bloodshed is worse. I too have spoken with Dr. Steck, and I believe he is a good man. We must end the killing because the People are getting the worst of it. I for one am ready to try peace."

A few others nodded in agreement, but Mangas Coloradas felt no rancor toward them. Then Victorio rose, and everyone turned to the rising star of the People, the Victorious One.

"There can be no peace," he announced, "because foxes and wildcats don't live together. I think we should leave for the land of the *Nakai-yes* Mexicans and be warriors again. Why surrender when there are still places where we can go?"

There was silence, then Mangas Coloradas replied, "Victorio has spoken wisely. Let us go out of the land of the *Pindah-lickoyee,* and journey to the land of the *Nakai-yes,* where we can be as in the old time, in harmony with the mountain spirits."

A schism developed among the People that afternoon. Some announced their intention to cooperate with Dr. Steck, while the wild ones determined to cut out for Mexico. And no one dared speak the awful truth that the White Eyes were driving them from their ancestral mountains.

After duty hours, Fletcher Doakes often walked to Santa Fe, sat on a bench, and watched the crowds pass by. He looked just like another semi-inebriated soldier, but he especially enjoyed scrutinizing women from beneath his hooded eyelids. I am the monster they fear most, he thought with satisfaction. We are all murderers in our hearts, but only I have the courage to act. At least I'm honest.

Doakes noticed a busty woman walking toward him, a leather satchel suspended over her shoulders by a black leather belt. He'd ridden in the stagecoach with her and remembered she was owner of the Silver Palace Saloon. If I could catch her right, she'd have her throat snapped before she could think about it.

But they'd organize a posse if I killed a respectable woman. It's best to stay with the tried and true, my friend, he told himself. The Mexican woman appeared confident and unafraid, inspiring Doakes to wonder how she'd look with his cord around her throat. A faint smile appeared on the face of the lone soldier sitting in front of the general store, blending into the background.

Chapter Nine

At dawn, Jocita rode with Running Deer into the wilderness, he sitting before her on her horse. "I am going to teach you something very important today," she said.

The boy was eager to learn, for his father was Juh, chief of the Nednai, and his mother was a warrior woman of high renown. He could think of no greater shame than disappointing his parents.

At midmorning, they stopped on a plain covered with chaparral, far from main trails. They dismounted, Jocita hobbled her horse, then kneeled in front of her son. "You are not big yet, but there is one thing you must learn. A time may come when enemies are about, and you must be quiet."

The boy nodded dutifully, although he wasn't sure what she meant. She lay him in a thicket, sat before him, and said, "Don't move until I tell you."

The boy flinched as an insect bit his leg. His mother slapped his face. "I said don't move."

"It hurt."

"If enemies were about, and you made noise, I or your father would have to kill you. The lives of the People are more important than that of one noisy little boy. Do as I say."

The boy's face stung, but his mind had become focused. He lay on the ground and closed his eyes.

"Don't fall asleep," admonished his mother. "Keep your eyes open at all times. You must melt together with the ground and think of other things."

He lay like a prairie dog, eyes scanning from side to side. His body became still and his skin color blended with the foliage. He soon became bored, but didn't want another slap. He felt like crying, but his mother was never moved by tears. He took her advice and tried to merge with the ground, as if his hands and feet grew roots. It seemed that long periods were passing, but he remained immobile. At odd moments, he wondered if his mother had died, for she didn't move a muscle. The sun passed the midday point and started going down. The boy's arms and legs ached, but he knew his mother would care for him. He became hungry, thirsty, irritable, yet refused to surrender. He believed his mother's training could save him from a bullet in the face.

Suddenly she started, and Running Deer found himself flying through the air. She covered him with kisses while massaging his limbs. "You are a good learner," she said. "Our enemies do not know how to be silent, and that gives us an advantage. In time to come, I will teach you other methods of superiority. You are everything I hoped you would be, my son. From this day onward you are learning to become a warrior."

A black shellacked open carriage rolled down a magnolia-shaded roadway near Charleston, South Carolina. Nathanial sat in the passenger seat, gazing at the white two-storied mansion with Georgian columns sitting contentedly at the end of the drive. The West Pointer was attired in a freshly cleaned uniform, his left hand resting on a wooden cane whose handle had been carved in the head of a wolf.

He admired neatly trimmed lawns, gardens, strategically placed trees, benches to rest upon, and an ornate white gazebo. Nathanial had telegraphed ahead from Atlanta, so Johnny's parents would be expecting him. Removing the gold watch from his pocket, he raised it to his ear; it still ticked merrily.

The carriage halted in front of the mansion, the front door opened, and a uniformed slave marched outside. "You must be Lieutenant Barrington."

"Yes—who are you?"

"I'm Raymond, suh. I'll have the bags removed to your room at once."

Raymond gave orders to other slaves, who carried Nathanial's bags into the mansion. Nathanial then followed Raymond inside. "I'll tell Mr. Davidson that you're here, suh."

Nathanial sat in the parlor and gazed at paintings of prominent Davidsons. One showed Johnny in his West Point uniform, similar to a painting of Nathanial that hung in his mother's home. A Negro maid arrived with a tray of pastries and a pitcher of lemonade.

The opulence reminded Nathanial of homes in New York City, yet Johnny Davidson had chosen harsh army life, just as Nathanial, and that made them brothers of the sword. Unfortunately, swords were of no use against the Apache, and if the arrow had flown eighteen inches to the left, Nathanial's bones would be lying in the Embudo Mountains.

Presently an elderly man in a white suit entered

the parlor, accompanied by a woman wearing a pink summer dress. "Lieutenant Barrington," said Samuel Davidson. "Welcome to our home."

Nathanial reached into his pocket and took out the watch. The bereft mother accepted it, tears rolling down her cheeks, while the father thanked Nathanial in a shaky voice. "I can see you're not completely recovered from wounds," said Mr. Davidson. "Perhaps you might want to lie down."

The maid said, "I'll take you to your room, suh."

Nathanial followed her up the spiral staircase, noticing that she was a healthy dark-skinned woman, good posture, probably selected for her physical strength, worth top dollar at any slave auction. White people were murdering each other over her in Kansas.

She opened the door to a guest room, raised the window, then turned to face him, waiting expectantly for his next command. He was tempted to tell her to remove her clothing and lie upon his bed, but instead, said, "What's your name?"

"Belinda."

"I'm Nathanial."

They examined each other carefully, then averted their eyes. He thought he saw fear in hers, because he was the white man with the power of life and death. "I'm from New York," he said. "We don't have slaves there."

"I wish I could go to New York," she replied. "Must be wonderful."

He didn't know what to say. Should I buy this slave and cut her loose in New York City? he asked himself. She sensed his change of mood. "If you need anything, suh, just call Belinda." With a polite smile, she departed the room.

He removed his clothing, thinking that he'd never made love with a Negro woman. It seemed the most exotic act imaginable. Is she a roaring jungle beast or a cuddly little black kitten? he wondered.

He couldn't simply say, "Let's go for a walk," or "May I escort you to the Academy of Music on Saturday night?" I'd better not try anything with her, he ordered himself, because I'm here to comfort the parents of Johnny, not fall in love with a slave. I'm liable to get lynched, if I'm not careful.

Despite lush bougainvillea, rose-filled gardens, and a tastefully appointed mansion, he detected vague menace lurking beneath the veneer of Southern gentility. It was his impression, based on experience with Southern army officers, that they were more apt to take notions of honor seriously, and duels were a way of life among them.

I'm not here to rile delicate sensibilities, he reminded himself. If I want to make a fool of myself with women, I'll have to wait until I return to New York City.

The lawyer was a tall bald man with a mustache and an unctuous manner. "What can I do for you, Mrs. Barrington?"

"I'd like a divorce," replied Maria Dolores.

They sat in the lawyer's bright, airy office on the second floor of an adobe building on San Francisco Street in Santa Fe. Nothing surprised the lawyer, for he'd spent his career observing the darkness that lives in the human soul. "I take it you've tried to reconcile with him?"

"I cannot very well reconcile with him if he is never home. From what I last heard, he is not even in New Mexico anymore. He has deserted his family."

"The first step is notify him of your divorce action."

"How long before I can marry again?"

"Depends on two factors: whether your husband will respond, and if he does, whether he'll contest your filing. Do you think he will?"

"It is difficult to know what my husband will do because he is completely loco. If he doesn't respond, what then?"

"Your divorce will be granted in approximately a year, Mrs. Barrington. And now, if I may be so crass, I think the time has come for a discussion of my fee."

Nathanial sat on the back porch of the mansion, sipping a tall, frosty glass of lemonade, while in distant fields fifty-odd slaves picked white balls from verdant bushes. Nathanial wore a thin white shirt with tan pants, but perspired in the shade of the porch. He could imagine how uncomfortable it was to bend in hot sun and dust, under the watchful eye of the whip-carrying overseer.

Nathanial hated moralistic sermonizing, but slavery had never felt right to him. It permitted some to live with good books, fine wine, feasts, balls, hunts, and all the accoutrements of the English manor, but it rested on the backs of other human beings.

"May I bring you anything else, suh?" asked Belinda.

He could sense her dusky body beside him. "Were you born on this plantation?"

"Yes, suh."

"I guess it must be an honor to work in the house, instead of those fields."

"Yes, suh." She had a blank expression, as if speaking what was required.

"Are you married?"

"No, suh. Are you?"

"My wife and I are estranged. I guess you knew Johnny pretty well."

"We sort of grew up together. Everybody liked Master Johnny."

She spoke almost like an educated Southern belle, evidently because she'd been serving them all her life. He turned his gaze to the slaves picking cotton in the fields. "Do you think the slaves out there liked Johnny?"

"Master Johnny never went to the fields, suh. He had to study so he could be a great man. Instead he is dead, and his parents aren't taking it so well."

"Do you know his lady friend, the one who wouldn't marry him?"

The maid frowned. "That's Jennifer Butler."

"What can you tell me about her?"

"I shouldn't say, suh."

"Why not?"

"If it hadn't been for her, Johnny would be alive, suh."

"It's not her fault that she didn't love him, is it?"

"Jennifer Butler doesn't love anybody but herself, suh." Belinda took a step backward as the bereaved parents appeared around the corner of the porch.

Mrs. Davidson sat beside Johnny and said, "We're

most grateful that you brought back Johnny's watch.
Please stay as long as you like. There's a wedding tomorrow and we hope you'll attend with us."

"I'd be honored, ma'am."

Mr. Davidson sat on his other side. "A wedding
means new life, and we must try to look ahead, I
suppose." The old man had a vague lost look in his
eyes. "Sometimes"—his voice caught—"I think I've
killed my son by encouraging him to enter the Army."

"Johnny loved the Army," replied Nathanial, "and
he would've made it his profession no matter what
you said."

"Please feel free to use the horses, carriages, or
anything you please," said Mr. Davidson. "I also have
a library if you care to read. It's wonderful to have
you here with us, because you remind us so of
Johnny."

Later, Nathanial decided to accept Mr. Davidson's
offer of a horse. He selected a chestnut stallion at
the steep-roofed stable. The animal was saddled by a
slave, then Nathanial rode the lively beast among
palmetto trees and tulip bushes, headed for the
fields. He wanted to see for himself how slaves were
treated.

The flower gardens and lawns of Rolling Hills
were tended by several sullen slaves who paid no attention to Nathanial as he passed. They wore simple
clothing and appeared stupefied by their abject condition, or at least that was Nathanial's impression.
He came to a wooded area that reminded him
vaguely of a certain encounter with Apaches in the
Santa Rita Mountains, August of '51. But there were
no Apaches in South Carolina, so he urged the horse
forward, soon finding himself in cool shade, with red

cardinals flitting from branch to branch above him. What would happen if the slaves revolted? wondered Nathanial.

At the edge of the forest, Nathanial saw rows of cotton as far as the eye could see. A group of slaves stooped in rows not far from him, plucking cotton balls and stuffing them into gunnysacks they dragged behind them.

Nathanial removed his wide-brimmed plantation hat and wiped perspiration from his forehead with the back of his arm. It was warm upon his horse, but nothing like those furrows from sunup to sundown. Is slavery worse than soldiers building barracks on the desert, or fighting for their lives in the Embudo Mountains? wondered Nathanial. A slave glanced sideways at Nathanial, and the New Yorker thought he saw naked hatred in those eyes.

He came to slave shacks amid a grove of trees and brought his horse to a halt in front of an old gray toothless Negro man sitting on a bench and watching him carefully.

"I'm a friend of Johnny Davidson's," announced Nathanial. "I wonder if you'd let me look at where you live."

The old Negro said, "Go right ahead, suh."

Nathanial entered the shack. Wooden bunks were lined along the wall, similar to the Army, and everything appeared clean. He didn't see cabinets or closets because apparently the slaves didn't own anything. Children and the old man followed him in. Nathanial noticed one light-skinned lad, his hair not quite so nappy as the others.

"What're you looking for?" asked a darker boy.

"Nothing special."

"Are you a Yankee?"

"I live in New Mexico."

"Where's that at?"

"Far away," replied Nathanial. "Do you go to school?"

The boy became afraid as a dark shadow came over the room. A brawny clean-shaven white man stood in the doorway, blocking the sun. "And who might you be?" he asked.

"I'm a friend of Johnny Davidson's."

"What're you doin' in the slave quarters?"

"I wanted to see how they live. Who're you?"

"My name's Clanton, the overseer. It's not so bad hyar, eh?"

"Not much different from an army barracks, I don't suppose."

"I was in the Army myself," Clanton said proudly. "General Pillow's brigade. Come on outside—let's have a talk. Was you in Mexico?"

"I was on General Taylor's staff."

"Them was the days, eh?"

They emerged into the sunlight, the overseer's horse next to Nathanial's. The Negro children no longer crowded around. "Looks like they're scared to death of you," said Nathanial jokingly.

"I don't tolerate no shit from nigras, and I suggest you don't leave nothin' valuable around 'em 'cause they'll steal it in a minute." Clanton placed his fists on his hips and cocked his head to one side. "I guess you'll go North and tell about how bad we treat the nigras."

"You don't treat them so bad, but they're not free to come and go. There's something I'd like to ask you, Mr. Clanton. One of those children has light skin, and he wouldn't be yours, would he?"

Something twitched in Clanton's cheek, but otherwise he was perfectly calm. "You don't know no better, suh, but we don't talk about them things hyar."

"I wonder why," Nathanial replied sarcastically.

"What if I was to tell you he was Johnny's son?"

Nathanial was stunned. "I'd ask you to prove it."

"It gives you comfort to think I'm lyin', but it's true."

Nathanial made a movement toward the boy, but Clanton got in his way. "Don't start trubble, suh."

"Who's the mother?"

"None of yer bizness, and keep yer mouth shut. Mr. and Mrs. Davidson done cried enough for that son of theirs, who got hisself killed when he should've been hyar helpin' run this plantation."

Nathanial wanted to lay him out, but gentlemen of his class didn't crack canes over the heads of inferiors. "Good day," he said curtly.

He took one last look at the light-skinned child, dragged his game leg toward his horse, then rode toward the manor house. He wondered what kind of man would take an overseer job. Like certain other Southerners, Clanton wasn't worried about the Rights of Man.

Soon Nathanial was back in the Garden of Eden, blossoms and greenery surrounding him, the day pleasantly warm, while behind him in the fields, slave women wore thin, clinging cotton dresses and colorful bandannas wrapped around their heads. It was a bucolic scene, with a white-porticoed mansion on the hill surrounded by oaks. Nathanial was reminded of paintings by Boucher and Fragonard, but demons poured forth if you scratched the surface.

He returned the horse to the stable, then made his way to his room, where he sat on a chair beside the open window, overlooking weeping willow trees, lily gardens, and the gazebo.

There was a knock on the door. "It's Belinda, suh. Can I get you something?"

"Come on in."

She stood before him in her immaculate gray-and-white uniform, as if waiting for his order.

"Have a seat."

She appeared confused, but dutifully dropped gracefully to a chair opposite him.

"I just heard a little rumor," he said, "and I want to know what you think. There's a little mulatto boy in the slave quarters and somebody said he was Johnny's son. Is it true?"

She thought for a few moments, then said in a low voice, "Yes."

"Who's the mother?"

"Works in the fields."

Nathanial was flabbergasted. How could a decent man like Mr. Davidson let his grandchild grow up a slave? "Is there any whiskey around here?"

"This is Rolling Hills, suh. We've got anything to drink that you might want."

"Bring me about a half glass, if you don't mind."

Their eyes met, and Nathanial had to admit that she was gorgeous. He admired her rounded figure and upright carriage as she walked to the door. No mournful shuffling slave, neither was she free to catch the next train to New York City. This is a very strange society, he said to himself.

* * *

Dr. Michael Steck, Commissioner of Indian Affairs for New Mexico, rode a horse through the Apache farm established beside Fort Thorn. Grimly he calculated that the Apache crop wasn't sufficient for the winter, but he couldn't supplement it. If the Apaches wanted to survive, they'd have to take up traditional pastimes such as raiding.

A Pennsylvanian, Dr. Steck had moved to New Mexico for the sake of his wife's health. Then he'd grown tired of looking down people's throats, or up their anuses, and managed to secure the position of Indian commissioner through political connections. He truly wanted to bring peace to New Mexico, but Apaches were leery of the White Eyes, due to the brutality of military campaigns, while settlers were terrified of Apache raids. Mistrust, hatred, and vengefulness dominated the discourse, and all Dr. Steck could do was attempt to reason with all parties.

The vast majority of Apaches was running wild, and it didn't escape the good doctor's attention that the most important Apache leaders had never deigned to speak with him. I'm making little progress, he admitted as he watched a group of drunken Apache men lolling about in front of a wickiup.

That evening, he sat in his office and wrote a letter to his superior in Washington, D.C., George W. Manypenny, Commissioner of Indian Affairs.

Dear Mr. Manypenny,

I'm cognizant of your many responsibilities, and I know that Apaches aren't the only Indians with whom you must concern yourself, but it is my duty to report that much blood will be shed in New Mexico unless the federal government acts quickly.

For the past year, approximately two hundred Apaches have been entirely pacific, and some property stolen by them has been returned.

They raise corn with sharpened sticks, because they have no hoes. Unfortunately, their crops and supplementary rations aren't enough to keep them alive. Much has been promised them, but little actually has been delivered. This proud people is enduring semistarvation to remain at peace with us.

If you reversed positions, and placed the white man in a starving condition, he too would steal. *Self-preservation is the first law of nature.*

Dr. Steck puffed his corncob pipe as he studied what he'd written. It wasn't the first time he'd sent such a letter, and wouldn't be the last. But senators and congressmen didn't care about people who didn't vote, such as Apaches.

The next day, Nathanial rode in a carriage with Mr. and Mrs. Davidson to a wedding at a neighboring plantation. It was Sunday, day off for the slaves. Nathanial engaged in civilized conversation with his hosts, but couldn't help remembering the grandson in the slave quarters and the daughter-in-law in the fields. No wonder Johnny joined the Army, he reflected. He remembered Johnny as a friendly easygoing officer, well-liked by his men, with a sense of duty and the willingness to try anything, including planking a certain slave and getting her pregnant.

Nathanial's sharp officer's eyes spotted a conglomeration of shacks on the far side of a cotton patch.

He could hear vague strains of a hymn being sung, as somebody strummed a guitar.

"The darkies sing so enchantingly," said Mrs. Davidson with a sigh.

The carriage turned a bend, and ahead lay a Grecian-revival white-columned castle, with its own special array of flower gardens, leafy trees, and chairs. It reminded Nathanial of a medieval land populated with gallant cavaliers and elegant ladies in ornate gowns. The carriage came to a stop in front of the mansion, where a liveried slave opened the door and helped Mrs. Davidson down.

"This way," said Mrs. Davidson, taking Nathanial's hand.

She led him up the steps to the wide veranda that surrounded the house. Seated at tables, ladies and gentlemen imbibed beverages in the shade, while children chased each other among trees. Uniformed slaves of both sexes carried trays of beverages and hors d'oeuvres to hands reaching out of the air. If you don't have to pay the help, you can live very well indeed, thought Nathanial.

The bride and groom met guests at the rear of the veranda, with the Ashley River glittering in the distance. Nathanial was introduced to strangers. He shook hands and struggled to remember names. Some were attired in uniform, but he didn't recognize army friends. The bride was a freckle-faced young lady of approximately sixteen, her husband a few years older.

The Davidsons spoke with elderly friends, while Nathanial retreated toward a chair against the wall. He'd been on the frontier so long, he'd forgotten what it was to be a wealthy man.

"Champagne?" asked a male uniformed slave, who looked like an elegant black beetle holding out a tray.

Nathanial removed a glass from the silver tray, then the slave continued along the passageway, offering his wares. I wonder what he thinks about all this, mused Nathanial.

"Cigar, suh?" asked another slave, holding out a box of panatelas. Nathanial selected one, which the slave lit with a match.

A man could get used to this sort of thing, figured Nathanial as he observed three belles advance across the veranda, headed toward the bride and groom. Nathanial couldn't help admiring their gowns.

He watched the belles kiss the friend who'd managed to snare a husband. Young, unsullied, the bride and groom were unaware of bitter arguments they'd doubtlessly have seven or eight years down the road, with children screaming in the background.

The cigar in one hand, a glass of champagne in another, Nathanial decided to take a walk. With a pronounced limp, he made his way to the stairs, descended them slowly, and headed in the direction of the river. He felt at peace with himself, because he didn't have to worry about an Apache stabbing a knife into his back. Sitting on a chair at water's edge, he sipped his champagne.

"Hello."

Nathanial glanced at an attractive honey blonde about twenty-five years old, possibly younger. She wore an orange chambray gauze dress trimmed with flounces of Bruges lace, and carried a red parasol. "May I sit?"

"By all means."

She dropped daintily beside him, spun the parasol, narrowed her eyes, and said, "I'm Jennifer Butler."

Nathanial stared at the woman who'd indirectly caused Johnny's demise. "How do you do?"

"I imagine you don't think much of me," she began, "but I've known Johnny all my life and am very sorry he's gone. I never realized he'd transfer to the frontier, and get . . . killed."

She said the last word in a whisper, so difficult it was to confess. He couldn't help admiring her thin waist and long slim legs outlined by her gown.

"He didn't blame you for anything," said Nathanial. "Love cannot be controlled."

"Some people never find love," she said in a faraway voice. "I'd rather be single than unhappily married."

"How fortunate the gentleman who finally captures you."

He watched her eyes as they roved his face, measured his shoulders, and dropped momentarily below his waist. "What do you think of South Carolina?" she inquired cheerfully, in an effort to change the subject.

"In a way, it's paradise."

"I live down the road, if you ever care to call. It was very nice speaking with you."

She walked toward the main house, swinging her hips easily. Now wait a minute, Nathanial cautioned himself. Johnny's barely cold in his grave, and it wouldn't be right if I pursued Jennifer Butler. Besides, Mother is waiting in New York and I've got to get a move on.

"Champagne?"

It was another slave with a tray of libations. Nathanial accepted a glass as the sun sank toward the Ashley River. He wondered if Johnny was in the sky, laughing at him.

Maria Dolores sat behind Cole Bannon's desk in the Silver Bannon Saloon, checking his books. "You're doing a fine job," she said as she totaled a column of figures.

It was late, and he'd taken a few drinks to bolster his courage. "Running saloons is second nature to me."

"There are some people who don't understand business, such as my husband, and others who play it like a game of cards, like you and me, Cole. By the way, I've spoken with a lawyer. It might take a year, but I'm divorcing my husband."

Cole thought she'd passed a hint. It's now or never, he told himself as he took a deep breath. "Do you think, after your divorce is final, you might want to marry again?"

There were several uncomfortable moments as she scratched the pen on paper, then raised her eyes and calmly evaluated him. That he was relatively handsome there could be no doubt. The swashbuckling Texas Ranger excited her, and she didn't feel like an abandoned wife and mother of two in his presence. "We both know how painful marriage can be. We mustn't do anything rash."

"Of course not," he replied, his eyes leveled at her breasts.

She closed the books. "We've completed enough work for today. I'm going home."

"May I accompany you?"

They arose inches apart. Close up, she liked his

angular jaw, the resolute expression on his lips, the rugged weatherbeaten visage. My God! she thought as he embraced her. He wasn't as brawny as her husband, but was strong nonetheless, his hands roving her back.

"Don't," she whispered.

He touched his tongue to her throat. "But I'm mad about you."

"We must be sensible," she protested, weakly trying to push him away.

"Don't you know that I dream about you?" He smothered her throat with kisses, as one of his hands cupped her left breast.

"We shouldn't," she whispered as he lowered her to the sofa.

His tongue inserted between her lips, something exploded within her, and she realized how starved she'd been for love. Why not? she asked herself as he unbuttoned her dress.

A lifetime of churchgoing was obliterated by the touch of his lips to her ear. He was pressing himself against her, just what she needed after many lonely anguished nights. Nathanial was unfaithful to me, so what am I worried about? she asked herself. There wasn't much room on the sofa, but lovers always find a way. "I worship you," he whispered into her ear as he drew up the hem of her dress.

Maria Dolores writhed with him on the narrow space. My husband does whatever he pleases, she thought. So do my children, and I deserve some fun too, don't I? But she knew, deep in her Jewish-Catholic heart, that one day she'd pay dearly for her shameless brazen lust.

* * *

Not far away, in a dark corner of the Silver Palace Saloon, Fletcher Doakes sat with a mug of beer and a copy of an old Cleveland newspaper. He held it before his face, pretending to read about the crisis in Kansas, but was hiding his face from everyone in the vicinity.

Doakes wanted to be alone, because he believed the monster within was becoming visible to the naked eye. Sometimes he imagined faces of his victims tumbling through his mind, as they strained against the killer cord.

His face was slick with sweat while his heart pounded loudly. He wanted to vomit disgust onto the floor or scream at the top of his lungs. The world was wicked, hateful, and incomprehensible, based on his experience.

Slowly he lowered the newspaper and gazed at expensive prostitutes flirting with customers. His eyes narrowed with desire as he imagined choking the life out of them, one after another. Perspiration soaked his underclothes and he knew the time had come for another sacrifice.

He drained the mug of beer, then headed for the door. No one paid attention to the soldier, and no one could spot the monster lurking behind his placid nondescript face. Doakes didn't realize that he was utterly mad, because his rage felt normal; he'd been living with it all his life.

He saw himself covered with fur, his ears pointed like a werewolf's, and his tail wagging behind him as he casually gazed at a pretty young prostitute in skimpy clothes, wiggling her butt and jiggling her breasts, corrupting the minds of men in the vicinity as Eve had tempted Adam. Was it not woman who introduced suffering to the world? Doakes asked himself.

His capacity to justify his behavior was exceeded only his need to inflict pain. He stepped outside, looked both ways, then headed toward Whore Alley, his right hand fingering the cord.

Nathanial returned to Rolling Hills after midnight, accompanied by Johnny's parents. They wished each other good night in the parlor, then departed to their respective rooms.

Nathanial had drunk a fair quantity of champagne at the wedding party, but had paced himself like the longtime saloon veteran that he was. No longer was he willing to pass out cold in public.

His room was dark, the window was open, and white curtains floated on the fragrant summer breeze. He lit the lamp and noticed that the maid had turned down the covers of his bed. A bottle of whiskey and a glass sat on a tray, so he poured himself one last drink, then sat on the chair near the window.

All the wedding guests had been extremely kind to the Yankee soldier, and nobody spoiled the fun with mention of Kansas. Nathanial didn't hate Southerners and neither was he contemptuous of them. Do we really have any choice about what kind of people we become? he asked himself.

There was a knock on his door, startling him. "Who is it?"

"Belinda," said the voice on the other side.

"Come in."

She entered the room, attired in her usual gray-

and-white uniform. "I was wondering if you wanted anything, suh, before you went to bed."

He looked at her full breasts and shapely hips, but decided against churlish remarks. "I hope you haven't been waiting up for me."

"I want to make you comfortable, suh."

A faint smile played on her lips, and he wondered if she was trying to tell him something. "You've thought of everything. Thank you."

"May I help you take off your boots, suh?"

"That won't be necessary."

"I'd be happy to help, suh." She kneeled before him, reached for his left boot, but he pulled back.

"I can take off my own boots. Please get up."

She appeared uncomfortable as she arose. "Did you enjoy the party, suh?"

"I met Jennifer Butler. She's quite beautiful, and I can understand why Johnny was in love with her."

A smile played on the maid's face. "Yes, she sure is beautiful, suh."

"What's wrong?"

"Nothing, suh."

"What are you laughing at?"

"I just thought of something."

"What?"

"My secret."

"Do you ever have any fun, Belinda—or are you always doing other people's dirty work?"

"Sometimes I have fun, suh."

"I'll bet you wish you could get out of here."

She shrugged. "There's no way."

"What if I bought you?"

"Why would you do that?"

"I'd turn you free when we got to New York."

"The Davidsons'd never sell me, suh. They even taught me to read, so's I can read to Mrs. Davidson before she goes to bed." She lowered her voice. "But I could run away and meet you in Charleston. If anybody asks, you can say you bought me to help your poor sick wife. Doesn't she need help in the kitchen?"

"What if you get caught?"

"I won't."

"I've heard they beat the hell out of slaves who run away."

The corners of her mouth turned down. "I know you—Mr. Yankee Man. You pretend to be all worried and concerned, but you're not gonna really risk something, are you?"

"You'll be taking the big chance, not me."

"I didn't think you'd help me," she said bitterly. "You're all talk—just like a Yankee." Then, all of a sudden, she burst into tears. Nathanial stared at her in alarm as she struggled to control herself.

"Have a drink," he said, reaching for the bottle of whiskey.

"All the fine gentlemen drink their troubles away," she replied bitterly. "I thought you were different." She pulled a clean white handkerchief from her sleeve, daubed her eyes, then blew her nose. "I've dreamed about being free since I could think. They've got organizations in the North that help runaway slaves. If you took me away, I'd do anything you say." She raised her hand and unfastened the top button of her dress. "Anything."

He placed his hand upon hers. "Don't."

"What's the matter, Mr. Yankee Man?" she asked

with a wry smile. "A darkie isn't good enough for you."

"I was thinking that you're as pretty and well-spoken as any belle at the wedding."

"What you think'll happen after Mr. and Mrs. Davidson are dead? I'll end in the fields, because Clanton wants my black ass out there picking his damned *cotton!*"

Nathanial stared at her as she sobbed before him, her normal servile composure gone. "What do you know about Jennifer Butler?" he asked.

Her eyes widened with fear or surprise, he couldn't be sure. "Nothing, suh."

He held her shoulders in his strong hands. "You expect me to save you, but you won't tell me the truth."

"I'll tell you everything if you help me escape," she replied, smiling through her tears.

Chapter Ten

In the hour before dawn, not even a stray cat disturbed the main street of Esquinita. In a few hours the dusty thoroughfare would teem with wagons, carriages, and vaqueros, but now children slept in their beds, cattle lowing in pens. A small town in Chihuahua and hub of a vast but sparsely populated ranching and farming region, Esquinita lay peacefully in the dawn.

The citizens had no reason to be alarmed, because a company of soldiers was garrisoned among them. Its commander, Lieutenant Fernando Rodriguez, was sleeping off a hangover at the home of his girlfriend, Damaris Souza, while guards dozed in front of the barracks.

Apaches left Esquinita alone, thanks to an "arrangement" that had been reached between both sides. For the occasional payment of a few head of cattle, ammunition, and other articles, the Apaches left Esquinita alone. No treaty had been signed, but that's how it worked.

The provisions of the treaty were about to change unilaterally, as a lone head appeared behind a yucca cactus five hundred yards from the edge of town. It was Victorio, subchief of the Mimbreno people, heir apparent to Chief Mangas Coloradas. Victorio examined pens of horses and cattle, then his sharp eyes scanned barracks and their sleepy guards.

He knew there were sixty-two soldiers, because Esquinita had been under surveillance for some time. Victorio looked to his right, where his Nednai and Bedonko brothers waited for his signal. To his left were his best Mimbreno warriors. Together, he held two hundred men under his command.

Among them were famous subchiefs and warriors such as Delgadito, Ponce, Cigarito, and Victorio's brother, Coyuntura. Their tactics had been practiced in advance, the war dance held in accordance with tradition, and now the time had come to fight.

Victorio pointed his forefinger at the stables, and thirty warriors began racing on foot in that direction. Then he pointed to the east, where another thirty warriors ran toward adobe homes. Victorio aimed his right hand straight ahead, then the remainder of his force rushed the barracks.

The warriors hit the town like a cyclone, shrieks filled the air, and soldiers came pouring out of their barracks, carrying rifles, suddenly wide awake. Even tubby Lieutenant Gonzalez fired his pistol wildly as he ran back to his headquarters, flaming arrows flying through the air.

Time and again Victorio charged the Mexicans, drawing their fire. When their muskets were empty, he rampaged among them with his war club, cracking skulls. No one could stop him, bullets whizzed around him like angry gnats, and his warriors followed him everywhere.

Soldiers and citizens were pressed back by marauding Apaches, as smoke from burning buildings obscured the view. Lieutenant Gonzalez prayed the sound of battle would draw soldiers from other towns, but then an arrow pierced his throat and he was dead before he hit the ground.

A tough old sergeant took command, received an arrow through his arm for his trouble, but soldiers could barely see the constantly moving Apaches. It appeared that massacre was on the menu, then the sergeant realized the Apaches were withdrawing.

"Hold your fire!" he bellowed.

It became silent, then the townspeople and soldiers cheered. "We fought them off!" somebody yelled.

Buckets of water were carried from wells and splashed on burning homes, while a doctor tended the wounded. It was discovered that all horses and cattle were gone, the attack on citizens and soldiers merely a diversion. The fires were doused by noon, then the priest held Mass in the town square. Despite hymns, incantations, and the transubstantiation of wine into the Most Precious Blood, every person in Esquinita would hate Apaches until the day he or she died.

Nathanial sat surrounded by luggage at the Charleston railroad station. He'd have to change trains about five times before he reached Washington, a trip of several days. The train was due in a half hour.

He glanced up from his Charleston *Mercury* as two men with constable badges entered the railroad station, a slave woman between them. She looked like Belinda, thought Nathanial, and then noted that she *was* Belinda. The constables headed for him, grim expressions on their faces. Nathanial decided to face them on his feet.

One of the constables wore a rust-colored goatee. "Sorry to bother you, Lieutenant, but this slave says she belongs to you."

"Of course she belongs to me. I have the bill of sale right here."

Nathanial reached toward his suitcase, hoping they wouldn't call his bluff, but the constable placed his hand on the West Pointer's arm. "That won't be necessary, suh. We take your word for it."

Nathanial turned to Belinda. "Where've you been, you worthless wench!"

She appeared confused. "I got lost, suh."

"I told you to stay behind me."

"I'se sorry, suh."

"Goddamned dumb nigra," said Nathanial gruffly.

The constable grinned. "Yer a Yankee, ain'tcha?" Then he balled his fist. "This is the only thing a nigra understands."

"Thanks for finding her, Constable."

The constable saluted. "Happy to be of service, suh."

The constables strolled off, and Nathanial figured they were veterans of the Mexican War, susceptible to the power of officers' insignia.

Nathanial and Belinda sat opposite each other in a corner of the railroad station. "I told Mrs. Davidson my sister was sick," said Belinda softly. "She won't know I'm gone till tomorrow, and might not report me for a few days. I'm sure they think I'm drunk or lying with some man."

"We've got a long way to go, but I don't suppose we can travel together."

"Lieutenant Barrington, you have a right to take your slave wherever you please. Don't you need me to do things for you?"

Nathanial noticed an elderly woman being attended by her slave not far away. "Oh boy, do I ever."

Belinda stowed their baggage over the seats, and he realized she was an actress like every other woman he'd known. When finished, she sat next to him and took out needlework.

"Don't look so worried," she muttered. "They'll never do anything to you if they catch us. They might hang me, but I'd rather take a chance on being free."

"Do you have a weapon by any chance?"

"An old pistol. Guess who taught me how to work it?"

"Johnny?"

"That's right, and there's something I never told you. Do you remember that light-skinned boy you saw at the slave quarters?"

"He's yours?"

She appeared astonished. "How'd you know?"

"Just a guess. I'll buy his freedom after we get to New York."

"I'm sure the Davidsons would be glad to get rid of him." Her big brown eyes burned into him. "The first time I saw you, I knew you were the man who'd save me."

"Were you in love with Johnny?"

"Sometimes."

The front door opened, then a rotund man in a blue uniform appeared, like an officer of the U.S. Dragoons. "The four-thirty train for Richmond is arriving, ladies and gentlemen," he announced. "Your tickets, please."

Nathanial heard the whistle's anguished call, the train puffed into the station, Nathanial boarded and selected a back seat, with his slave facing him. No one else sat nearby, so Nathanial leaned forward and said, "It's time to tell the truth about Jennifer Butler."

Belinda fluttered her eyelashes, pretending to be a dizzy Southern belle. "But, Lieutenant Barrington," she said in a high-pitched voice, "whatever makes you think she'd do anything wrong?"

If Nathanial closed his eyes, he's never know the difference. "I figure she's getting it somewhere. What's his name?"

"Guess."

"I don't know any of those people. How can I guess?"

"But surely you have suspicions."

"It's somebody who can't marry her because he's married already."

"Wrong."

"Her beau doesn't have enough money?"

"You think a Southern belle would marry for dirty ole money?"

"A belle can't meet a man at a tavern. Is there a male houseguest?"

"You're getting closer."

Nathanial wrinkled his brow. "Don't tell me it's a . . . relative, like a brother or father?"

"No."

"Is she carrying on with a house slave?"

"Which house slave?"

Nathanial's jaw dropped open. He'd heard of white

Southern men sleeping with Negro women, but never white Southern women sleeping with Negro men. The notion disturbed him for a reason he couldn't fully comprehend. "I don't know—the one who polishes her father's boots, or maybe one of those young bucks in fancy uniforms who carry the trays of champagne around."

"Who could walk into her room anytime, day or night, and no one would get suspicious?"

"Her maid?"

Belinda winked.

Nathanial's mind sought to encompass the impossibility. Johnny's great love was a woman of Lesbos, and that's why she'd never married. Nathanial had heard vague stories about lesbians, but never a white woman and black woman. The very thought seemed incredibly thrilling to a man who adored the gentle sex.

He wondered about the rebellion of the bedroom, where slaves subjugated masters and mistresses on clean cotton sheets. It seemed erotic and weird to a man who himself had enjoyed a one-night romance with an Apache. Again, he caught a glimpse of the deceptive South. How long can this house of cards stand? he wondered. He and his slave looked out the window at Charleston blurring past as the thundering vehicle gathered speed.

"We'd better rehearse our stories," she said, "in case we run into slavecatchers."

"If they ask for the bill of sale, I'll say I lost it. I don't think they'll dare take you by force, but maybe the war between the North and South will start on this very train."

The iron horse lumbered toward Richmond as

darkness came to the Southland. Nathanial and his
slave ate sandwiches that she'd packed, and after
supper, most passengers moved to the sleeping car. It
was time for Nathanial to retire, but he didn't want
her to go to the car reserved for darkies, because
somebody might molest a pretty slave.

"You'd best stay with me," he said.

"But darkies aren't allowed on the sleeping car."

"I need the assistance of my faithful slave, due to
the infirmity of my recent war wounds, etcetera.
Come on."

They carried their bags to the sleeping car, where
several male and female passengers were preparing
for bed under the watchful eye of the conductor. No
one complained about Belinda's presence because
other slaves also had accompanied their masters and
mistresses to the sleeping car.

"Make believe you're busy," Nathanial whispered.

She opened one of the bags and appeared to be
looking for something, then crawled onto the bed
where she arranged sheets and blankets. Nathanial
observed other passengers disappearing into their
bunks while the porter wrote on his notepad and
slaves departed the sleeping car. Nathanial nonchalantly climbed into bed with Belinda. Their shoulders touched as they tried to get comfortable in the
narrow space.

"What are you doing?" she asked in a whisper.

"You don't expect me to sleep in my clothes, do
you?"

"Don't get any ideas."

"All I want is to sleep, I assure you."

It was a warm summer night, a breeze whistled
through the open window, beyond were vague out-

lines of eastern mountains, but they looked like little bumps compared to the Sangre de Cristo range near Santa Fe, or the Mimbres Mountains of New Mexico. Belinda unbuttoned her dress, then removed and folded it neatly at the bottom of the bunk. Clad in a white cotton slip, she lay beside him.

"The hardest part was leaving my son," she said. "I hope it's for the best."

"You'll be with him soon. Be patient." He held up his Colt .44. "Nobody's taking you anywhere."

"Do you sleep with it in your hand like that?"

"Where else? We've got a long day tomorrow, so go to sleep."

"I know I shouldn't do this, but . . ." Impulsively, she kissed his cheek.

He looked at her in dim moonlight filtering through the blinds. "But, Belinda—what if I fall in love with you?"

"How will you explain me to your mother?"

Remembrance of that lady jolted Nathanial to a keener awareness of his situation. "I apologize," he replied, moving away.

They tried to make themselves comfortable on the narrow jiggling berth, and it wasn't long before two exhausted people were fast asleep. Wheels clanged beneath them as the steam engine pulled mightily toward freedom.

In New York City, Amalia Barrington sat in her front parlor, reading *The New York Daily Times*. A spare woman in her sixties, she could hear children laughing in Washington Square Park across the street. How wonderful to be innocent, she thought.

Amalia Barrington's husband had left her for another woman, after being unfaithful many years. Her beloved older son was a drunkard, patron of prostitutes, and officer in the U.S. Army. Now her hopes rode with her youngest son, Jeffrey Barrington, a student at the Pembroke School, and her adopted son, Tobey, at the same institution.

Jeffrey wanted to go to West Point and continue the family's military tradition, but Amalia had hoped he'd become a lawyer, stockbroker, or shipping executive, like other members of her family. She had encouraged Nathanial to attend West Point, believing that he'd needed the discipline, but now thought military life had been the ruination of him.

Tobey, on the other hand, intended to become a lawyer. A former street urchin whom Nathanial had brought home one day, Tobey was the most level-headed member of the family.

"Hello," called a voice from the street.

A friend named Myra Rowland stood on the sidewalk with a young blond woman whom Amalia took to be her daughter. Amalia led a reclusive life, but had been trained in hospitality from an early age. "Won't you come in for a glass of lemonade?"

"Love to," said Myra.

The front door was opened by Shirley Rooney, Amalia's aging maid, and the guests led to the parlor.

Myra Rowland was stout in contrast to her slightly taller and lean daughter. "You remember Clarissa?"

"How she's grown," said Amalia, who remembered Clarissa as a withdrawn serious child.

They sat in the parlor and were served lemonade, small sandwiches, cookies, and a wedge of cheddar cheese.

"Are you in school?" Amalia asked Clarissa.

"Not anymore," said the young woman, who sat with her back perfectly straight. "I'm studying music with a private teacher."

"She's a very accomplished pianist, I'll have you know," replied her mother proudly.

"Perhaps she can play something when she's finished her lemonade."

Clarissa appeared well-mannered and proper to Amalia's coolly evaluating eyes, and she wore an engagement ring. "How old are you, dear?"

"Eighteen."

"Who's the lucky man?"

"Ronald Soames."

Amalia knew of the Soames family. A sensible alliance. "You're a lovely girl and I'm sure you'll be very happy."

"Have you heard from Nathanial?" asked Myra.

"I've recently received a telegram from him, as a matter of fact, and am pleased to say he's on his way to New York even as we speak."

"The city has changed in recent years—he'll barely recognize it. Is he bringing his wife?"

"No," replied Amalia. "She has extensive business interests in Santa Fe, I'm told."

"How can anyone have 'extensive' business interests in Santa Fe. It's just a frontier village, isn't it?"

"It's quite a bustling place, according to Nathanial, and don't forget that Manhattan once was a frontier village too."

Clarissa sat quietly, sipping lemonade. She vaguely recalled meeting the notorious Nathanial Barrington when she'd been a little girl, and had heard gossip about him all her life. He'd disgraced his family on numerous occasions, and presently was married to a

Mexican woman. Unlike most men of their class, he'd joined the Army and nearly been killed in action several times. Clarissa always had been curious about him.

"Do you think you could play something, Clarissa?"

The trim young blonde crossed the carpet as Amalia admired her perfect posture. Why didn't Nathanial marry somebody like that? she wondered.

Clarissa sat at the piano, unlimbered her fingers, practiced a few chords, and then performed a Bach partita. Her fingers raced nimbly over the keys as her passionate longings filled the air in the form of music. Since childhood, music had been the outlet for emotions she dared not express verbally. An occasional movement of her shoulder or toss of her head were the only indications that depths resided within the young woman.

Amalia closed her eyes, transported by the beauty of Clarissa's soul. Many amateurs played the piano acceptably, but Clarissa obviously was especially talented.

"How exquisitely you play," said Amalia after the last note had been struck.

"Your piano is out of tune," replied Clarissa. "I can fix it for you, if you like."

"She has her own tools," said Myra proudly. "My daughter doesn't trust anyone to touch her piano. She's a perfectionist."

What a wonderful young woman, thought Amalia after the Rowlands had departed. Too bad Jeffrey and Tobey are too young for her.

* * *

Maria Dolores couldn't bring Cole Bannon to her home, because Santa Fe was a small town. Instead, a few nights every week, she visited his hotel room. Frequently she stayed until morning, confident her children were safe with maids, servants, and cooks

One morning she gazed at Cole Bannon's sleeping profile in the light streaming through the curtains. She thought he resembled a poet or professor, although he was a Texas Ranger. She'd seen him manage brawlers, bullies, and drunkards with ease, and men appeared to respect him.

Yet she didn't love him as she'd loved Nathanial in the early years of their marriage. On the other hand, she wondered if such passion could exist for a mature woman such as herself. Should I marry Cole Bannon? she asked herself.

She didn't like sneaking around Santa Fe like a harlot or an adulterous wife. One must be cautious in the choice of mates, she warned herself. I don't want to make two mistakes in a row.

He opened his eyes, then gradually the sleepy expression transformed. "What's wrong?" he asked.

"I was looking at you."

He embraced her. "If only we could be together all the time."

"You would tire of me."

"No, I'll love you forever."

She recalled making the same ill-considered statement to Nathanial approximately six years ago, and now she lay naked in bed with another man. She thought she was betraying something, although she wasn't quite sure what.

* * *

That evening, Fletcher Doakes strolled through Santa Fe, contemplating his future. Should I head for California or go down to Mexico? He never liked to stay in one place too long, because sooner or later something went wrong.

On the other side of the street, he spotted the Mexican woman with whom he'd ridden in the stage-coach, the one who owned the Silver Palace Saloon. She was married to an army officer stationed at Fort Union. I wonder what it's like to sleep with that? he asked himself.

Doakes wished he could have a woman waiting in a nice home somewhere, but it seemed as far as the moon. The followed her to church, and out of curiosity stepped inside the twin-towered adobe house of God. Candles illuminated gaudy statues and light streamed through stained-glass windows as his quarry lit a candle before the Virgin Mary, then dropped to her knees.

Doakes snickered inwardly. How can a virgin give birth to a child? he asked himself. They invent God to tolerate their stupid pathetic lives. Doakes felt superior to the worshipers. People like this don't deserve to live, but I can't kill them all.

He chortled at his private joke, then the Mexican woman rose and crossed herself. He stood beside a statue of Saint Jude and tried to appear innocuous as she passed only tantalizingly inches away. He felt her feminine emanation, then followed her out of the church. She was taller and stronger-looking than some of the men she passed.

He followed her to the Silver Palace Saloon, where she disappeared through a corridor at the rear of the establishment. Doakes couldn't afford a trip to the bar, so he retreated from the noisy crowded saloon. He sat on an empty bench in front of a hardware store and imagined himself in bed with the Mexican woman, she telling him how handsome he was. The dusty street was crowded with wagons, carriages, and riders floating in a cloud of dust.

"Howdy, Doakes."

The fugitive became terrified at the sound of his name, but it was only Sergeant Berwick standing before him, hands on his hips. Doakes tried to smile. "Evening, Sergeant."

"What're you doing?"

"Taking it easy, you might say."

The sergeant appeared about to move on, when he had second thoughts. "You're a strange one, Doakes. Always alone." The sergeant sat on the bench beside the private. "Is somethin' botherin' you, soldier?"

"No, sir," replied Doakes as he fought rising panic. "Just like to be by my lonesome, that's all."

The sergeant placed his hand on Doakes's shoulder. "I guess you can't talk about it, but if you ever want to get it off your chest, they say I'm a good listener. Buy you a drink?"

"Not right now, Sergeant."

"Well, I'll be moving along, Doakes. Don't let life get you down."

The sergeant crossed the street, heading toward the Silver Palace. *I must appear odd to him,* Doakes realized. It was as if Doakes had a long hairless tail that had become visible.

It was night when the warriors returned to their hidden camp in the Alamo Hueco Mountains. Women and children rushed to meet the heroes, but the boy named Running Deer stood by himself before his mother's wickiup, watching them solemnly. Dirty, tired, and bloody, the warriors sang victory songs as they passed among the campfires, heading toward the wickiup of the great Chief Mangas Coloradas.

He was waiting for them, arms crossed, a smile creasing his weathered features. Victorio dismounted and bowed. "The raid was successful, my chief. We have many splendid horses and you would do us honor if you selected your favorites among them."

"I require no more horses," replied Mangas Coloradas. "But I need more Victorios!"

The warriors cheered as Mangas Coloradas embraced his heir. The boy watched wide-eyed, for glory went to he who performed great deeds. Then Running Deer spotted his mother trudging toward him out of the mass of cheering warriors. Leaves covered the gash on her shoulder, her eyes half closed as she dropped to her knees and hugged him. "My boy," she said in a barely audible voice.

She held him so tightly he had difficulty breathing. Then she loosened her grip. "I hope you have been good."

"What is wrong, Mother?"

"Oh—I am tired, I suppose. But I have many horses and your belly will be full for a long time." She patted his stomach with the back of her hand.

Other warriors had fires waiting for them, built by their wives, but Jocita was a wife herself. She stacked twigs and branches, then borrowed a burning stick from another fire. Running Deer watched as she dropped to her knees, bent low, and blew flames to life. Then she loaded on heavier logs.

The odor of roasting meat filled the air as meals were cooked in fires across the campsite. Jocita sat beside her hunk of horsemeat and hoped she wouldn't fall asleep, she was so tired. She and the others hadn't eaten or slept for three suns. The meat dripped fat into the fire as her son stared at her in awe.

Cheers and shouts of joy went up around the campsite, someone was playing a lute, and then, out of the shadows stepped Chief Juh, a playful smile on his face. He dropped beside Jocita, placed his hand on her shoulder, and squeezed. "You are a great warrior, my dearest one. Not even men much larger than you could fight you off." He smiled. "I would hate to have you aiming one of your arrows at me."

"How could I aim an arrow at the father of my child?"

She looked significantly at her son, then Juh turned toward Running Deer. "How are you doing, my boy?"

Running Deer stood shyly before the great chief and was unable to speak.

"He is afraid of you," said his mother. "Because you never play with him."

"But I am busy . . ."

"You have plenty of time for your other children," she said coldly.

Neither dared to say the truth about Running Deer's parentage, so Juh was forced to reply. "You are right. Come here, Running Deer."

The boy cautiously stepped closer, and Juh could see that the boy was terrified of him. Juh hated the light hair and strange green eyes before him, because they reminded him of the White Eyes war chief who'd seduced his wife. But Juh had to admit that the boy was not to blame. He wrapped his arms around his putative son. "One day soon I shall take you for a ride and show you many things. But now it is late and I would like to speak with your mother alone."

Running Deer walked off to visit friends, leaving Jocita and Juh beside her fire.

"You are a great chief because you have a great heart," said Jocita. "You understand that a boy needs his father."

Juh glanced up at her. "But his father needs his wife."

"You have so many wives—you can take your pick."

"You are the one I really want."

"You should have thought of that before you married Ish-keh."

"If I can love your bastard son, why cannot you love me?"

"But I do love you, my husband."

"I want you to love my body, not my kind deeds."

"Never again, because you have broken a solemn vow to me."

"You have broken one as well with me." He gestured with his head in the direction that Running Deer had gone. "We're even."

Sometimes Jocita experienced certain thoughts about men that drove her to distraction, and now it was happening with her husband. She lowered her eyes demurely. "Perhaps it is time to forgive and forget past crimes," she said.

"May I come to your wickiup tonight?"

"Not yet," she replied, pushing him away. "You have not yet suffered enough."

"Why must you torture me?"

"You deserve to die for what you have done to me."

"But you have done the same to me!"

"You were the first traitor, not I."

"Can I help it if I wanted sons? It is right for a man to want sons, but wrong for a woman to go with another man. A few times I even thought of killing you, but I cannot kill her whom I adore."

She looked at his bronzed muscles rippling in the firelight. He was her first love, and his generosity to her son tipped the scales. "Not tonight," she said. "But soon."

Chapter Eleven

The locomotive clanged into Washington, D.C., shooting steam beneath iron wheels. Nathanial and Belinda gazed out the window at the distant capitol dome in the red effulgence of the setting sun.

They debarked from the train, then porters carried their bags to a waiting carriage. The officer and his slave viewed stately hotels, private mansions, and sprawling government buildings as they headed toward the Emory Hotel, an out-of-the-way brick structure favored by military officers. It looked run-down since Nathanial had visited last, but the same whorehouse sat across the street.

The desk clerk looked up from his *Intelligencer*, and wasn't surprised to see an officer and a slave, for slavery was permitted in the capitol of the United States. But it was unusual for an officer to travel with a female slave, arousing the clerk's suspicions.

"I'd like to rent adjoining rooms for me and my slave. Could I send a message?" Nathanial wrote on the scrap of paper:

Dear Father,
When and where can I visit?

He scrawled an address on the envelope, the clerk handed it to a messenger, then hotel porters carried the officer's and his slave's luggage to their rooms. Nathanial was pleased to note that the Emory had installed indoor plumbing since last he'd stayed.

Alone, the West Pointer opened a leather bag and removed his scissors. He carefully trimmed his blond beard as the porcelain tub filled with warm water. Then he lay in it and tried to prepare himself for the reunion with his father.

Nathanial was apprehensive about meeting the man with whom he hadn't spoken for seven years. Last time they were together they'd come to blows over Nathanial's effort to meet his father's paramour, a beautiful octoroon. But now the errant son was more mature, soldierly and steady under fire. He didn't want his father to smell anything on his breath, so he didn't order whiskey.

Instead he reclined in the tub and smoked a cigar. When his fingers shriveled, he dried himself, dressed in his best uniform, and looked at himself in the mirror. A hardy combat commander peered back at him.

There was a knock on the door. "Come in."

Belinda entered, wearing her uniform. "This just came for you."

She held out an envelope, and he saw his father's handwriting.

Dear Son,
    I'll be home the rest of the day, waiting for you.

"Bad news?" she asked.

"I'm going to see my father." He thought how nice her blackness would look against the red bedspread.

"While you're gone, I'll take a walk."

"A slavecatcher might drop his net over you. I suggest you stay in your room."

"I'm not staying in any room," she said.

He sat at the desk and wrote:

My slave Belinda is simpleminded and sometimes
wanders off. If you find her, please return her to me
at the Emory Hotel. Reward.

He signed with a flourish. "I hope this keeps you out of trouble."

"Yas, suh," she said, shuffling toward the door. "Yas, suh."

He hailed a carriage at the corner of New Jersey Avenue, then told the driver to take him to Georgetown. The carriage rolled past the Mall, where the Washington Monument and Smithsonian Museum were being constructed by teams of workmen. His father's home was a two-story red brick building on a gaslit block. The ambiance reminded Nathanial of Washington Square, as he limped from the carriage toward the front door. His father had retired from the army in 1852, after more than forty years of service.

Nathanial hit the knocker and it wasn't long before a uniformed elderly Negro maid opened the door. "You must be Lieutenant Barrington," she said warmly.

"Indeed I am."

"I'm Mattie. Right this way."

Nathanial wondered where his father's octoroon mistress was as the maid led him to a parlor. Above the fireplace hung a full-length oil portrait of his father as a captain of infantry, with barracks and soldiers in the background, painted by Theodore Sydney Moise.

Studying his father's painting, overcome with conflicting emotions, he heard footsteps behind him. "I was about your age when that painting was done," said his father.

Nathanial's first impression was that the colonel had become old and somewhat shrunken. They embraced, and his father felt almost frail against him. Nathanial's voice choked in his throat, because he didn't know what to say.

"Can I get you something to drink?" asked his father.

"A cup of coffee, if you don't mind."

The colonel relayed the order to Mattie, then father and son sat on two chairs facing each other. For a few moments neither could speak, then his father said matter-of-factly, "You're wounded again."

Nathanial nodded, there was silence, then the younger Barrington realized he couldn't just sit like a porcelain statue. "How are you feeling, Father?"

"Quite well. How do you like New Mexico?"

"I like it a lot, except for the Apaches."

"I've been following your career. Evidently you're something of a drunkard, and you've been involved in fisticuffs with fellow officers. Is that more or less correct?"

"I've cut down on my drinking, sir, and have become much more conciliatory in my relations with others."

His father smiled. "To tell you the truth, my boy—I'm proud of you. Because it all comes down to combat command, and you've acquitted yourself well in a number of scrapes with Apaches."

"Maybe, but I'll probably be a first lieutenant until the day I die."

"Don't you think it rankled when I was a colonel and many of my contemporaries became generals? All soldiers have is their duty, but I'm sure I've given this lecture before. How's your wife?"

"She's thrown me out." Nathanial's voice caught in his throat, when he realized that his mother eventually had thrown his father out also. Is this becoming a fine old family tradition? he wondered.

His father raised his hand. "You needn't speak the details. I understand."

Nathanial felt closer to his father now that they'd both committed similar transgressions against womanhood. "Are you still with . . ." The son couldn't finish the sentence because he couldn't bring himself to say the octoroon's name.

"She's out right now." His father's facade cracked for the first time. "It's rather awkward, isn't it?"

Nathanial didn't know how to respond, so his father continued. "When we're young our passions carry us along. I'm not the man I was, not that I ever was much. I can't tell you how happy I am to see you." His father leaned toward him and narrowed his eye. "Are you staying at the Emory alone?"

"No, I have a slave. Bought her in South Carolina, and I'm going to turn her loose once we get into New York. In case you're wondering, I'm not having a love affair with her."

"For some reason I believe you. Yes, you have changed, Nathanial. There's nothing like mortal combat to mature a man, and you've seen your share.

I admit I haven't been much of a father, but perhaps we can be friends after all. In fact, I have an idea. Tomorrow we'll go to the War Department and I'll introduce you to some friends. You're right—it's time you made captain, and perhaps I can help with your promotion."

Eighteen hundred miles to the west, in the foothills of the Sierra Madre Mountains, the great chief Mangas Coloradas lay among rocks and cacti, observing a column of Mexican cavalry passing in the distance. The old chief's eyes weren't as sharp as previously, but he could perceive the Mexican officer riding in front, followed by one hundred and fifty-odd soldiers armed with rifles, pistols, and knives.

Mangas Coloradas was accompanied by twenty-two Mimbreno subchiefs and warriors, not enough to take on the Mexicans. The chief and his tribe had fled south to Mexico to escape the American Army, but now the Mexican Army was hunting them. He felt trapped beneath tons of enemy soldiers.

Then Cuchillo Negro arose, shook his head, and spat in disgust. The oldest fighting subchief among the Mimbrenos, he was even older than Mangas Coloradas himself. "It is no use," said Cuchillo Negro in a deep, resonant voice.

The chiefs and warriors were silent, because they appreciated their predicament. They could become farmers, like Tomaso and his band, or join forces with the Chiricahua People to the north, but their usual haunts were no longer safe.

Mangas Coloradas said, "My heart is against planting seeds in the ground. I am going to our brothers, the Chiricahuas."

"But must we leave our homeland forever?" asked Delgadito.

"I do not know" replied Mangas Coloradas.

Then Victorio arose, and all eyes turned to the next chief of the Mimbrenos. "We are the children of the Lifegiver," he declared. "He will remain with us no matter where we go."

Cuchillo Negro shook his head in disagreement, but he was from the old time. "There is no separation between the homeland and the Mimbreno. It is the place that Yusn has given us to inhabit forever. If we abandon it, it means we have abandoned Yusn, who made us all. Yusn did not want me to be a Chiricahua. He wants me to be a Mimbreno. If I must plant seeds—so be it."

Delgadito, another old-time warrior rose to his feet. "I do not know about you, Cuchillo Negro, and I mean you no disrespect, but I do not believe Yusn wants me to walk bent over all day long, pulling weeds out of the ground." Everyone laughed as Delgadito mimicked a farmer tilling the land.

Cuchillo Negro replied, "I have participated in many battles, and I have seen many friends killed. I also have heard women and children weeping, and it is more than I can bear. I believe that Yusn has given us life so we can be happy, and not run this way and that, trying to elude enemies. Dr. Steck is a good man and I trust him." Cuchillo Negro pointed toward the Mexican soldiers. "If we do not change our ways soon, there will be a river of blood flowing through this land, and most of it will be ours."

Belinda stood across the street from the Congress, staring at it in wonderment and delight. It was the largest most splendid building she'd ever seen. She'd read mention of the Congress in newspapers and magazines, and now she actually was seeing those immense walls, hundreds of windows, and the cupola. Walking up and down the stone steps were congressmen, senators, lawyers, businessmen, and clerks, as a never-ending stream of carriages rolled to the front entrances.

She imagined great debates taking place in hallowed chambers, for she understood well the significance of the Kansas legislation. The fate of slaves like her was being decided within that imposing edifice, and she wanted to tell her story to congressmen and senators, but Southerners would laugh while Northerners would never actually do anything. The North wanted peace, she knew, and would make any compromise necessary to preserve it, no matter how many darkies were worked to death every day, or whipped, kicked, raped, and shot.

"What the hell're you doin' hyar, nigra?"

Her blood nearly backed up as she turned toward two bulky men wearing badges. "Is you talkin' to me, massa?" she asked, and her trembling wasn't completely pretend.

"Who'd you run away from?" asked one, wearing a wide-brimmed straw hat. "And if yer lyin', I'll whup yer black ass myself, get me?"

"I ain't no runaway, suh." She opened her purse and withdrew the note from Nathanial. "Look at that, suh."

The constables examined Nathanial's note. "I figgered there was somethin' wrong with her head," declared the other constable, who puffed a corncob pipe. "Belinda, do you know which way's the Emory Hotel?"

She pointed. "That way, suh?"

"No, you goddamned fool, the other way." He aimed in the opposite direction. "You'd better git a move on, and if I see you wanderin' around again, I'll throw yer ass in jail, hear me?"

"Please don't tell my massa, suh. 'Cause he'll hit me, he will."

"It's just what you need, but I'll let you go this time. Get a move on."

He slapped the back of his hand against her fanny, and she wanted to put a ball of lead between his eyes. Instead she bowed humbly, stuttered, muttered, and shuffled away like a frightened ignorant slave.

The slavecatchers were named Jim and Bob, and they watched her go with more than passing interest. "Not a bad-looking nigra bitch," said Jim. "How'd you like to toss one into her, Bob?"

"A little dark meat never hurt nobody," replied his slave-catching partner. And he knew whereof he spoke.

A few blocks away, Secretary of War Jefferson Davis gazed at a map of Russia, Turkey, Austria, and Greece mounted on the wall of his office. Davis was a slender, severe-looking man of forty-six, and former senator from Mississippi. It appeared that the next great war was about to break out in central Asia. He intended to send military attachés to report from the area, so he could adapt the lessons to his own impending reorganization of the U.S. Army.

Davis planned to replace musketoons with rifles,

while tests with the latest breechloaders were underway in the Ordnance Department headed by Henry Craig. A pay raise was in store for all officers and men because one ex-soldier, Franklin Pierce, sat in the White House and another in the Department of War.

One of the most famous heroes of the Mexican war, Colonel Jefferson Davis, knew how victory crowns he who fights with fanatical fire. His favorite new project, which he kept secret from everyone except his wife, was an elite military unit. He didn't dare call it "elite" in public, because the rest of the Army would be jealous, and it would be commissioned with no special fanfare, as if it were just another regiment. He couldn't name it the First Cavalry, because *First* would imply special favor, so he intended to call it the Second Cavalry, with the best man in every slot. If most happened to be Southerners, so much the better. The former Colonel Davis could see that ultimately the slavery issue would be settled in blood, and he wanted the South to have as many advantages as possible.

His wife had told him that morning that their two-year-old son Samuel had been feverish during the night. It was a hot summer day and the father thought he might go home early for once, to see how the boy was doing.

He put on his jacket, for Jefferson Davis would never be seen in public without his jacket. Proceeding down the hall, he headed for the front door of the War Department.

He couldn't see well out of his left eye because it was covered with thin white mucus which doctors couldn't cure. His range of vision had narrowed and he couldn't spot the source of a voice calling out to him. "Secretary Davis, may I have a word with you?"

Jefferson Davis turned toward Colonel Barrington, whom he'd met at military functions over the years. Standing next to Barrington was a tall, beefy army officer wearing a short blond beard and holding a cane.

"May I present my son, Lieutenant Nathanial Barrington. He's stationed in New Mexico and this is his first trip East in six years."

Jefferson Davis noticed the clear expression in the younger officer's eyes. "What happened to your leg, Lieutenant Barrington?"

"Apache arrow, sir," said Nathanial matter-of-factly.

Jefferson Davis was one of the few Washingtonians who knew about the Apache Wars, because they fell within the purview of his duties. "It appears that you fellows have the situation pretty well in hand."

"I wouldn't go that far, sir. The largest and most warlike tribes are still on the loose."

Jefferson Davis took a step backward, as erect as if on the parade ground at West Point. "It's rare that I meet junior officers who actually fight the nation's battles. I'd like to speak with you more about Apaches, Lieutenant Barrington. Could you drop by my office tomorrow?"

"Yes, sir." Nathanial tossed off a smart West Point salute.

Jefferson Davis continued down the corridor, light from the front door outlining his body. Retired Colonel Barrington leaned toward his son and murmured, "Just what I was hoping for. You make a good impression on him tomorrow, you'll be getting your captain's bars before long."

* * *

Amalia Barrington sat in her study, reading *The New York Daily Times*. The first U.S. Consulate was under construction in Japan, following the Treaty of Kangawa signed in March by Commodore Matthew C. Perry. Amalia wondered about the strange exotic island nation whose emperor was descended from the sun and now had been forced at the point of guns to open his ports to the world.

There was a knock on her door, then Otis, her Negro footman, appeared. "Your mail, Mrs. Barrington. There's a letter on top from Santa Fe."

She appeared placid as Otis withdrew from the room. The moment the door latch clicked shut, she pounced on the letter. She'd been about to tear it open, when she realized the letter was addressed to "Lt. Nathanial Barrington," and the return address was a Santa Fe lawyer.

Amalia wondered what was in the letter, and of course would never, under any circumstances, tear it open and read the contents. Is he being sued? she wondered. Perhaps he's killed somebody and the lawyer wants to get paid for defending him. She wouldn't put anything past her firstborn son.

She carried the envelope to the kitchen, where her elderly maid, Shirley Rooney, was preparing supper. A kettle of boiling water sat on the stove, and Amalia casually held the envelope over the steam.

Shirley never said a word, although everyone in the household was curious about the mysterious letter. Gradually the wax softened and Amalia was able to open the envelope. Her eyes widened at the words:

Dear Lieutenant Barrington,

It is my unpleasant task to inform you that your wife, Maria Dolores Barrington, wishes to dissolve the union that presently exists between you.

Amalia stared at the document as Shirley and Otis read over her shoulder. Amalia had never seen her grandchildren, and it appeared she never would. Nathanial had been in trouble with women since his teens, and she wouldn't be surprised if he married an orangutang.

The door chimes went off, startling everyone. Otis rushed toward the vestibule to see who it was. A young blond woman stood on the doorstep, carrying a carpetbag. "I'm Clarissa Rowland and I'm here to see Mrs. Barrington."

"I'll tell her you're here, missy. Please have a seat and she'll be right with you."

Clarissa sat in the parlor and looked at paintings of distinguished Barrington ancestors. Then Amalia Barrington strolled into the room. "You're right on time, my dear. May we get you something?"

"I'd as soon get to work," replied the young woman.

She opened her carpetbag and took out her piano tuning tools. Then she opened the front of the piano, exposing hammers and strings. She sat at the keyboard, hit a few notes, then made adjustments with a wrench. When finished with one key, she tuned the next. "They lose their tension so easily," she explained. "You should have this done at least once a year."

"I love the piano," said Amalia wistfully, "but play so seldom now."

"I don't know what I'd do without music," replied Clarissa.

Amalia sat quietly and watched the young woman work. Clarissa was attired in a plain light blue cotton dress, no cosmetics or jewelry, and a navy blue ribbon held her blond hair. She appeared deeply concentrated and thoroughly professional, yet also had the air of an earnest child.

Amalia remembered when she'd been young, but then her husband betrayed her with other women, and she'd banished him from Washington Square. There'd been days when she'd thought of killing herself, but stayed her hand for the sake of her boys. Tears came to her eyes when she realized that once she'd been pretty like Clarissa Rowland.

When finished, Clarissa sat on the bench and played a selection from Franz Liszt's first Hungarian Rhapsody. She hit the last note triumphantly and said, "Perfect tune."

"You're so talented, and how lovely you are."

Clarissa looked at the floor, "I wish I could be a great lady like you, Mrs. Barrington, instead of the fool I sometimes am."

"Don't judge yourself too harshly, dear. There are plenty of others who'll do that for you."

"Isn't Nathanial supposed to arrive soon?"

"He's in Washington with his father."

"I've heard so much about him. My fiancé is one of his friends, and says he's the most wonderful person."

"Sometimes," said the mother. "And at other times he's been extremely thoughtless."

"Marriage generally makes men more mature, according to my mother. Maybe he's changed."

"Extremely doubtful," replied Amalia, the letter from Santa Fe in her hand.

In Santa Fe, Zachary Taylor Barrington was nearing the end of his patience. Nearly four years old, he constantly tried to be a good little boy, but gained no advantages.

He was playing with his sister while two maids on the far side of the nursery conversed about men. His mother was gone most of the time, his father had totally disappeared, and everybody was always saying how cute his sister was.

The more he tried to be good, the more he was ignored. If being good wasn't getting what he wanted, he picked up a vase of flowers in both little hands and waited for the reaction.

"Zachary—put that down!" shouted one of the maids.

He let it go, it crashed onto the floor, water splashed in all directions. Carmen looked up and smiled, because she copied everything her brother did. She grabbed one of his toy soldiers and threw it across the room. Zachary ran toward the bookcase and began pulling volumes onto the floor. The maids swooped down on him, but he wrestled, squirmed, and managed to punch one in the mouth. It wasn't a powerful blow, but without thinking she hauled off and delivered a backhander to the side of his head.

He went flying across the room, rose immediately, balled both fists, and charged the maid, who was three times his size. She'd either have to kill the determined boy or get the hell out of there. She chose the latter course, leaving the other maid alone with the children.

"You'd better behave yourselves," she said, looking at them from on high, wagging her exceptionally long finger.

Zachary kicked her in the shin, she wanted to strangle him, but instead said, "These children are impossible, and I quit!"

She too fled the room, to be replaced by other maids, who tried to mollify the children, giving them cake, cookies, and candy, as one maid ran for Maria Dolores.

Belinda awakened Nathanial at the crack of dawn. A pot of coffee sat on the dresser while a tub of hot water waited in the bathroom. He gulped coffee, soaked for a half hour, then dressed in his best uniform and inspected himself carefully in the mirror. He couldn't allow one hair or thread out of place in the meeting with Jefferson Davis.

The lieutenant climbed into a carriage waiting in front of the Emory Hotel. "The War Department," he called out to the driver, a dour man with a nose like a turnip.

Nathanial sat erectly in his seat, hands resting upon his cane. He passed consulates, legations, the offices of lawyers, the Bureau of Patents, the post office. On sidewalks, government clerks and officials raced about purposefully, while the nation sank deeper into chaos.

What America needs, thought Nathanial, is a strong man to hammer out a fair solution to the slavery situation. The lieutenant of dragoons had no idea what the resolution should be, but easily could imagine himself in General Scott's job as Commanding General of the Army, or even a senator, possibly the

President himself. I couldn't do any worse than Franklin Pierce, he mused.

The carriage stopped before the War Department, a two-story red brick edifice. I could even become military attaché to France, if I play my cards right, thought Nathanial, climbing the steps to the front door.

He entered the building and limped down the main corridor, reminding himself never under any circumstances to mention his antislavery sentiments to Jefferson Davis. I'd seal a bargain with the devil himself, if I could make captain.

He came to a sign that said:

SECRETARY OF WAR
Jefferson Davis

He knocked on the door; a sad-faced clerk opened it a few moments later. "May I help you, sir?"

"I'm Lieutenant Nathanial Barrington, First Dragoons. I have an appointment with Secretary Davis."

The clerk looked at the floor. "Evidently you haven't heard, sir. Secretary Davis's baby boy has died during the night, and he won't be in today, nor I suspect for a good many days to come."

Juh and Running Deer rode on the same horse across a mesa covered with paddle cactus and aloe vera bushes. The boy sat in front of the saddle, his head turning from side to side as he studied the terrain, his body loose against the belly of Juh.

Juh had more important duties to perform, but would do anything to return to the wickiup of his first wife, Jocita. He thought he could accomplish his goal more easily if he was kind to her son, so this was their first day together.

It touched Juh to know that the boy trusted him, although Juh occasionally felt like choking the little bastard. It had been a tremendous defeat when he'd learned of Jocita's infidelity.

Why do I love her? he often asked himself. But he'd been obsessed with Jocita since they were children growing up in the Sierra Madre Mountains. She'd always wanted to play with the boys instead of girls, and had been considered exceptional from an early age, like himself. They'd been destined to marry, but the mountain spirits had played a cruel trick on Juh. Jocita had been barren with him, but produced a son for the White Eyes war chief. Will it be worth it when she admits me to her wickiup? wondered Juh. Perhaps I love her too much, like a sickness.

They came to a region of thorns and weeds, dismounted, and Juh opened his saddlebags. The boy wrinkled his nose in distaste as Juh unwrapped a rotting chunk of beef. "Come with me," said Juh. "We are going to kill the lion."

Juh hobbled his horse, then plunged into the foliage on his hands and knees. The boy followed dutifully, although sharp thorns made red marks on his body. Finally they came to a small clearing. "If you want to catch the lion," taught Juh, "you need bait."

He lay the meat on a clump of gama grass, then withdrew, covering their tracks carefully. Finally they took positions behind a thick creosote bush. "You must be still," said Juh.

"What if the lion does not come?" asked the boy.

"Every hunt cannot be successful, but the lion

lives in this place and I have killed him here before. Ssshhh."

The boy had learned from his mother how to be still. He lay belly down, scanning from side to side as Juh examined him. *He thinks I am his father, and how strange if he succeeds me as chief of the Nednai.*

They lay side by side for a long time, the sun baking them and insects crawling over them, yet they refused to move. The sun rolled across the sky, shadows changed formation, the boy became thirsty, but had been taught to deprive himself. It felt good to be with his father, who was bigger and stronger than his mother, and a better warrior. The boy didn't understand his mother, but had no difficulty with his father. He felt honored to be with the great man.

Juh touched the boy gently with his elbow. Running Deer narrowed his eyes, then noticed a leaf trembling. A few moments later, the head of a great cat appeared cautiously. It snarled as it spotted the meat, showing long fangs, then his bloodshot eyes glanced back and forth. Running Deer felt the beam of the beast fall upon him, but didn't flinch. Then the lion advanced to the lump of meat, looked around once more, and lowered his head.

Juh silently drew back the bow, and the boy saw muscles standing out in his putative father's arms. Juh closed one eye and let fly. The lion dug his teeth into the meat as an arrow pierced his heart. In the midst of chewing, he fell to the ground.

Knife in hand, Juh approached carefully. "Stay where you are," he said to the boy. "He may still be alive."

A ribbon of blood rolled out of the lion's belly as

Juh dived onto him and cut his throat. The boy advanced as Juh skinned the animal with quick, sure strokes. "His fur is very soft," said Juh. "It will make a beautiful shirt for you, my son."

Running Deer's heart swelled with pride when he realized that his father was giving him a present! Juh peeled the last length of fur off the lion's back and held up the unblemished coat. The boy touched it thoughtfully as flies buzzed around the red carcass.

Juh placed the wet fur over the boy's shoulders, then stood and drew his arm across gleaming expanses of desert. "You are not an ordinary boy, but the son of a great war chief. One day you may succeed me as leader of the Nednai, and all this will be yours. I have felt this about you since you were in your mother's womb. You are one who shall transform the world!"

The words embedded themselves into the child's growing bones as his gleaming eyes opened wide. Paradise stretched before him, its rays bombarding his skin as lion power energized his soul. "All this will be mine," he whispered, holding out his little arms.

What does it matter if it's not true? wondered Juh as he led the boy back to the horse. *It is better for him to have great dreams, especially if they win me favor in the eyes of Jocita.*

Next day during the siesta hour, Cole Bannon lay in bed and pondered his future. *Do I really want to marry a woman who's richer than I?* he asked himself. He knew what the bullwhackers and vaqueros were saying behind his back, that he was Maria Dolores's lapdog.

Cole didn't like to take money from a woman, even if he worked hard for every penny. It wasn't easy to run a saloon, but she made the final decisions. It rankled to be placed in an inferior position to a woman, dependent upon her whims. It made him less attractive to himself.

The sun dipped toward the Jemez Mountains, time to return to the saloon. He sat in front of the window and pulled on his boots, then glanced out the window, surprised to see Maria Dolores approaching through the back alley in broad daylight. He was surprised to see her that time of day, because she worried about her reputation.

Then Cole noticed a soldier at the far end of the alley, as if he'd followed her. She entered the hotel; the soldier stopped cold, then turned and walked away. *I wonder if he's the strangler, or just a fool soldier wandering around?*

Cole was buttoning his shirt when she knocked on the door. He bade her enter, and she appeared agitated as she said, "I have been having terrible *problemas* with Zachary, and you must help me, Cole. I will increase your salary again if you manage *all* my businesses and investments for a few months. You are the only one smart enough to do it, because I must spend more time with my children."

"Did you notice anyone following you here?" he asked. "I saw a soldier in the alley just now."

She looked out the window. "Santa Fe is full of soldiers and I am even married to a soldier, but not much longer. My husband must have received the letter from my lawyer."

I hope not, thought Cole, less eager to marry a

woman with two brats. "Sure, I'll run your businesses for you, but I'll need help."

"Hire anybody you need, but no women prettier than I."

She reached for him; he didn't push her away. She was, after all, an extremely lovely woman, and he a lonely man. Together they sank to the mattress while removing each other's clothing.

Even in the throes of passion, she felt as if she was using his body. The mattress squealed in protest as they struggled to recapture the halcyon hours of their first encounter, but the past is gone forever.

Chapter Twelve

The train arrived in Jersey City on a hot July day. Nathanial paid a porter to transfer his bags to the ferry boat, then he and his slave boarded with other passengers.

Belinda gripped the rail and stared in amazement at the spectacle of New York City across the river. Sulphurous fumes arose from distant chimneys, as tall buildings gleamed dully in the summer haze. It looked far larger than Washington, D.C.

The ferry rumbled across the Hudson River, filled with high masted ships and paddle wheelers. Nathanial had a lump in his throat as he surveyed the city in which he'd been born. At the pier, an army of porters begged to carry luggage. Nathanial selected a big fellow with a wheelbarrow, then headed toward the row of two-horse hackney coaches waiting at the curb.

The luggage duly loaded, the driver flicked his reins. Murray Street was filled with wagons, coaches, riders on horseback, scarlet and yellow omnibuses, producing a percussion symphony on cobblestones, everyone in desperate haste.

The closer the coach advanced toward Broadway, the more the noisy dockside commercial district

gave way to fashionable shops and hotels. Now they
were nearing the heart of the city, Belinda's eyes like
saucers. She appeared overwhelmed as the coach
turned left on the most famous main artery in America.

Broadway was filled with conveyances of every
type, all inching toward their destinations. The noise
was deafening and Belinda was tempted to block her
ears, but didn't want to appear unsophisticated. They
passed luxury hotels, palatial restaurants, theaters,
and vast emporiums of fashionable clothing and jewelry.

Nathanial pointed to a large white building in the
midst of a vast lawn. "That's City Hall. And across
the street is where the newspapers are printed, on
Printery Row."

Never had she seen such pandemonium, and in
the midst of it all were ornate barouches and cabri-
olets transporting well-dressed and wealthy ladies on
shopping tours. That's the life I want, thought
Belinda.

They passed A. T. Stewart's famous store at the
corner of Chambers Street, facing Taylor's Restaurant, one of the finest in the city. On sidewalks, men
in suits carried satchels filled with documents, passing women ogling store windows. On the next corner, Nathanial spotted a ragged newsboy. "Stop the
carriage!" he ordered.

The driver pulled back his reins, Nathanial
jumped to the cobblestones, lost his balance, nearly
pitched onto his face, and landed in front of the
newsboy. He bought a *Tribune,* climbed back into
the coach, and eagerly read:

TERRIBLE ASSAULT
WITH A DEADLY WEAPON

Last Sunday night at a late hour, Andrew Hoffman, who keeps a lager beer shop at No. 127 Avenue A, was struck on the head with a club or stone in the hands of one James Morris, and injured in such a fearful manner that Death may result.

Hammering came to Nathanial's ears as he turned toward a new building under construction on Thomas Street. He realized that nothing had changed, people were killing each other as was customary in New York, buildings were being torn down and built up, and beautiful ladies entered or departed stores in unending streams.

He wondered if Layne Satterfield was still in town, and how many children she had. She'd been his first true love, they'd even been engaged, but Layne Satterfield decided to marry an Astor, and thus had ended the initial great romance of Nathanial's life.

The coach turned left on Waverly Place, they passed two- and three-story brick and stone residences, then came to Washington Square, an acre of grass and trees surrounded by homes on three sides, with the University of New York and the Reformed Dutch Church on its eastern border. "This is where I live," Nathanial said to Belinda.

Her ears still rang with the tumult of Broadway, the people had seemed mad, but Washington Square was serene, children played in the park, dogs daintily sniffed trees. The faint odor of rotting garbage was in the air as the sun beat down on America's largest city.

The coach came to a halt before a three-story mansion on the north side of the square. Nathanial helped Belinda to the ground, then unloaded the luggage, the driver making no effort to help. Nathanial paid him, then climbed the stairs and was about to knock when the door opened suddenly, revealing a wrinkled and stooped old lady, Shirley Rooney, his mother's maid.

"We've been a-waitin' fer you," she said, then screwed up her eyes and recognized the black woman standing next to Nathanial. At first the elderly woman appeared shocked, as if Nathanial had brought home a new scandal for the family.

"Shirley—this is my slave. Her name is Belinda."

The slave appeared well-mannered to Shirley's rheumy old eyes. Then a familiar voice came from the far end of the vestibule. "Your slave?" asked his mother.

Nathanial was shocked at how gray and wizened she'd become. My God—she's going to die soon, he realized as he limped toward her. They met in the middle of the corridor, and she was a scarecrow beneath her crisp tan summer dress. "May I present Belinda, whom I met in South Carolina. I'm going to set her free as soon as I speak with a lawyer."

The mother looked at her son askance, because he'd performed bizarre acts in the past, such as marrying a Mexican woman. "You're not having a love affair with her, I hope," she whispered into Nathanial's ear.

"How can you think such a thing?"

"You're limping. Oh, Nathanial, I do wish you'd be more careful."

A dark figure appeared in back of his mother, and Nathanial recognized Otis, another of his former slaves. The two men shook hands. "Glad to see you, sir," said Otis.

They'd been in Santa Fe last time they'd talked, Otis a raggedy-ass downtrodden slave, whereas now he seemed like a gentleman of means in his black suit. If it hadn't been for Nathanial, his owners would've sent him to the cotton fields of Georgia. "Do you think you can find a room for Belinda? She's come an awfully long way."

Otis and Belinda studied each other, then Otis lifted her bags and carried them to the servants' quarters. Shirley headed for the kitchen as Amalia led her son into the parlor. The mother was shaken by how much her son had aged, with a haunted expression in his eyes.

"Oh, there's a letter for you," she said. "I'll get it."

"Are my brothers home?"

"They're spending the summer on Cortlandt Lake."

She climbed the stairs to her sitting room while he dropped into his father's old easy chair. Above the fireplace hung a painting of Nathanial's great grandfather on his mother's side, in the uniform of the Continental Army. Nathanial gazed at familiar polished wood cabinets and plush furniture, but he missed the purple-and-orange mountains of New Mexico, with the fragrance of sagebrush in his nostrils. Is this my home, or that? he wondered.

His mother descended the stairs, holding out the letter. He looked at the return address, saw the name of a lawyer in Santa Fe, and murmured, "Uh-oh." His eyes widened as he read the first few lines, then refolded the letter and returned it to the envelope. "My wife is divorcing me, and I can't say it surprises me."

"I hope you're not planning to marry that Negress."

"Do you think I'm insane?"

"Sometimes I've had that thought, I admit, but now you're free to marry someone new, someone more appropriate to your station. I've never been able to understand exotic marriages, but I suppose they carry a certain novelty at the beginning."

"Is Layne Satterfield still around?"

"She has three children and I believe she's away for the summer. By the way, has anyone mentioned the cholera epidemic? Be careful what you eat and drink, because there were fifty-seven deaths last week, and the toll is climbing every day."

In the servant's quarters, Otis escorted Belinda to an empty room. "You can stay here," he said.

It was small, the walls covered with beige wallpaper. There was an oaken bed, a dresser and a chair.

"Did Nathanial buy you too?" she asked.

"Yes, but in those days he was drunk practically all the time. Where'd he find you?"

"South Carolina, and actually he hasn't bought me yet. I'm still a fugitive but he's going to buy me and my son."

"You'd better be careful when you go outside, because this city is full of slavecatchers. You might be able to get a job right here, 'cause old Miss Rooney is on her last legs, as you can plainly see." Otis winked. "These folks have got nothing but money, but they don't work you too hard. When I first came to New York, I didn't know what to make of it, but now I can read and write and I'm a free man. By the way, are you and Nathanial . . . ?"

He let the question hang in the air, but she knew what he was talking about. "No, he just felt sorry for me."

"Is he still drinking?"

"Yes."

"I don't understand why they didn't drum him out of the Army, and he even got into fights with his best friends." Otis looked into the hall to make sure no one was listening. "Everybody wants him to quit the Army, but he won't listen. If anything happened to Nathanial, it'd kill his mother. He's the strangest man I've ever known."

Belinda leaned against the doorjamb, thought about Nathanial for a few moments, and then said, "I agree."

Running Deer sat cross-legged near the fire, watching his mother making a bow. Many suns ago, she'd selected a branch of mulberry wood as long as two arrows, then stripped and rubbed it with horse grease, shaping it roughly into its final position. Then she let it dry for many more suns, followed by more rubbing and shaping. Now she strung the bow, tightening it to its final curvature. He watched avidly as she lay the bow upon hot coals.

Pungent smoke filled the air as the bow was hardened and purified. She flipped it with a stick and when satisfied that all excess liquid had been evaporated, removed it from the fire.

"Is it finished?" asked Running Deer.

"We must cure it for six suns, and then I will put on a new string. After that, we shall test it."

He smiled as he touched the still-warm bow. "I like it."

"Once you went on a raid with me, when you were in my belly, remember?" She leaned toward him, eyes gleaming mysteriously.

He vaguely recalled the shooting of arrows and guns, but it was buried far below. "A little."

She wrapped her arms around him. "You were a warrior before you were born, and you will be a warrior until you die. That is your sole destiny and you must never deny it."

He gazed at her wide-eyed. "Why are *you* a warrior, Mother? Not many other women are."

"The mountain spirits have offered a special gift, which I bequeathed to you. Don't ever let me hear of you planting seeds in the ground, like the *Nakai-yes* and the *Pindah-lickoyee*. Greatness will be yours if you cherish the holy Lifeway. But if you betray the mountain spirits, you will be cast down."

The boy pondered her words as footsteps approached the fire. It was Chief Juh, his father, one hand behind his back. "Is it the little warrior that I see?" the chief asked, a smile on his face.

The boy rose to his feet and said simply, "Yes."

Juh withdrew his arm from behind his back and showed a lion fur shirt. "Remember this?"

It was a simple garment with no sleeves, sewed up the sides with deer sinew. Juh helped the boy put it on, then took a step backward and observed him. "Perfect."

The boy felt lion emanations, as on the day they'd

hunted the beast. He touched his hand to the fur. "I like it."

"Go—show your friends."

The boy wandered off, leaving his mother and Juh at the fire. "You were kind," she said. "It makes me happy."

He dropped to one knee in front of her, peered into her eyes, and said, "When?"

She thought for a few moments. "Tonight."

"Where?"

"Not in front of the boy."

"In the desert then."

She lowered her eyes. "So be it."

In the alley, Private Fletcher Doakes stared across the yard at lights blazing in the Barrington home. He glanced both ways, then advanced stealthily, finally arriving at a window of the parlor. He removed his hat, peered around the sill, and saw her sitting on the floor, reading to her children.

Doakes wished he could join a real family, because his mother usually had been busy with men. He'd believed she didn't like him, and he'd spent most of his childhood sleeping. His father evidently had been a swine who made babies and then moved on.

Doakes smiled as he watched the beautiful woman with her children, both of whom appeared fascinated by the story. They'll grow up smart, thought Doakes. But I grew up stupid.

His eyes felt salty as he watched the mother hug her children. They squealed with delight, wriggling in her arms, covering her face with kisses. Doakes imagined himself being cuddled by the Spanish woman.

"Don't move!" said a voice behind him.

Doakes froze. He'd been caught looking into somebody's window! Frantically he searched for an alibi.

"I'm a Texas Ranger and I do believe you're the man I'm looking for. Raise your hands real slow. What's in your pockets?" The ranger took a few coins out of one and a dirty handkerchief from another. The culprit's right trouser pocket appeared empty, except Cole's fingers touched something unusual. He pulled out a length of cord.

Cole was certain he'd caught his strangler, while Doakes contemplated trying to take the gun away from him.

"What's this for?" asked Cole.

"Just a piece of string."

"What do you use it for?"

"You never can tell when you might need a piece of string."

"Especially if you want to strangle a prostitute?"

Doakes nearly choked, because it was the last thing he'd expected the ranger to say, while Cole saw the change of expression on his face.

"What's your name?" asked the ranger.

"Fletcher Doakes."

"That your real name?"

"Sure."

"Start walking to the jail, Fletcher Doakes, or I'll blow your head off."

Nathanial went to bed around midnight, but couldn't fall asleep on his first night in Manhattan. Finally, he decided to take a walk to Broadway. He rolled out of bed, selected a pair of light blue linen trousers, a white shirt, and a dark blue jacket.

He put on a pair of civilian shoes, but they were too tight so he had to wear army boots beneath his trousers. Then he made his way toward the stairs, where a door opened at the end of the hall. "Is that you, Nathanial?" asked his mother, standing wraith-like in moonlight.

"Thought I'd take a little walk."

"We're not going to do anything we'll be ashamed of, are we?"

"Of course not, Mother."

Washington Square was deserted except for a few derelicts and idlers sleeping on benches or among foliage. Nathanial walked east on Fourth Street, his path illuminated by gaslit lamps on poles, with additional light spilling from the odd tavern or oyster cellar.

Broadway was crowded with people and carriages when he arrived, for many New Yorkers venture outdoors only after the sun goes down. He came to the Saint Nicholas Hotel, a six-story white marble palace with lights blazing in windows, filling the block between Spring and Broome streets. On the next block, three pretty prostitutes approached. They gave him knowing looks as he and his cane drew closer, but he continued his nocturnal wandering. Suddenly, out of the night, he heard a voice say, "My God—it can't be."

A corpulent gentleman with a walrus mustache approached on the sidewalk as Nathanial recognized his old friend, Reginald van Zweiñen, scion of one of the city's prosperous old Dutch families.

"How long have you been in town?" asked Reginald, leaning first to the left and then to the right.

"Just arrived a few hours ago. Where are you going?"

"To meet some friends. Why don't you come along? You look as if you've been hurt."

Before Nathanial could escape, Reginald dragged him down a flight of stairs into a small subterranean room crammed with diners. The fragrance of roasted or fried oysters filled the air, overlaid with lager beer. A circular table lurked in a corner, surrounded by gentlemen and ladies engaged in noisy discussion, empty plates of oysters before them, and everyone had his or her mug of beer handy.

"Make way," growled Reginald as he dragged two empty chairs to the table. "Ladies and gentleman, may I present an old friend, Nathanial Barrington, recently returned to New York from . . . where?"

"New Mexico," replied Nathanial.

Reginald introduced his friends as waiters carried trays of roast oysters, fried oysters, oyster stew, oyster on the half shell, and mugs of beer past them. Raucous conversation reverberated off walls as a couple in a corner shared a brief but affectionate kiss.

"What's New Mexico like?" asked an unusually handsome dark-haired man sitting on the far side of the table, his arm around the shoulder of a red-headed woman who smoked a cheroot and wore a dress that revealed the upper portion of her breasts.

Nathanial found himself staring at those two tempting melons. "Mountains and semiarid plains," he replied. "Not much population."

"Is the frontier as lawless as we've heard?"

"Worse."

The waiter arrived, Nathanial ordered roast oysters and a mug of beer. Conversation returned to its former din, individuals hollering at each other across the table in order to be heard. Reginald turned toward Nathanial and said, "I've never been able to understand how an intelligent man could remain in the Army."

"Are you still drama critic for the *Post*?"

"Do you think actresses would look at me if I weren't? This isn't a position one gives up easily."

Nathanial found his eyes drawn repeatedly to the redhead sitting on the far side of the table. She'd been introduced as Patricia, and he assumed she was a theatrical lady who found life on the boards amenable to her loose living habits and virtually nonexistent morals. They pretended to be sisters of the footlights, but would step over each other's dead bodies to win a cherished role.

Patricia leaned toward Nathanial and stage-whispered across the table, "You look as if you don't know where you are."

"I've been away six years."

"I've always wanted to go West, but they say living conditions are quite primitive."

"Are you in a play that I should know about?"

"Only a small role in *Old Heads and Young Hearts* at Wallack's Theatre."

"I'm sure you light up the stage."

"You're very kind," she said in an offhand way, as if accustomed to compliments.

The gentleman to her left sought to engage her in conversation, and Nathanial figured he was protecting what he considered his property. The waiter arrived with a plate of oysters sizzling in butter, with fried potatoes, two fat slices of white bread, and a mug of beer.

Nathanial proceeded to consume the meal as he studied his companions. Patricia was engaged in hushed disagreement with her boyfriend, while the others ignored them, absorbed in their own cacophony of opinions. Then suddenly Patricia's boyfriend curtly excused himself and left the oyster cellar. "I don't know why you bring him around," said one of the other actresses. "He's such a bore."

"He has his uses," replied Patricia.

He probably pays the rent, thought Nathanial. The chair beside her now was vacant. Without hesitation or doubt, Nathanial carried his plate to her side. "Mind if I sit down?"

Across the table, a dark-haired woman with golden earrings said in a tone of amusement, "An army officer doesn't waste time, I see."

Nathanial resumed his meal as Patricia watched him with an flirtatious smile. "Do you know any Indians?" she asked.

"A few."

"Are they as bloodthirsty as I've been told?"

"Killing white people is their favorite pastime."

She leaned toward him and asked, "Have you ever slept with an Indian woman."

"Once," Nathanial admitted. "Perhaps you'd like me to demonstrate later, purely in the spirit of scientific discovery, of course."

She leaned closer and whispered into his ear, "I've often wondered what it was like to be an Indian."

Suddenly the door of the oyster house was flung open. Her paramour returned, the one she'd expelled only minutes ago, but now he wore an angry expression. "So!" he said as he arrived at the table, pointing at her. "I can see you've found your next fool, eh?"

Nathanial rose unsteadily, his belly full of oysters and beer. He couldn't let anyone talk like that to a lady, even if every word was probably true. "I think you'd better walk on out of here," he growled.

The rejected lover's eyes widened. "Who do you think you're talking to?"

"You," replied Nathanial.

Suddenly the oyster cellar became very still. Nathanial realized too late that he wasn't in Santa Fe anymore.

The threatened gentleman tried to smile. "You're not planning to fight me, are you?"

"Up to you."

"But you can barely walk."

"Leave the lady alone."

"What lady?"

A greasy frying pan came down onto the gentleman's head from behind, and he collapsed to the floor. Standing behind him was a cook in a white jacket. He and the Negro dishwasher grabbed the gentleman and dragged him toward the back door. Diners looked at each other curiously for a few moments as Nathanial returned to his seat. Conversation soon returned to its previous volume, because New York night owls are the most jaded in the world.

"Where are you going?" asked Ish-keh.

"To look at the horses," replied Juh.

"You are not fooling me. You are going to see *her*."

"Quiet, woman."

Juh crawled out of his wickiup, then glanced around the encampment to make sure no enemies

were about. He headed for the chaparral, aware that
Ish-keh knew precisely what he was up to. Let her
nag, he thought. I don't care.

He was willing to endure anything if he could get
his hands on Jocita again. He paused at the edge of
the encampment, then continued into the wilderness. Trying not to think of Ish-keh, he knew she
would insult him intensively in days to come. He
was destablizing his domestic life but would worry
about that some other time.

His legs felt enlivened as he made his way toward
the agreed meeting place. He thought of Jocita
writhing naked in his arms and nearly fainted with
desire. What if she doesn't come? he thought. I will
kill her if she disappoints me.

Silently he moved through the wilderness, musket
in hand. A coyote sang mournfully in a far-off cave
as a bat flew across the face of the full moon. Juh
came to a grove of cottonwood trees, where Jocita sat
at the side of a stream.

"You are late," she said.

He kneeled in front of her. "I have dreamed about
this moment."

So had she, but never could admit it. Instead, she
had to appear that she was disinterested. "I want to
show my gratitude for what you have done with Run-,
ning Deer."

"I will give him a lion shirt every day to please
you."

"Be his father, Juh, that's all I want."

"What do I get?"

She reached to the hem of her deerskin shirt.
"Me."

She pulled it off, then he gazed at those rich

breasts denied him for so long. He pressed his lips against them as she reclined on the ground. "At last," he whispered.

She felt his muscular body against her and no longer could pretend disinterest. She hated him and loved him at the same time as she sank her teeth into his shoulder.

"Easy," he said.

They clutched each other desperately, tearing at each other's clothing. They wrestled to determine the top position, but he defeated her easily, pinning her wrists to the ground.

He was her first lover since the bluecoat officer, and it was all she could do to prevent herself from shrieking with joy. They rolled into the stream during their exertions, but not even frigid mountain water could stop them.

Chapter Thirteen

Nathanial awakened at noon, and at first thought he was with his wife in Santa Fe. An arm lay across his chest as Patricia snored softly into the pillow. The frontier officer opened his eyes on a small room with three dolls sitting on the dresser, looking at him dolefully as carriages rolled past in the street outside. It had been an educational night for both, but he needed to see his lawyer. Gently he removed her arm from his chest and rolled out of bed.

"Where are you going?" she asked, one eye half open.

"I have business."

"So early?"

He dressed, smoothed his hair in front of the mirror. She'd fallen asleep again, the sheet dropped from her shoulders, exposing nipples big as twenty-dollar silver coins. He kissed one of them, and said, "Bye."

She barely stirred. He placed money on the dresser, and with one last glance at his sleeping beauty, was out the door.

She lived on Rivington Street, not far from the Bowery. He jumped into the first empty coach he could find, then told the driver to take him to the corner of Pine and Pearl. Why get married? he asked himself as he rode down the colorful Bowery. It's so much easier this way.

He bought a *New York Daily Times* from a corner newsboy, and on the front page, he read:

IDIOTS AND THEIR INSTRUCTION

The number of idiots or feebleminded people in the United States is much greater than previously supposed. The census of 1850 provided (for the first time) for the enumeration of idiotic persons, and the number reported was 15,787.

Is this why America can't settle the slavery issue? he asked himself. We've got too many idiots? He laughed at his little joke as his coach came to a halt at a gray stone building. He climbed to the law offices of Soames and Soames, where a clerk led him to a door at the end of the corridor. "He's waiting for you, sir."

Nathanial found his old friend Ronald Soames sitting behind the desk, studying a legal brief. Soames glanced up and presented the old familiar dimpled chin, black mustache, bushy eyebrows. "Nathanial, old boy—it's great to see you. I've just received an invitation from your mother, by the way."

Nathanial was taken by surprise. "An invitation to what?"

"A party for you at Cortlandt Lake. Haven't you heard about it?"

"I'm sure my mother intends to tell me. What's new?"

"I'm getting married to a wonderful woman who plays the piano like an angel. A man can only pursue tarts for so long, and then it becomes a chore, wouldn't you say?"

"That's exactly what I've come to talk with you about." Nathanial reached inside his jacket and pulled out an envelope. "It appears that my dear wife wants to divorce me."

Soames accepted the document, adjusted his eyeglasses on his long thin nose, and made strange murmuring noises as he read. "It's all perfectly straightforward. What would you like to do?"

"If she wants the divorce, she can have it."

"What about your children?"

"She can have them too."

"What about property?"

"Anything she wants."

"You're certainly an easy client to represent. Any other problems?"

"I'd like to buy a couple of slaves, so I can set them free."

Soames appeared surprised. "Where are these slaves now?"

"One is in New York, the other in South Carolina. The one in New York is technically a fugitive."

"In other words, you've more or less stolen him."

"*Her.*"

Soames widened his eyes. "What does she look like?"

"Absolutely beautiful."

"Are you . . ."

"Of course not."

"I hope you don't intend to marry her!"

"What if I did?"

"I'll have to look at the statutes. Buy why destroy your reputation for a woman? I mean—there are so many of them. In fact, I'll bring several likely prospects to your party, all well-bred, each a certified virgin."

"It's too soon to get married again. For God's sake, I'm not even divorced."

"My advice is find a well-behaved youngish woman, and if she plays a musical instrument, so much the better."

"We'll see if you sing the same tune after five years with Miss Whatever-Her-Name-Is."

"You're bitter, Nathanial. Do you really shoot at Indians, and they shoot at you?"

"Sometimes."

"What a strange profession," sniffed Soames.

At dawn, Fletcher Doakes wondered if they were going to hang him or merely put him before a firing squad. He'd read about townspeople breaking into jails, taking out prisoners, and literally tearing them to pieces. Doakes broke into a cold sweat as he contemplated possible dismemberment.

The next cell contained a drunkard asleep on a cot, while farther down the row a burglar paced back and forth nervously. A door opened, then footsteps approached. A civilian wearing a green suit and black string tie came into view, with a deputy sheriff sporting a tin badge pinned to the front of his indigo canvas shirt. "That's him right there," said the deputy, pointing toward Doakes.

The civilian grinned, showing tobacco-stained teeth. He had a bald pate, long, scraggly gray hair hanging over his ears, and was built like a cadaver. "My name's Chester Lovey," he said to Doakes. "I'm your lawyer."

"But I can't afford a lawyer," sputtered Doakes.

"You'll find money someplace, otherwise you'll hang. What's your side of the story?"

"I don't know."

"You're on trial for your life, Doakes. Make no mistake about that. You'd better come up with the right answers." The lawyer winked.

Is he asking me to lie? thought Doakes. Why the hell not. With renewed hope, he testified, "I was just walking along, minding my own business, and some loco son of a bitch threw me against a wall, told me I was under arrest and walked me to jail. Hell, I'm an innocent man."

"And a soldier too. Serving your country with distinction, I'm happy to note. What else happened?"

"I carry a piece of cord in my pocket, because we often have to tie things together in the Army."

The lawyer read the affidavit. "The Ranger said it's the murder weapon."

"Who am I supposed to've killed?"

"About ten women."

Doakes appeared surprised. "Why would I do such a thing?"

"You ever see the Ranger afore?"

"He's the manager of the Silver Palace Saloon."

"You have any arguments with him?"

"Never talked to him in my life."

The lawyer smiled, his breath like a dead gopher's. "When I get finished with that Texas Ranger, he'll wish he was never born."

The preliminary hearing was held at ten o'clock in the chambers of Judge Henry Hoskins, a bony, dour man with deepset eyes. He sat at his desk and read charges against Fletcher Doakes as the lawyer of record and arresting officer stood before him.

Judge Hoskins suffered from a stomach ailment that made him irritable. "What's this about?" he asked.

"It's nonsense," replied lawyer Lovey indignantly. "An honest American soldier was taking a walk, and this Texas Ranger arrested him for the murder of ten women. Can you imagine?" Lovey made it sound like the most preposterous notion in the world.

"Your Honor," replied Cole Bannon, "I have reason to believe that Fletcher Doakes has killed prostitutes all over Texas and New Mexico. And he wasn't just taking a walk, as this lying lawyer said. He was looking through a window at a certain woman, and if I hadn't come upon him, no telling what might've happened. Moreover, all his victims were strangled with a thin cord, and I found a length in his pocket. I realize it's circumstantial evidence, but it seems pretty solid to me."

"Solid?" asked the lawyer, an expression of astonishment on his face. He reached into his pocket and withdrew a length of cord similar to the one Cole had confiscated. "What's wrong with carrying a length of twine? Even I do it because you never know when you might need to fix a harness, or make a splint on a broken bone. Your Honor, there is no merit whatever to these charges, and this Texas Ranger obviously is as ignorant of the law as a mule. If that's not enough, he manages saloons when he's not arresting innocent citizens on trumped-up charges."

The judge turned to Cole. "What's your side of it?"

"I saw him following the lady in question once before, Your Honor, and the man committing these crimes is the sort who follows women and kills them."

The lawyer raised his finger in the air. "Only prostitutes, not decent married ladies like your friend, Mrs. Nathanial Barrington, the woman with whom you are consorting, isn't that correct?"

Cole became flustered. "She's my boss."

"Don't you cohabit with her from time to time?"

"What does that have to do with it?"

"Perhaps you fear a rival in Private Fletcher Doakes?"

"A rival!" exploded Cole. "I have no . . ." He realized that he was losing control, so he struggled to settle himself down. "What about those dead prostitutes?"

The lawyer faced the judge. "Your Honor, I've been in every whoop and holler west of the Pecos, and so have you. You and I know that these women are getting kilt all the time, sometimes by their husbands and boyfriends, other times by customers or even each other. What makes this ranger here think it's all the same man? He has no evidence, no testimony, no nothin'. I think this case should be dismissed."

The judge turned to Cole Bannon. "This is New Mexico Territory, and next time you arrest somebody in these parts—you'd better have proof. Case dismissed."

The coach came to a halt before a three-story stone residence on Washington Square. Nathanial told the driver, "Wait for me—I'm moving some things to the Saint Nicholas Hotel."

Nathanial nearly fell out of the coach, climbed the

steps, and the door was opened by Otis, his former slave. "We thought you'd been hurt, sir."

"I know how to take care of myself, Otis. How can you doubt me?"

A tall, spectral figure stood at the end of the vestibule. "What are you two plotting?" asked Amalia Barrington.

Nathanial kissed his mother on the cheek. "Sorry I stayed out late, but I ran into a friend."

"What was her name?" she asked, furrowing her aquiline nose in distaste at the perfume on his clothing.

Nathanial looked into her eyes. "My dear mother, I'm a grown man and I don't need to account for my activities to anyone."

"You will as long as you're living in this house."

"That's why I'm moving into a hotel."

Nathanial packed his clothes, then Otis helped him carry the luggage downstairs, where his mother was waiting. "I disapprove of your behavior," she said coldly.

"Mother, there's something I've always wanted to ask you. What makes your opinions the standard for the world?"

"Because they are. By the way, I'm having a party for you at Cortlandt Lake next Saturday night. I expect you to be sober, do you understand?"

He traveled to the Saint Nicholas Hotel, where he booked a suite of rooms on the top floor. He hadn't eaten all day, so he went down to the dining room, which was shaped like an oval, with murals and maroon draperies providing a frame for busy Broadway. The waiter led him to a table near the middle of the floor. Nathanial sat and studied the menu.

"Anything to drink, sir?" asked the waiter.

Nathanial was about to request whiskey, but he'd been drinking whiskey for six years. "What do you recommend?"

"Many prefer gin slings this time of year, sir."

"That's what I'll have, plus the leek soup, broiled haddock, and mashed potatoes with beef gravy, stewed beets plus a bit of steamed broccoli."

"Right away, sir."

Nathanial's mouth watered in anticipation of his feast, for the Army didn't offer many fresh vegetables, and salt water fish was unheard of in New Mexico Territory. While waiting for the food and drink to arrive, Nathanial opened his *Tribune*.

He discovered that the red weevil was destroying wheat in western Virginia, there was a revolution in Nicaragua, and anti-Nebraska rallies had been held in Ohio and Illinois. Twenty-three citizens had died of cholera the previous week, but Horace Greeley advised New Yorkers they'd be safe if they avoided "gross inpudence of eating and drinking."

"Your gin sling, sir."

Nathanial sipped the cold fruity beverage. It was difficult to imagine that alcohol had been included except for an odd warm sensation as the mixture descended his parched throat. It tasted so delicious he polished off the glass before he knew it, but a waiter was on hand to take his order for another.

Across the dining room, Myra Rowland glanced up from her blueberry pie and stared a few moments. "If I'm not mistaken," she said, "that's Nathanial Barrington."

Clarissa Rowland was seated opposite her mother, enjoying a slice of chocolate cake. She saw a well-tailored, wide-shouldered man in a short blond beard trying to read the paper and eat soup at the same time. "He looks funny."

"He's a disgrace, but quite a few women were head over heels in love with him when he lived here. They say his mother turned him out of the house one Christmas because of his drinking."

"It sounds like a story that everybody believes, but never really happened."

"His downfall supposedly was a certain woman. To forget her, he volunteered for frontier duty. According to his mother, he was nearly killed by Indians on numerous occasions, then he married a Mexican woman, but now she's divorcing him. Every mother's worst fear is that her daughter will run off with an amiable drunkard like Nathanial Barrington. Fortunately, that hasn't happened to you, my dear. You've always been so sensible."

Every time Doakes heard a loud sound in the street he thought the mob was coming for him. His tail appeared longer as it thrashed from side to side on the floor. He was growing whiskers and his ears felt pointed.

I'm becoming a rat, he realized as he sniffed with his tiny upturned nose. Mother, how disappointed you must have been when you received a rat for a son, not a pretty baby. Perhaps you thought God played a trick on you, but He really played it on the rest of the world.

The door to the jail opened and Doakes jumped to his feet. A jailer approached, accompanied by Lawyer Lovey puffing a cigar and grinning.

"I got you off scot free," said the lawyer in his nasal twang. "I'm surprised the judge didn't make that ranger get down on his knees and apologize."

Lovely laughed as the jailer unlocked the door. Dazed, the rat followed his lawyer to the street. "Good luck to you, Doakes," said the lawyer, shaking his hand, "and by the way—you owe me ten dollars."

"I only earn eight dollars a month."

"A few dollars every now and again will be fine till the debt is paid." The lawyer leaned closer to Doakes, narrowed an eye, and asked softly. "Did you really kill them whores, soldier?"

"Course not, sir."

The lawyer laughed derisively, then puffed his cigar and strolled away as Doakes blinked in the bright light of midday. He thought about stealing a horse and fleeing to Tucson, but the ranger would be hot on his trail. *I've got to go back to Fort Marcy, but I haven't done anything wrong. I'm only the victim of an ambitious Texas Ranger.*

Fletcher Doakes sauntered toward the post, wondering if the word had gotten around that he'd been caught peeking into a lady's home, but he had his alibi worked out, thanks to the assistance of his lawyer.

Doakes had learned a valuable lesson during his incarceration. He wasn't the only liar in the world, and not the best by any means. He entered the orderly room and found Sergeant Berwick behind his desk. "Guess what happened to me, Sarge?"

"You got arrested," growled the first sergeant. "What'd you do?"

"Some crazy Texas Ranger hauled me in when I was taking a walk. Son of a bitch must be crazy. Anyway, the judge let me go. He said the case was so dumb, there wouldn't even be a trial."

"I heard you was lookin' into some woman's window."

"It's all in the ranger's mind because he's screwin' her. I heard she's an officer's wife. Name's Barrington."

"When the cat's away, the mice'll play. Anyways, there's a pile of work accumulating on your desk. You might as well get started."

I've just got away with murder, thought Doakes with satisfaction as he sat upon his chair.

After the hearing, Cole Bannon returned to the Silver Palace Saloon, walked to the bar, and said, "Whiskey."

The bartender was surprised because Cole seldom drank on the job. The Texas Ranger carried the full glass to an empty booth against the side wall, sat heavily, and drank half in one solid gulp.

It hit his guts like a cannonball, just what he needed to slow him down. Why am I so inarticulate? he wondered. That lawyer made me look like a fool, and nobody cares about strangled old prostitutes.

Cole was certain Doakes had committed the murders. At least I've thrown a scare into him, and maybe he won't kill for a while. If he deserts the Army, I'll follow wherever he goes. He fooled the judge, but he hasn't fooled me.

The Texas Ranger continued to drink during the rest of the day, wishing there was a way to let off steam. After supper, an army sergeant walked toward his table. "Are you Cole Bannon?"

"So what if I am," growled the Texas Ranger.

It was Sergeant Berwick and he too had imbibed a few whiskeys. He was annoyed by the extra work he'd been forced to do while his clerk was in jail. "You arrested one of my men on trumped-up charges, that's what. A man can't take a walk without some-body comin' down on him. Who the hell do you think you are?"

"Pass on," said the ranger in an ominous tone.

"You're nothin' but a glorified bartender and a fancy man."

Cole Bannon exploded out of his booth as Sergeant Berwick flung a stiff left jab. It glanced off Cole Bannon's forehead, but the ranger kept coming, bringing a left jab with him. It landed on the front of Berwick's noggin, whereupon the sergeant responded with a right hook to the ranger's liver.

Cole seemed to fold, the sergeant prepared to fin-ish him with an uppercut, but unfortunately had opened his right side. Cole hit him with another hook, then caught him on the mouth with an over-hand right.

It connected on the sergeant's nose, which crunched beneath the ranger's knuckles. Berwick went stumbling backward, tripped over a cuspidor, and fell on his butt.

Soldiers saw the sergeant sprawled semiconscious on the floor. Shame came over him, so he reached for the nearest bottle, smashed it onto a table, and came up with the jagged edge.

From his boot, Cole Bannon deftly withdrew a Comanche knife with a seven-inch blade. Both men stared at each other, the ante just raised dramatically. They realized that perhaps they'd let things get out of hand, but a man can't back down in front of an au-dience. The two combatants circled each other war-ily, searching for openings and wishing they'd gone to bed. Each knew he might die in the moments to come, over nothing at all.

"That'll be enough!" shouted a raucous fellow plowing through the crowd. It was Sheriff Roger Boneham, a Colt .36 Navy Model in his right hand, his mustache twitching with determination. "Drop them weapons!"

A knife clanged to the floor, followed by the crash of a bottle. The sergeant and Texas Ranger heaved sighs of relief as the sheriff marched them to jail.

Clarissa Rowland sat at the piano in her home and played Mozart's 41st Sonata in E-flat minor. The mellifluous sounds transported her to Austria, and she imagined herself a Hapsburg princess sitting in a castle on the Rhine. She practiced piano not out of obligation, but she loved music deeply. It elevated her to heavenly spheres and made her feel she was more than an awkward and inexperienced young woman.

She was content to make music, and her upcoming marriage would permit her to continue its study. There was talk of her performing in public, although she didn't think she was ready.

Sometimes, while playing the piano, she experienced fantastical conceptions. She recalled the notorious Nathanial Barrington downing one gin sling after another in the Saint Nicholas dining room as he consumed what had appeared a prodigious amount of food and read the newspaper front to back.

She was destined to meet the culprit, for her family had been invited to the party at Cortlandt Lake. She and her mother planned to depart New York tomorrow for their cottage in the Hudson highlands. Clarissa looked forward to riding her horse and listening to the music of the forest.

Everything was sound to Clarissa Rowland, and she believed every person gave off a musical aura. A mysterious tune had come to her across the potatoes and squash in the Saint Nicholas dining room, and she was curious to hear it again. Just because I'm getting married, it doesn't mean I can't talk with interesting people, she advised herself. Marriage isn't prison, I don't think.

Sheriff Boneham locked Sergeant Berwick into a cell on one side of the jail, and Cole Bannon across the corridor in another. "Do you remember that soldier you arrested?" the sheriff asked Bannon. "This was the cell he occupied, and now you're in it. It has a certain logic, wouldn't you say?"

The sheriff chortled as he departed the cell block. Cole Bannon and the sergeant stood behind bars and glowered at each other. "Stupid son of a bitch," muttered the sergeant.

"Birdbrain," replied Cole Bannon.

It was embarrassing for a Texas Ranger to end in jail, caught in the act of trying to stab someone. Cole cursed his bad temper and other shortcomings, but most of all cursed Sergeant Berwick. The disgraced ranger sat heavily on his wood cot, no mattress. "A killer is walking around free and nobody gives a damn."

"You arrested a man fer takin' a walk," replied Sergeant Berwick. "You probably want to put half the population in jail."

"How well do you know Doakes?" asked Cole.

"Well enough to know he's innocent."

"He showed up in Santa Fe about two months ago, so you can't know him that well, idiot. If he killed those women, you don't think he'd tell you."

"But you can't arrest a man for nothin'," protested Sergeant Berwick.

"I saw him looking into a woman's window. Maybe I can't prove it to you, but I know what I saw. What can you tell me about him?"

Sergeant Berwick shrugged. "He's a good worker, minds his business."

"Where's he from?"

"Someplace out East. Hell, I don't know anything about most of the soldiers, but that don't mean they're all criminals. Besides, if he's killin' so many women, why haven't I read it in the papers?"

"Like I said, nobody cares about whores. I wonder what they ever did to him? He talk about women much?"

"Never."

"When I was in the Army, that's all the men talked about."

Sergeant Berwick knew that women were the main topic of barracks conversation, and now that he thought of it, it was odd that Doakes never said anything. "Maybe I'll ask him sometimes."

"I'm sorry I punched you, but this case has got me baffled. If you care about dead women, why don't you see if you can dig up some information on Doakes? Maybe he's innocent, but it wouldn't hurt to be sure."

"I'll think it over," replied the sergeant, "but now I want to sleep."

Cole stepped to the rear of his cell and looked out

the barred back window at privies, sheds, and barrels of trash in the backyard. He wished he had a cigarette, but the sheriff had taken his personal belongings. He lay on the hard cot, placed his hands behind his head, and wondered if it would be possible to sleep.

He noticed a message carved into the adobe wall next to the cot. Sitting upright, he tried to read it in the dim moonlight filtering through the window. It had been carved with a sharp object, possibly a belt buckle, and declared:

I AM THE SCOURGE OF GOD

Chapter Fourteen

Nathanial selected a russet gelding with lean Arabian lines at the stable of his Uncle Jasper, then tied a bedroll behind the saddle. The saddlebags contained cheese, wine, and bread, courtesy of the Saint Nicholas dining room. Nathanial was on his way to Cortlandt Lake in the far northern reaches of Westchester County, where the party in his honor would be held Saturday night.

He rode up Fifth Avenue, lined with extravagant mansions and private clubs. The grid pattern ended in the fifties, then Nathanial came to squatters' shacks, bone boiling works, swill mills, and hog farms. He steered his horse left to the Bloomingdale Road, which was the upper extension of Broadway, and rode it past farms to the Harlem River, where he crossed the bridge into Westchester County.

He thought it delightful to travel through lush wilderness without fear of a stray arrow from the bow of an Apache. He'd been a frontier officer so long, he'd forgotten how pleasant civilian life could be. There's something to be said for resigning my commission, he thought.

Through branches and leaves he made out the Hudson River, then the Jersey palisades came into view. He brought his horse to a halt, sat at the base of a tree, and watched sailboats and paddle wheelers traveling the mighty river.

He wondered how it had looked to Henry Hudson when that great navigator first sailed by in 1609. Possibly an Algonquin Indian sat on this very spot and watched the passage of that ship, thought Nathanial.

The warm summer sun created an emerald haze while the blue waters flowed steadily to sea. Nathanial saw the relentless passage of history, the transformations of lives and continents, while the river itself offered no judgment.

His sharp frontier officer's eyes detected movement to his right. Another rider came into view a hundred yards away, on a sunny patch of moss and ferns. The rider stepped down from his horse, then looked around suspiciously. He had blond hair, stood with his hands on his hips, and stared at the river for a long time.

Nathanial felt like a voyeur, but didn't want to disturb the other fellow's meditation. Then, with his back to Nathanial, the rider removed his shirt. He turned around, and Nathanial was shocked to realize that the rider was a woman in man's clothing!

She arranged her shirt upon the ground, then lay upon it, to sun herself. Silently, as if Apaches were in the vicinity, Nathanial returned to his horse, removed his brass spyglass from a saddlebag, focused upon his quarry, and his heart quickened as he saw two smallish breasts standing straight up, blond hair cascading about her head. A nymph of the woods, he thought, licking his chops. He'd spent the previous night with Patricia, but the girl with bare breasts shook him to the depths of his being, perhaps because she imagined she was alone.

Nathanial realized that he was salivating like a hound dog. He felt ashamed of himself as he led his horse away from the clearing. There are some splendors a man should never see, especially if they encourage conduct unbefitting an officer.

Wickiups stood empty and abandoned as Mimbrenos packed their few belongings onto horses and mules. One faction, under Mangas Coloradas and Victorio, would head west toward the Chiricahua Mountains, while the rest would follow Cuchillo Negro to Fort Thorn, where they'd try to live in peace with the *Pindah-lickoyee*.

There was much embracing and crying, for families were coming to the parting of the ways. Brother was separated from father and daughter from sister. It was a great tragedy for the People, but no one could reconcile opposite positions.

Finally the time came to move on. Cuchillo Negro and Mangas Coloradas embraced, for they'd been friends and warrior brothers practically all their lives. There was nothing more to discuss, for the fine points of disagreement had been debated in council many times. Cuchillo Negro believed in peace, while Mangas Coloradas knew it was impossible.

A red-tailed hawk floating on updrafts watched the strange spectacle below, as a group of two-leggeds split in half, one headed toward the land where the sun arose, the other to where it set. At the head of the Western group, Victorio rode beside Mangas Coloradas. The subchief's heart was heavy, for he knew that the people were weakened by the loss of Cuchillo Negro's band.

"Do not despair," said Mangas Coloradas, lifting his great mane of gray hair. "The People will survive this."

Victorio stiffened his spine and held his chin higher. "I fear a terrible outcome for Cuchillo Negro. His heart is for peace, but the White Eyes are murderers."

"The White Eyes have not yet invaded the Chiricahua Mountains, and perhaps never will. But if they do, the combined warriors of the Chiricahuas and Mimbrenos surely will stop them. I have seen it in dreams."

"Do we defeat them, great chief?"

"That I was not permitted to see."

Mangas Coloradas and his foremost disciple rode side by side, the mountain breeze cool on their bare chests as the Mimbrenos retreated from the land promised them by their gods.

Cortlandt Lake was a mile long and a half mile wide, fed by streams and springs, owned by the Rutherford family. Several members had built elaborate log cottages on cliffs overlooking the lake, while other cottages were at the water's edge.

It was late afternoon when Nathanial arrived at Uncle Jasper's compound. He'd spent summers here as a child, learning to swim, playing soldier among elm and maple trees, and paddling an old Algonquin canoe.

A wiser Nathanial left his horse with a servant, slung his saddlebags over his shoulder, and headed for his mother's cottage. Well-rested and stone cold sober, Nathanial intended to continue healing amid the balm of green leaves and clear lake water.

The front door of the cottage opened, then two young men appeared on the porch. Nathanial wondered whether they were servants, but was jolted by the realization that they were his brothers! He stopped in his tracks, while they stared at him as if he were an apparition, for this was their heroic older brother who'd fought in the Mexican War, the idol of their young lives.

Nathanial shook hands with both of them, then lied, "I've thought of you often. I trust you're doing well in school?" He cocked an eye, like the commanding general before his stripling brothers.

"I've applied to West Point," blurted out Jeffrey, a hale and hearty lad of sixteen, with curly blond hair. "Did you know that General Scott is coming to the party?"

Nathanial thought his heart would stop, because General Winfield Scott was the real Commanding General of the U. S. Army. "How come?"

"He's visiting with friends in Dobbs Ferry, and he knows Uncle Jasper. They say he loves to eat."

Nathanial harbored one primary ambition: to swap the single silver bar of first lieutenant for the twin silver bars of a captain. "I look forward to meeting the general," he said. "And I understand many pretty girls will be in attendance as well. Has anybody told you two rascals about women, and how babies are made?"

The boys looked at each other and laughed. "Of course," replied Jeffrey.

"Have you ever . . . ?"

"Sure," stated Tobey, black-haired and lean, also

sixteen. "Uncle Jasper took us to a place on Mercer Street."

As he took me, thought Nathanial. My God. "Well," he said cheerily, "I'm sure we have a lot to talk about."

They sat on the front porch of their mother's cottage. Nathanial glanced about nervously, but no words came to mind. These were his brothers, not fellows he'd met in a Santa Fe cantina. He wanted to impart his hard-earned knowledge to them, although he wasn't certain he'd learned anything.

Jeffrey smiled. "Relax, Nathanial. There's nothing you have to do here. Let's have some liquid refreshment." He snapped his finger.

An Irish manservant appeared around the corner of the porch. "And what might I get you boys?"

"Would you have a gin sling?" asked Nathanial, who then noticed expressions of disapproval on his brothers' faces. "No—make that lemonade instead."

The servant walked off with the order, reminding Nathanial of his Irish soldiers at Fort Union. He wondered how they were getting along without him.

Tobey looked his older brother up and down. "How badly are you hurt?"

"Getting better every day."

"How'd it happen?"

Nathanial wanted to remain flippant, but caught a flash of the hell that had been Embudo Canyon. His throat tightened as he recalled the arrow piercing Lieutenant Davidson's chest. "An ambush," he said gruffly. "I happened to be in the wrong place."

The boys looked at each other significantly, then leaned forward. "How does it feel to be in a real battle?" asked Jeffrey.

"After you're in the Army awhile, you perform your duties by the numbers."

Tobey shook his head incredulously, just as he had in his bitter days as a street urchin. "Why join the Army in the first place? I don't understand the both of you. I prefer to make my contribution in The Law, because you can't have civilization without law."

"You can't have law without the Army," Nathanial reminded him. "Those who disapprove of soldiers and armies generally change their minds when threatened by outside forces. The people in New Mexico love the Army because we keep the Apaches off their backs."

"Is Santa Fe much of a town?" asked Tobey.

Nathanial smiled as he recalled his years at Fort Marcy. "Santa Fe is mostly saloons and cantinas. The climate is pleasant but it's filled with the worst criminals in America, and I wouldn't be surprised if somebody was getting killed there even as we speak."

Private Fletcher Doakes walked through the mess hall serving line, holding out his tin plate. Orderlies on the other side served him bacon, beans, bread, and the usual mug of thick black coffee. He carried the meal to a vacant table and sat by himself.

The tables were lined carefully, with salt and pepper shakers in their appropriate positions. Everything was neat, clean, organized, and best of all, as headquarters clerk, he never had to pull mess hall duty. He ate his food in small bites, as his mother had taught him, and wondered if she'd be proud to know he was a soldier.

Occasionally he imagined he was normal, provided he didn't think about dead women. He was tired of army rigamarole and wanted to go where he could kill with impunity. They say a life isn't worth an enchilada down Mexico way, he thought. Maybe I should head south, where nobody knows me.

He'd escaped the gallows of Santa Fe, but one man was on his trail. Should I desert? wondered the stranger. The bloodlust was coming on again, Doakes's hand trembled, his eye developed a tic. He barely recovered from one murder when compulsion to commit another started arising.

"Mind if I sit down?" asked a voice above him.

Doakes was jolted by the sight of Sergeant Berwick. "Go right ahead, First Sergeant," he said with a smile.

Sergeant Berwick lowered his tin plate to the table. "I've been thinking about you, Doakes. You're the kind who minds his business but always ends in trouble."

"Ain't it the truth?" asked Doakes. "If I'd been the usual drunken son of a bitch, it never would've happened."

"I knows what you mean. Some of these lawmen, you pin a badge on 'em, they think they own the world."

Doakes noticed his tail whipping around on the floor. He couldn't understand why the sergeant didn't see it writhing in front of his eyes.

The sergeant examined Doakes's face and it appeared that Doakes was struggling to keep his cork from popping. The sergeant knew the feeling, having popped a few himself over the years.

"Are you all right, Doakes?" he asked gently. "Yer sweatin' like a horse that just run ten miles."

"Hot in here," replied Doakes, fighting rising panic. He's seen through my mask, he realized.

"What's it like where you're from?"

Now he's researching my past, reckoned Doakes. Well, I'll give him the ride of his life. "It gets pretty hot this time of year."

"What town?"

"I lived in lots of towns."

"How come?"

"Ask my daddy."

"Where's he now?"

Doakes narrowed his eyes as he looked at the sergeant. "With all due respect, I thought it's bad manners to ask about a man's past."

"A good worker comes along, I can't help wonder how he got that way."

"My father was a minister," lied Doakes. "He taught me right from wrong."

"And your mother?"

"I'll never forget her after a performance . . . ah, I mean, after one of my father's sermons. Her face fairly seemed to glow, like an angel."

"Sounds like you loved her very much."

"She was everything to me, but she died."

"How?"

"Just wasted away, and in the end she was nothing but skin and bones."

The tail flicked on the floor. What am I talking about? wondered Doakes, his private world undermined by the questions of the Sergeant. "What about your mother?"

"Ran off with a hardware salesman when I was four years old."

Doakes brought his last crust of bread to his

mouth, for he'd been eating frantically throughout the conversation to provide an excuse for leaving. "I've got boots to shine," he said nervously. "Nice talking with you, First Sergeant."

Doakes fled toward the dish bucket, not daring to look back. I'll bet that damned ranger has put a bug into his ear. Doakes dropped his plate into the bucket, surprised to see a face looking at him from within the suds. It was his mother, screaming as he stuck the knife into her belly. His hair stood on end as his heart stumbled in his breast. Glancing sharply away, he headed for the door.

Doakes crossed the parade ground swiftly, imagining Sergeant Berwick watching from the windows of the mess hall. The killer turned a corner and found the gloom behind the stable. He sat on the ground, shivered, and scratched his arms, wishing he could vanish.

Chapter Fifteen

The sun dropped behind the Shinnemunk Mountains as Nathanial's head broke the surface of Cortlandt Lake. It was late afternoon, he could smell meat roasting on the grounds of his uncle's estate, and many guests already had arrived for the celebration.

Nathanial heard his brothers splashing behind him, but he was a far stronger swimmer. Cortlandt Lake was cool, sweet, crystal clear, and he needn't worry about an Apache throwing a hatchet at him. He stroked toward the dock, reached for his towel, and Uncle Jasper sat on a nearby chair, studying the battle scars on Nathanial's body. "Don't you think you've been in the Army long enough?"

"Maybe," Nathanial replied truthfully as Jeffrey and Tobey climbed the ladder.

Nathanial pondered the question as he walked with his brothers to their mother's cottage, where they entered their respective rooms. There aren't any advantages to army life, he admitted to himself as he selected a white suit, blue shirt, and black necktie.

He dressed carefully, because he knew how important appearance was to his mother. He was tempted to take a shot of laudanum, but Cortlandt Lake wasn't Santa Fe, where he could behave as badly as he pleased. He combed his beard, noting a bright gleam in his eye, in contrast to his usual cynical glaze.

One of the carriages pulling up to the main cottage contained Clarissa Rowland. She wore a peach organdy gown with a high-buttoned green bodice and puffy sleeves, her blond hair combed into a bun behind her head.

The grounds were heavily wooded, with more structures barely visible through the foliage; the air smelled like smoke and sap. She followed her family into a spacious well-lit parlor furnished with wooden chairs. Guests conversed in little groups as her parents led her to a jolly old elf, Jasper Rutherford, Nathanial's uncle. "Welcome," he said, taking Clarissa's hand. "Congratulations on your engagement, my dear."

She made a curtsy as he turned toward the next guest. Her social obligations terminated, Clarissa was curious to see the lake. She descended steps leading to the carpet of pine needles between the veranda and the water's edge. The clean odor of the forest filled her nostrils; she raised her dress so she wouldn't sweep up beetles and ants. When she was halfway to the lake, someone began playing a violin.

The main cottage became hidden behind trees and shrubs of the seemingly enchanted forest. She continued toward the water, its musky odor enveloped her, and finally she came to a halt at its edge.

Wavelets lapped the shore as stars blazed brightly

overhead. She knelt and touched her fingers to limpid water, thinking how enjoyable it would be to swim naked across the lake.

"I'll watch your clothes, if you like," said a male voice behind her.

She spun around. Nathanial Barrington walked toward her, a faint smile on his tanned features. "I've been swimming here since I was a boy," he said, "and can recommend . . ." His voice caught in his throat as he drew close to her.

"Are you all right?" she asked.

"Do you like riding, by any chance?"

"What a strange question. I love riding—do you?"

"In point of fact, a few days ago I was riding in the Hudson highlands just south of here. I stopped to rest my horse, and then noticed movement in a clearing just downwind. I took out my army spyglass, and to my astonishment it was a young woman with hair the same color as yours, dressed like a man. T'wasn't you, by any chance?"

She was unable to speak for several seconds, her face turned bright red, and finally she declared, "No gentleman would ever mention such a thing."

"It's a remarkable coincidence, wouldn't you say?"

"You should have left the person in question alone, and walked noisily away."

"It was a vision of loveliness that I dared not disturb with idle movement."

"I suppose you sat and watched for a fairly long period of time?"

"As a matter of fact that's true."

"If I were a man, I'd shoot you."

"Just for looking?"

She glanced around him and said suddenly, "There's something out there!"

He turned quickly, like an army officer in Apache territory, and reached for his Colt Dragoon, but it was in his dresser drawer. She pushed firmly, his hands flailed through the air, an expression of panic came to his face, and he choked off the scream about to issue from his lips. A tremendous splash ensued, the frontier warrior disappeared, and with a victorious laugh, Clarissa held her skirts and ran back toward the main cottage.

Why that little bitch, thought Nathanial as he rose through the turgid water. He saw her fleeing toward the house, heard her merry laughter, and shook his head in disgust. How could I fall for that tired old Indian trick? A fish nibbled his finger as his clothing threatened to drag him beneath the waves.

He swam to shore, praying no one had seen him. Otherwise they'd say he got so drunk he fell into the lake with his clothes on, providing another Nathanial Barrington scandal for decent folks to discuss in the privacy of their homes, exactly the outcome he'd been trying to avoid.

He arrived at the shore, crept onto land like a giant snail, and made his way laboriously around the main cottage, utilizing lessons of stealth and concealment he'd learned from the Apache wars. If my mother saw me like this, she'd kill me.

He snuck into the back door of her cottage and was horrified to see her enter the parlor from the other door. She stared at him dripping onto the floor, muck and dirt clinging to his white suit, and a leech fastened to his left pantleg. "My God—has it come to this?" she asked no one in particular.

"I was walking on the dock," he said, "and tripped over something."

She advanced toward him and sniffed about his face. "Are you drunk?"

"It was an accident."

"Everybody's been wondering where you are. Don't you intend to make an appearance at your own party?"

"It'll only take a minute to put on another suit. I'll be right with you, Mother."

"You'd better be sure of your footing when you're introduced to General Scott. If you make a good impression, he might transfer you to his headquarters."

"He can keep that nest of rattlesnakes. I just want to make captain."

"Don't try to impress him. Just be yourself—no—that's not a good idea either. Please don't talk too much, don't mention politics and whatever you do, don't insult him."

Nathanial returned to his room and put on a black suit, white shirt and purple necktie. He examined himself in the mirror as he combed his hair and beard. He couldn't stop thinking about the girl who'd thrown him into the lake.

He considered her delicious with her flaxen hair and dramatic features. Some might say her nose was too pointy, or she was too frail, but she reminded him of strawberries, tart and sweet at the same time. Besides, he'd always been attracted to women who wouldn't tolerate his horseshit. She actually pushed me into the lake, he reflected with a smile. If I'd had my wits about me, I would've dragged her in with me.

There was a knock on the door, which was opened before Nathanial could respond. "What are you waiting for?" asked Jeffrey, a perplexed expression on his face.

"Don't be angry at me, little brother."

"Why are you always upsetting Mother?"

"I had an accident."

"But you have so many of them, Nathanial. Have you ever stopped to think you're the cause?"

Nathanial suspected his little brother of possessing more intelligence than he as they crossed the yard to the main cottage. They passed through the entrance, where guests in the parlor burst into applause.

At first Nathanial thought they were showing appreciation to the fiddler, but then realized the adulation was for him! His mother stepped forward to kiss his cheek, and he dutifully bent toward her like a dancer in a ballet. Then she reintroduced him to nearby relatives, thus beginning his slow journey through the cottage, shaking hands with gentlemen he barely remembered, receiving kisses from elderly aunts he'd totally forgotten, kissing children who'd been born after he'd last been in New York, seeing old friends who'd become covered with fat, mothers who'd been damsels when he'd last seen them, and hordes of children pressing forward to view the great Indian fighter.

Negro servants brought trays of food and drink, but Nathanial waved them away as he passed from room to room. A distinguished-looking distant relative leaned toward him. "If there's anything I can do, Nathanial—just let me know."

Nathanial realized that his family loved him, although he'd been a disgrace most of his life. They saw him as an outstanding individual when all he'd done was nearly get killed by Apaches.

On the veranda, Reginald van Zweinen stepped out of the crowd and pressed his hand. "You look splendid, Nathanial."

Nathanial wanted to converse with his friend, but then Uncle Jasper arrived with much embracing and kind words. Next came another gaggle of lady relatives, saying how wonderful and handsome he was. He received so much praise he was starting to believe it.

He spotted Belinda standing against a wall, a tray of small sandwiches in her hands, an amused expression on her face. He recalled the night they'd slept together chastely on the train. *The North isn't so different from the South,* he realized. *Everyone has his own secret concerning Negroes, including me.*

The lawyer Ronald Soames gripped Nathanial's hand. "How's your vacation going?"

"So well I've been thinking about resigning my commission."

"By the way, have you met my fiancée? Clarissa!"

A blond head turned around, and Nathanial's knees nearly buckled. "Yes, we introduced ourselves at the lake. You're a lucky man."

Soames placed his arm around her shoulders and hugged her closer. "You should hear her play the piano."

Nathanial turned toward her. "What's your favorite piece?"

"Handel's *Water Music*."

Nathanial recalled how she'd appeared without her blouse, and then remembered that his friend and lawyer was marrying her. "When's the wedding?"

"October," said Soames, "and we hope you'll be able to attend."

Nathanial was about to say "I don't know," when his mother came into view, a sombre expression on her face. "He's here," she formed with her lips.

Nathanial realized that the Commanding General of the Army had arrived. The first lieutenant wanted to flee to the nearest mirror, to make sure his appearance was flawless, but then a crowd of guests stepped out of the way. A hulking mountain with slabs of wrinkled flesh upon his face rumbled into view.

It's him! thought Nathanial. He stared in open wonder at the illustrious hero of countless battles and the general who'd marched his army through two hundred fifty miles of jungles, mountains, and Mexican soldiers to capture Mexico City.

General Scott had run for President on the Whig ticket in 1852, while Nathanial's uncle had contributed generously to Whig causes. So that's how you make captain, calculated Nathanial. General Scott owes a favor to my family. The Commanding General appeared grotesquely corpulent, awkward and logy in his movements, and it was rumored he no longer could mount a horse without help.

The time had come for the grand performance. Nathanial squared his shoulders, sucked in his stomach and drew his chin close to his chest. What am I afraid of? he asked as he advanced toward the commanding general. He's on Uncle Jasper's payroll.

Uncle Jasper smiled as the frontier officer drew closer. "General Scott, I'd like to present my nephew, Lieutenant Nathanial Barrington."

Nathanial raised his arm in a regulation West Point salute. "I'm honored to meet you, sir."

Sixty-eight-year-old General Scott was a mass of blubber encased in a white linen suit, his eyes set behind massive gray eyebrows, with his jaw like a boulder. "Didn't you work in my department for a time?" he asked in a gravely voice.

"Yes sir, during '49."

"What are you doing now?"

"I'm at Fort Union, sir."

"Apache country. How are you getting along against them?"

"Not very well, sir."

General Scott frowned. "What's wrong?"

Nathanial noticed his mother turn pale, so he framed his words very carefully. "In a nutshell, we don't have enough men for the job."

"That's going to change soon, but I'd be interested in your assessment anyway, since you're an eyewitness. Why don't you stop by my office next week?"

General Scott turned toward another potential contributor, and Nathanial stepped out of the light of the great man. Uncle Jasper winked at his nephew, and Nathanial could feel the bars of a captain upon his shoulders. He was certain his whole view of life would change if he made captain.

Excusing himself, he headed toward the lake. A captain was a real officer, whereas lieutenants merely moved small numbers of men around, not much different from sergeants. Maybe, by the time I'm fifty, I might even make major.

He stood on the shore and gazed at the moon floating through massive constellations. Are captains more attractive to women than lieutenants? he wondered. He'd wanted to become a captain for so long, it had become an obsession. What does a man have to do to become a captain? If so many of my classmates have won their twin bars, why not me? If I were a captain, maybe I'd respect myself.

The full moon shone upon him as flames of ambition surrounded him. Just as Napoleon and Wellington were noticed by their senior commanders, my time had come. He closed his eyes and saw himself riding a white stallion down Pennsylvania Avenue after winning an imaginary war. Nathanial knew it was a dream, but he'd believed it practically from the day he'd entered West Point.

He heard something rustle behind him, reached for his Colt Dragoon, and realized again that he was unarmed. A peach organdy gown could be seen among boughs of pine trees. "My God—don't tell me it's you," he murmured. "I hope you're not going to push me into the water again."

She laughed into the back of her hand. "You looked so funny when you hit the water."

"It may have been funny to you, but he who laughs last . . ."

He made a lunge for her, which she successfully dodged. But she ran into the rough bark of a pine tree, skinned her nose, and before she could cry out, he'd scooped her in his strong arms.

He carried her onto the dock, she kicking wildly. "What do you think you're doing?" she asked as she pounded his massive shoulder with her tiny fists.

"I'm going to throw you in the water."

"You're an unprincipled beast! Let me go this minute!"

"It's not so funny when you're on the other end, is it?"

"I don't have an extra dress with me, and you were being cruel."

"Perhaps your dress will dry before you leave. Or you might want to stop fighting me, otherwise I'm liable to drop you by mistake."

She settled down immediately. "You're a very bad man," she told him, as she wiggled uncomfortably in his arms. "No true gentleman would ever watch a woman innocently expose herself."

"If you weren't engaged to marry my lawyer, I do believe I'd propose marriage to you. You're so magnificent, I'll never forget this moment."

"But you're already married, you fiend."

"I'm in the process of divorce."

"Who could live with a man like you?"

"Of all the places between Battery Park and Cortlandt Lake, we happened to be in the same little corner of the Hudson highlands. Why, it's enough to make a man believe in God."

"It was only a coincidence, and would you mind releasing me?"

"I'll bet there are other times when we've passed like ships in the night, but didn't recognize each other."

"As a matter of fact, I saw you at the Saint Nicholas Hotel dining room last week. I thought you were going to eat everything in the kitchen."

Moonlight illuminated her face, like the white marble statue of a Grecian goddess. "Do you understand how truly exciting you are?" he asked as he drew her closer.

She closed her eyes, he kissed her lightly. "I used to blame my bad manners on whiskey, but I haven't touched a drop for five days." Then he lowered her to the ground. "I'm sorry—I didn't mean to offend you."

She smoothed the front of her skirt. "It was better than being thrown into the water, I suppose. You really must gain control of yourself, Lieutenant Barrington. Another girl might've screamed to high heaven, and you've been trying so hard to impress General Scott. I'm surprised you didn't polish his boots with your nose."

"It's the only way to treat a general. You don't know much about the army, I see."

"Nor would I want to."

A voice came to them from the woods. "Clarissa?" It was Soames. "I'm over here!" she called out.

He emerged from the woods, a glass of potent-looking beverage in his hand. "It is rather nice down here, isn't it?"

"Do you think we could have a lake, Ronald?" she asked.

"I'll buy you all the lakes you desire, my darling, and by the way, you've been asked to perform. Could you?"

She followed him to the main cottage while Nathanial lingered near the lake. "What's wrong with me?" he asked, the moon floating overhead like a big silver serving bowl. He felt off balance, light-headed, and queasy in his stomach, as if he were acquiring an illness.

The faint sounds of a piano sonata came to him from the main cottage. He climbed the stairs to the veranda and observed her sitting at the piano, surrounded by thoughtful listeners, long elegant fingers dancing nimbly over the keys.

At Fort Thorn Dr. Michael Steck sat at table with his wife, dining upon braised ribs of beef, one of her specialties. They'd been married twenty years and felt comfortable in each other's presence, without the need to talk constantly.

Despite frontier hardships, they were happy at Fort Thorn. Rosalie's health had improved dramatically in the clean mountain air and she looked almost like a young woman again. I did the right thing by coming here, thought good Dr. Steck. But never did I realize the greatest obstruction to peace would be my own government, not the Apaches.

He tried not to think of professional responsibilities when home with his wife, but sometimes felt bedeviled by the contradictions of his position. He wished he could find another good-paying job, but pickins were slim in the region that had brought his wife back to health.

Impulsively, he leaned closer and kissed her cheek. She smiled and held his hand. Someone knocked on the door. Dr. Steck opened it, revealing Corporal Shanahan. "Sir, a bunch of Injuns just showed up at the gate. They said they want to talk to you."

Dr. Steck figured it was Tomaso making more requests that couldn't be fulfilled. He kissed his wife's forehead. "I'll be right back."

He was grateful she didn't throw a tantrum, as another women might. He placed his wide-brimmed hat onto his head and followed Shanahan to the gate. What can I tell them this time? wondered Dr. Steck. I've become a professional liar.

If he told the Apaches the bald truth, that the Great White Father didn't give a damn about them, New Mexico would have a bloodbath. Washington would rather spend a million dollars on a good war, rather than a few thousand for shovels and seeds.

Guards at the gate watched Apaches nervously, while other soldiers gathered nearby.

"Who's in charge here?" asked Dr. Steck.

"I am," replied the firm voice of a hefty officer wearing curly black sidewhiskers, Lieutenant Beauregard Hargreaves, who had been Nathanial Barrington's roommate at West Point.

"Dismiss your men."

"Not with those Apaches out there."

"They're from the settlement. You don't need to worry about them."

"They're not from the settlement. That's Cuchillo Negro with some of his top warriors. And there may be more in the chaparral."

Dr. Steck was taken aback. Cuchillo Negro was one of the foremost Mimbrenos, nearly the equal of the great Mangas Coloradas. Past the gate, Dr. Steck saw warriors, women, children, horses, as if an entire tribe had come in. An old warrior of great dignity stepped forward, a solemn expression on his face. Dr. Steck shook his hand heartily. "Chief Cuchillo Negro," he said, "welcome to Fort Thorn."

Cuchillo Negro touched his fist to his breast and

said solemnly. "I believe you are a good man, Dr. Steck. I have come for peace."

"Find yourself a plot of land," replied the Indian commissioner, "and tomorrow I'll bring whatever you need."

Cole Bannon sat at his favorite table against the wall, facing the cash register. His bartenders didn't know whether he was reading a newspaper, staring into space, or watching their hands dip into the till.

Maria Dolores stepped into the saloon; his sharp eyes spotted her instantly. He smiled nervously as she approached his table, then pulled out his watch. "Sometimes I lose track of time," he alibied.

"I waited a half hour."

"I was so tired—I couldn't move."

She sat beside him. "I remember when you couldn't be with me enough."

"I'm not in the mood for an argument."

"Are you coming?"

"I'm not finished with my drink."

"You can finish at the hotel room."

"Sometimes," he said without thinking, "I feel like a stud horse."

She recoiled as if he'd slapped her face. He placed his hand on hers.

"I'm sorry—I didn't . . ."

She pulled her hand away and rose from the table.

"But I didn't mean it, Maria Dolores."

"I am just a cow?" She made a hurt smile as she headed for the door.

He caught up with her on the planked sidewalk outside. "Please forgive me. I guess I've been working too hard."

"It has nothing to do with work."

He took her arm. "Please come with me to the hotel."

"Take your hand off me."

They gazed into each other's eyes from a distance of eight inches. It was one thing for him to sit with a mug of beer, and another to have the beautiful Mexican woman so close. He began to feel certain inspirations. "I can't live without you," he whispered as he touched his lips to hers. They embraced for a long time, then drifted toward his hotel.

It was two in the morning when Clarissa Rowland finally crawled into bed. She lay atop cool cotton sheets, and moonlight glittered upon the Hudson River less than a hundred paces away.

Her bedroom was on the second floor of her parents' cottage at the outskirts of Peekskill. All was still, the party receding into memory, and she realized it had provided a number of truly extraordinary experiences, most interesting of which was pushing the guest of honor into the lake.

She couldn't imagine what caused her to commit such a horrendous act, but couldn't help laughing softly. He'd been asking for it and she gave it to him royally. She'd thought of herself as Miss Clarissa Bland, who did what she was told and wouldn't say boo to a goose. She'd enjoyed standing up for her rights for once in her life.

If she'd pushed Soames into the lake, he probably

would've drowned, for he was a dissipated and physically weak man. And if he didn't drown, he might very well break off their engagement.

But the scoundrel Nathanial Barrington had threatened to throw her into the lake as revenge, then stole a kiss. Evidently the guest of honor felt attracted to her, despite her engagement to one of his best friends.

Nathanial Barrington is capable of any foul deed, she realized, but he also represented freedom, adventure, and fun to a woman who'd lived a narrowly circumscribed life. It was touching to watch him trying to please his family, while everyone knew he'd rather get roaring drunk in a tavern full of prostitutes. Nathanial Barrington had many facets and was the strangest man she'd ever met.

She felt weird as she recalled how he'd watched her half naked. What if he'd come over and taken me against my will, or worse, with my cooperation? She felt perversely honored that such a rascal had shown interest in her, but figured he pursued every skirt he saw. He's probably lying with somebody's wife at this very moment, because a man who'd threaten to throw a helpless woman into a lake is not to be trusted, although I pushed him in first.

When she placed Soames on one side of the scale, and Nathanial on the other, somehow Soames didn't have much weight. She was marrying for all the right reasons, and Ronald even made interesting comments from time to time, but she didn't especially relish the notion of sleeping with him every night, especially in comparison with a man like Nathanial Barrington.

* * *

"I want to show you something, Running Deer."

Jocita took his hand and led him to a sloping hill at the edge of the encampment. Older boys climbed the hill, while warriors at its base placed six-inch arrows into special shortened bows.

Jocita kneeled beside her son. "Pay close attention," she murmured into his ear. "You are going to learn something important."

Running Deer became serious as he looked at older boys waiting anxiously. Meanwhile, at the bottom of the hill, the warriors were lining up. The teacher for the day was old Nana, the *di-yin* medicine man of the Mimbrenos. "Are you ready?" he called to the boys.

They shouted that they were, then began darting about frantically as warriors at the bottom of the hill took aim at them. Running Deer stiffened, but his mother held him tightly.

"You will be up there one day," she said.

The warriors fired arrows at the boys, who leapt and pitched out of the way. The miniature arrows didn't fly as fast as regular arrows, which provided an additional second of time. Their mouths open and sucking wind, the boys remained in motion, dancing around arrows, twisting and turning, bumping into each other as they struggled to avoid those sharp points.

There was a scream, a boy fell to the ground, the game stopped, and everyone ran to help him. Jocita carried Running Deer up the hill and set him down in front of the wounded boy. An arrow had pierced the boy's left thigh, but he showed no pain as he lay still on the ground. Nana pulled the arrow, then someone placed a handful of leaves against the wound, but blood continued to pour down the boy's leg.

The warrior woman whispered into Running Deer's ear. "You must learn to be fast, my dear son. Otherwise that will be you."

Chapter Sixteen

Nathanial rode through the Hudson highlands, wondering if he was on a fool's errand. She'll never dare show up, after I admitted I'd spied on her, he told himself. This is a cosmopolitan woman of the upper classes, not an actress from an oyster cellar.

He wouldn't have given her a second thought if she hadn't pushed him into the lake. No woman had ever captured his attention so quickly and completely. A woman who'd do that would do anything, he calculated. I think she'll come here again, if not today then maybe tomorrow, but sooner or later, I, her ardent admirer, will see her.

If he ever told his friends, they'd laugh him out of town. But he was willing to wager a few days on the remote hope she was as much a romantic fool as he. The forest was cool, smelling of peat, with diamonds of light breaking through leaves. It reminded him of fairy tales about elves and goblins living beneath toadstools, while princesses reclined in distant castles.

He couldn't help contrasting the opulent greenery of the Hudson highlands with scraggly cactus, clumps of gama grass, and sad little mesquite trees on the endless plains of New Mexico. He'd seen vistas extending for seemingly hundreds of miles, whereas now he rode inside a sweet-smelling green cocoon.

What do I need the army for? he asked himself. What do I care about Apaches? Even if the South secedes from the Union, the Saint Nicholas Hotel dining room will continue to serve its varied cuisine.

He came to the promontory, dismounted, and loosened the cinch beneath his horse's belly. Then he lay on the ground with his spyglass, a few sandwiches, a bottle of wine, and a copy of *Moby Dick*, a recently published novel by a New Yorker named Herman Melville, recommended by his mother.

If I'm going to waste three days, I might as well get caught up on my reading, thought Nathanial. He found a comfortable spot and opened the book. Wouldn't it be funny if she actually showed up?

Moby Dick was written so vividly it gradually shanghaied Nathanial onto the *Pequod*, where he became a sailor chasing the great white whale. His eyes raced along, wondering how anyone could conceive such an unusual story, and he made comparisons between Captain Ahab and certain officers under whom he'd served, such as General Bull Moose Sumner.

The atmosphere below decks, with creaking hull, smell of bean suppers mixed with tobacco smoke and brine, was evoked superbly. It was a tale of adventure on the high seas, but also the story of one man's obsession with revenge, while the great primordial white whale kept swimming indifferently along, demolishing everything it found.

Sailing across the China Seas, Nathanial noticed movement out of the corner of his eye. Instinctively, he reached for his Colt. A woman with blond hair was riding into the clearing below. My God, thought Nathanial. She's done it.

His jaw hanging open, he watched her climb down from her horse. She tied it to a tree, then turned her back to Nathanial, who rubbed his eyes to make certain he wasn't hallucinating. It appeared she was unbuttoning her blouse! She wouldn't dare.

She peeled it off and spread it on the ground, then lay upon it, folded her hands upon her belly, and sunned herself. Nathanial yanked out his spyglass and focused on those two pink nubbins standing proudly in the air. It was as though the temperature had increased by at least twenty degrees. He reflected upon the heart of a woman who'd follow dreams to their illogical conclusions.

She's engaged to one of my best friends, but she and I are attuned on the deepest levels, he concluded. Hands trembling, he reached for his horse's reins.

Clarissa lay on her back, dozing to forest music. He's probably recovering from the drink he consumed last night, she thought. He's forgotten who I am by now, and I imagine he tries to kiss every girl he meets.

Then she heard the sound of someone approaching through the underbrush. She hoped it was he, not an illiterate mountain ruffian come to leer at the half naked girl lying brassily in the clearing. The sounds drifted closer, she was tempted to cover herself, and began to question what she was doing there. He probably thinks I'm insane.

She heard him stop before her, opened her eyes to

half mast, and it was the scoundrel Nathanial Barrington staring at her naked breasts. She thought he was going to dive on top of her, but instead he dropped to a cross-legged sitting position nearby and became pensive.

Self-consciously, she raised herself, then put on her blouse, buttoned it to her neck, but didn't bother tucking it into her riding pants. "Aren't you going to say anything?" she asked.

"If you believe in destiny," he replied in a faraway voice, "then you must believe we were meant to be together."

"Perhaps," she replied. "But I'm engaged to your friend."

"I hope Ronald doesn't challenge me to a duel, because I might have to kill him."

"I have always believed in destiny," she admitted. "Do you think we should get married?"

"Of course. And there's something I must tell you, so you won't suffer unpleasant surprises later. Army life is nothing like Fifth Avenue, or even Cortlandt Lake, so you'd better stay with Ronald if you require champagne and caviar."

"I've never liked champagne and caviar, and it'd be wonderful to have adventures for a change."

"There isn't much adventure on an army post, I'm sorry to say. You may be thrown together with people you may not like."

"I like nearly everybody," replied Clarissa. "Are we not all children of God? But you must promise one thing, before I give my consent. You must promise a piano wherever we go, no matter how remote the army post. Because I cannot live without music."

"You shall have as many pianos as you desire, even if I have to bring them in on the backs of mules. I never dreamed I'd be fortunate enough to marry a virtuoso pianist."

"In that case, I'll see Ronald tomorrow and give back his ring."

Major Stanfield Parks, executive officer at Fort Thorn, looked up from his desk as the sergeant major approached. "Dr. Steck would like to see you, sir."

Major Parks was second in command, but Colonel Hall had gone on a scout, ostensibly to show the Apaches that the Army controlled the territory, but actually to get away from the old lady for a few days. The major didn't want to talk with Steck, because Steck was a civilian authority. But neither could he refuse. "Send him in."

The door opened; tall, tanned Dr. Steck appeared, wearing rawhide pants and a rawhide vest over his blue shirt. "I'm sorry to bother you, Major," he said, "but Chief Cuchillo Negro and his tribe arrived last night, and I wonder if I can borrow some cornmeal and a few beeves."

Major Parks frowned. "But, Dr. Steck, we barely have enough for the men."

"Cuchillo Negro is one of the most important Mimbreno chiefs. It's cheaper to feed him than fight him."

"I can't take food from the mouths of American soldiers and give it to Indians who'll fill their bellies and then go out and kill a white man. We've had reports that Cuchillo Negro has been raiding in Sonora, or maybe he's the one attacking wagons on the

Journado del Muertos. How can I give you what I don't have myself?"

Cuchillo Negro examined the new campsite, as the women constructed wickiups. He was hungry, no animal tracks were in the vicinity, and they were far from mountains where mescal was harvested. This is a sacrifice I must make for future generations, he told himself.

He couldn't understand why food hadn't been offered, and it was almost midmorning. His warriors looked at him reproachfully, and he wondered if he was being foolish. Perhaps I should have stayed with Mangas Coloradas, but how can I gamble with the lives of children?

He sat by himself away from the others and wondered why the White Eyes were denying food. Perhaps they are testing our commitment to peace, he thought. But I know how to go without food.

"Steck is coming!" shouted one of his warriors.

Cuchillo Negro arose, a smile spreading over his wrinkled features. Dr. Steck sat alone on the front seat of a wagon. My fears were unfounded, thought Cuchillo Negro. Steck will take good care of his Indian brothers.

Cuchillo Negro walked toward the center of the encampment, followed by warriors, women, children, and dogs. They all looked expectantly as Dr. Steck came to a halt in front of them. The doctor appeared embarrassed as he climbed down from the wagon. The warrior known as Ponce looked inside and saw two bags of cornmeal.

"Welcome, brother," said Cuchillo Negro.

"I apologize," replied Dr. Steck. "We didn't expect

you, and you must be patient until we receive more supplies."

Cuchillo Negro saw his warriors unloading the paltry bags of meal. "But you promised . . ."

"And I shall live up to my promises, but even the soldiers are short of food."

"How do you expect us to live on that, Steck?"

Dr. Steck leaned toward him and said evenly, "Your alternative is the warpath where bluecoat soldiers will hunt you down and kill you."

"It is better to die like a warrior than starve to death, no?"

"Soon I will have more supplies. It has taken many years to make enemies of our peoples, and you cannot expect everything to be solved in a day."

Cuchillo Negro looked him in the eye. "Do not disappoint us, Dr. Steck."

The Indian commissioner raised his right hand in the air. "I will work hard to make you happy here, but I am not alone. The White Father in the East has many concerns, and the bluecoat soldiers are angry at your bad men, the ones who steal and kill, unlike you, great chief. And we too have our bad men. But you and I must work together so that peace can come to this land."

"I will do all you say," replied Cuchillo Negro. "It is not healthy to fill our bellies, because we only get sick afterwards."

That poor misguided Apache has faith in the U.S. Government, thought Dr. Steck as he walked to his office. A recalcitrant tribe could be subdued during one season of hard campaigning whereas pacification might take ten or twenty years.

Sometimes Dr. Steck thought of returning to the

medical profession, but it too was in turmoil, with doctors disagreeing over the relative merits of lancing, allopathy, phrenology, and massive doses of medications such as calomel, opium, quinine, arsenic, and tartar emetic.

He wished he could retire to a farm in Pennsylvania, but lacked *dinero*. It troubled him to reflect upon Cuchillo Negro's simple trust in the federal government. That old Apache will be disappointed many times, and I wonder how strong his peaceful convictions will prove to be. He'll be put to the test in the months to come, as will I. Perhaps, before he returns to the warpath, he'll kill the White Eyes who has deceived him.

The office of the Commanding General of the Army in New York City was far from the Department of the War in Washington, D.C. The reason was General Scott and Secretary of War Davis had been feuding via the mails and the press ever since Davis had been appointed to President Pierce's cabinet.

General Scott could not take seriously a man who'd been in diapers when he'd been wounded twice in the Battle of Lundy's Lane, War of 1812. General Scott had won so many honors and glories that sometimes he saw himself as a living monument, not just a man.

The Department of War ran the Army, while General Scott remained its figurehead. Occasionally he visited military posts, but usually could be found at his office near Wall Street, or at his home on Bond Street.

A few days after Nathanial's party, General Scott

was having lunch at Delmonico's with Major General Persifor Frazer Smith, commander of the Department of Texas. Smith had come east for a vacation, but actually to renew acquaintance with old army friends and perhaps win another star for his shoulders.

"In my opinion," said General Smith as he sliced into a perfectly cooked carrot, "if the South seceded from the Union tomorrow, three-quarters of the best officers would resign their commissions and fight against us."

General Scott wasn't surprised by the news. The Army was facing the worst crisis in its history, because like the rest of the country, the officer corps was split along proslavery and antislavery lines. "The news from Kansas couldn't be worse," he muttered. "Bull Moose Sumner refuses to fire a shot against abolitionists or proslavers without written permission from the White House, and naturally President Pierce is afraid to put his name on the dotted line."

"He tries to please everybody," replied General Smith. "A man's got to show backbone if he wants to sit in the White House. Why don't you run again, General Scott?"

"If I were nominated . . . how could I refuse to serve my country? But I don't intend to run for anything, and I wouldn't worry about the Army if I were you. There are plenty of fine young Northern officers that you never hear about, and in fact I met one over the weekend. His name's Nathanial Barrington and he's been shot up by Apaches. I'm supposed to see him tomorrow afternoon, in fact. Young officers are closer to the action, or at least this one was."

"Did you say Barrington, sir?"

"Yes, do you know him?"

"Perhaps I shouldn't say, sir, but ... I saw him when I was in the War Department last month. He's the son of Colonel Barrington, whom I believe is retired now, and Lieutenant Barrington was having a discussion with ... Jefferson Davis."

At the mere mention of the name, General Scott's bushy eyebrows knitted together, a scowl came over his face, and he grunted. "Evidently young Barrington is playing both ends against the middle, but this time he has outsmarted himself. Thank you so much for the information, General Smith. I know exactly what to do with the likes of Lieutenant Barrington."

Miguel Narbona of the Chiricahuas and Mangas Coloradas of the Mimbrenos smoked together every day, while pondering the future of the People. The Mimbrenos now resided in the Chiricahua homeland, but Mangas Coloradas longed to return to his own domain, the one that had been given his people by Yusn.

The two aging chiefs were observed by all members of the encampment, for everyone knew the fate of the People was being decided in those long conversations. Miguel Narbona and Mangas Coloradas were becoming old, sometimes they lost the threads of conversations, and both had become infected by cynicism, the most debilitating illness of age.

"I wonder," said Miguel Narbona, "why Yusn gave us this land in the first place?"

"We see that all things die," replied Mangas Coloradas, "from the creatures of the desert to the plants that grow on mountains. Perhaps the epoch of the People is coming to an end."

"I cannot believe it," replied Miguel Narbona, shaking his head. "Yusn would not play a trick on the People."

The two old war chiefs struggled with faith and the challenges of the future, while the younger generation turned increasingly toward Cochise of the Chiricahuas and Victorio of the Mimbrenos. Cochise was forty-four, Victorio twenty-eight, and both had distinguished themselves by great deeds of valor.

Cochise and Victorio had been measuring each other since the Chiricahuas had welcomed the Mimbrenos into their camp. Finally one dawn they rode off together to have their first private council. They sat silently in their saddles as their war ponies carried them to a secluded spot high in the Dragoon Mountains.

Upon their arrival at the selected plateau, each sprinkled sacred pollen to the four directions, then sat cross-legged and faced each other. Both wore scars from fights with the *Nakai-yes* and the *Pindah-lickoyee*, both were full-muscled and deep-chested, with Victorio two inches taller than Cochise. They peered into each other's eyes, trying to make contact with each other's spirits.

Victorio spoke first. "My heart is against the White Eyes," he said. "I don't trust them, but many Mimbrenos are tired of running. They desire peace."

Cochise stretched out both his arms, as if to encompass his surroundings. "There is peace here, and we Chiricahuas shall always have room for our Mimbreno Brothers."

In the distance, on a brownish red trail bordered by chaparral, a stagecoach and its escort could be seen. Other than it and a few isolated shacks there were no White Eyes or Mexicans in the Chiricahua homeland.

Victorio pointed at the stagecoach as the breeze lifted a few strands of his jet black hair. "That is the way it began for us, a few stagecoaches, a few soldiers. What will you do when you are engulfed by the White Eyes, as were we?"

"The Chiricahuas will fight for these mountains," replied Cochise. "Because there is no place else to go. Are you afraid to die, my brother?"

"No, are you?"

"What is there to be afraid of?"

"Then we shall fight together, the Chiricahuas and the Mimbrenos, against the invasion of the White Eyes."

"So be it," replied Cochise.

Each took his knife and cut a small gash in his forearm. Then they leaned forward and pressed arms together, commingling blood. This was the mutual defense treaty sealed between the Chiricahuas and the Mimbrenos in the Dragoon Mountains, during the season of Many Leaves.

The headquarters of the commanding general was an imposing three-story stone building near Wall Street. Nathanial's coach stopped at the front door, he climbed to the sidewalk, and was attired in a freshly pressed blue summer uniform, brass and leather gleaming. He limped slightly as he climbed the stairs, accepting salutes from two soldiers on duty at the entrance.

Nathanial entered the cool, dark building and made his way to General Scott's office, passing officers and clerks in the corridor. Stopping at the commanding general's door, he adjusted his uniform and made sure he was perfect. He knocked on the door, and after a brief interval it was opened by a slender officer around Nathanial's age, only he wore the bronze maple leaf of major on his shoulder straps. "May I help you, Lieutenant?"

"My name's Nathanial Barrington, and I have an appointment with General Scott."

"I'm sorry, but he's not available today."

"But . . . has our meeting been rescheduled?"

"Not to my knowledge."

"Would you speak with him about it?"

"If I were you, I'd write a letter. Now if you'll excuse me, I have work to do."

Major Thompson closed the door on the perplexed face of the lieutenant, then permitted himself to smile. He crossed the carpet and knocked on the door of the commanding general.

"Come in."

Major Thompson opened the door. "I've just got rid of that Barrington fellow."

"Excellent."

Nathanial frowned as he walked up busy Broadway. *Was I born beneath an unlucky star?* he wondered. *Why were Napoleon, Wellington, and Caesar promoted, but not I?*

Why does Lady Luck smile on one man and not another? he asked himself as he passed ladies gazing into the window of a jewelry store, while a few blocks away men competed for the right to pay the bills. At the same time, dragoons were scouting the Apache homeland, where death came suddenly, with no warning. The world seemed warped and out of balance to the frontier officer.

What do I lack? he wondered. He wanted to leave his imprint on history, but wasn't receiving cooperation from above. Is military life a roulette wheel? he asked himself. Winfield Scott fell into the commanding general slot while I dropped into New Mexico Territory.

Am I being vain? he mused as he paused at the window of another jewelry store. In fact, my record of accomplishments is dismal. Were it not for my family, I'd probably be a beggar, my bedroom a back alley of Five Points.

"Nathanial?"

He turned toward a tubby well-dressed woman with blond hair and a double chin. "Have I changed that much?" asked Layne Satterfield, his first great love. "Don't you recognize me."

"You haven't changed at all," he lied courteously, although she looked like somebody's mother, which in fact was the case. "I was hoping I'd run into you and am pleased to see you're lovely as ever."

"You were always so complimentary, Nathanial." She smiled. "I saw you limping—have you been wounded again?"

"No, I fell off a horse."

"You must be more careful." She became wistful. "You always were a hellion."

"How are your children?"

They exchanged polite information about the accomplishments of their progeny as Nathanial wondered what it was like to be married to a big lady. Must be comfortable on cold winter nights, he decided.

"Where are you going?" he asked.

"I have an appointment with my dressmaker around the corner."

"I was hoping to share a pot of coffee with you. We could talk further . . ."

She smiled. "I'm not sure I could manage the temptation, Nathanial."

"The only way to manage temptation is surrender totally. Do you believe in destiny?"

"Nowadays I believe only in my children and certain memories of when I was . . . young."

"I have a better idea. Why don't you come to my suite?"

She appeared delighted by his invitation. "But, Nathanial—I'm a married woman."

"And I'm engaged to get married, but we can't let that stop us. Haven't you ever wondered . . . ?"

She cut him off. "Of course I have."

"So why don't we?"

"Do you see that man standing over there, pretending to read a newspaper?"

"The fellow whose suit is too tight?"

"He's my bodyguard."

"It appears we've been saved from the sin of adultery."

"I must say that I'm flattered by your offer, for I'm not the woman I was."

"You're lovelier than ever, but I'm sure it's better being an Astor."

"Not always, because I can't be seen speaking for an extended period with a gentleman to whom I was formerly betrothed."

"Whom you unceremoniously tossed aside, as I recall, to marry the Astor millions. Your destiny ultimately was not mine, but perhaps it's best this way."

They were married but not to each other as they gazed into each other's eyes. Then they turned and continued on their respective Broadway strolls, as if they'd never embraced passionately in darkened carriages eight short years ago.

In Gramercy Park, Clarissa sat down to dinner with her parents, brothers, and sisters. A roasted haunch of beef lay in the middle of the silver platter, surrounded by roast potatoes and onions. Clarissa ate sparingly and seemed distracted as conversation swirled around her.

Finally her mother turned and said, "Are you all right, dear? You're hardly eating anything."

"I'm not hungry."

"I know when something's bothering you," thundered her father. "You can't fool me. Come on—out with it."

"I had intended to tell you after the meal," replied Clarissa.

Her father raised his eyebrows. "How can I enjoy supper when you're withholding a secret? What is it?"

Clarissa took a deep breath. "This may come as a shock, but I've decided not to marry Ronald Soames."

There was silence as her parents and siblings looked at each other meaningfully. "Have you so advised Mr. Soames?" asked his mother.

"I thought I should tell you first."

Her father shook his head in despair. "The wedding date has been set, Clarissa. The invitations have been sent. It's a little late to change your mind."

"I realize this is embarrassing, but I've decided that I don't love Ronald."

"Then why'd you agree to marry him?"

"He seemed clever and entertaining compared to men my own age."

"I always thought Soames was too old for you," admitted mother. "I never wanted to say anything, but . . ."

Father added, "There were many disreputable incidents in his past, but I kept my peace."

"From what I could see," said her younger brother Tim, "he was awful."

Her sister Marion, only nine years old, said, "He's ugly."

Clarissa shrugged. "If none of you liked Ronald, why didn't you say something before?"

"Who can stop you, once you set your mind on something?" asked her mother. "Now everyone will look at me strangely next time I go to A. T. Stewart's. If you ever consent to marry again, I hope your selection will be more prudent. No reputation can survive two such incidents in a row."

"As a matter of fact," said Clarissa, "after a decent interval, I intend to marry someone else."

It became silent at the table, and even little Marion was impressed. "Who?" she asked.

Clarissa looked at the ceiling, sighed, and said, "Nathanial Barrington."

A violent cough developed in her father's throat. His face turned purple, his wife clapped his back, and Tim passed him a glass of water. The patriarch caught his breath, then said, "Clarissa—have you lost your mind?"

"I know it sounds odd," she replied. "But we have fallen in love."

"Fallen in love with Nathanial Barrington?" asked her father. "Is it conceivable?"

"I'm sure his reputation has been greatly exaggerated," countered Clarissa. "It's obvious that you don't know him well."

"Neither do you," reminded her mother. "He just arrived a few weeks ago."

"Has the scoundrel actually proposed?" asked her father.

"Yes."

"I thought Ronald was one of his best friends."

"Not any more," uttered her mother.

Father shook his head sadly. "I knew it would turn out this way, because she spends too much time with her piano, and not enough with other people." He gazed levelly at his daughter. "You were bound to veer into eccentric directions, I now realize. Don't you understand that marriage is built on trust? It's not that the gentleman in question is wicked, but he has virtually no character, he's a morally wicked man, and does whatever he pleases, regardless of how much it hurts others."

Clarissa sat stalwartly, unwilling to surrender. "I know him far better than you," she replied coldly, "and I trust him completely."

"I wonder how many other nice girls said that," commented the matriarch.

Jocita picked pinyon nuts with other women as warriors searched for enemies. The children played in a clearing nearby, watched over by an old woman named Three Moccasins.

The People traveled to higher elevations for pinyon nuts every year at that time, just as they visited other locations to harvest mescal, berries, and prickly pears. Later, back at the village, they'd pound the pinyon nuts into a flourlike substance for bread.

Jocita's hands worked swiftly as she advanced among the bushes, dropping nuts into a sack. Every few minutes she glanced at the children, to make certain her son was safe. Heat pounded her, but she looked forward to eating bread.

Toward noon, she turned around and her heart nearly stopped when she realized that Running Deer was nowhere to be seen. She called his name but there was no answer. Then she ran toward Three Moccasins, as the others stopped work. "Where is my son?"

"I don't know," replied the befuddled old lady.

They organized, combed the chaparral, and it wasn't long before Chatto shouted. "He's over here, but there's a snake!"

Jocita dropped her bag of nuts and strung an arrow in her bow. Then she stalked toward Chatto, who was perched on one knee, aiming his bow and arrow into the thicket straight ahead.

"Let me," replied Jocita.

She took careful aim. Her son stood still in the small clearing where he'd wandered, and the rattlesnake appeared to be dancing from side to side in front of him, while shaking his tail.

"Don't move, my son," murmured Jocita.

The boy didn't flinch. He was entranced by the creature in front of him. He'd never seen a live rattlesnake so close before. The snake's forked tongue flitted and his fangs dripped with venom. The boy had been told to be motionless if ever he saw a rattlesnake.

He heard a *zzzzttt* sound, then an arrow pierced the snake's belly. The creature twisted and writhed as Jocita rushed forward, knife in hand. In a quick movement she pinned the snake with the arrow, then cut off his head.

The snake tied himself into death knots as Jocita turned to her son. "Why did you walk off?" she demanded. "The snake almost killed you." She wanted to slap him, but realized he was too young to understand everything. More importantly, he hadn't been afraid.

He stood defiantly, feet spread apart, a confident expression in his eyes, and reminded her of the golden-haired Pindah war chief in his blue army uniform, striding across the campsite near the Santa Rita Copper Mines. Jocita hugged her son.

"You are a brave boy," she told him, "but no warrior can afford to be foolish. You must be careful in the future."

"I knew you would save me," he said.

Nathanial climbed the stairs to his mother's sitting room as if on his way to the gallows. He'd fortified himself with a large meal of roast chicken and sweet potatoes, among other delicacies, but still feared the wrath of the woman who'd given him life. He knocked on her door.

"Come in, Nathanial," she said sweetly, for she'd seen him arrive in his carriage, plus every other item of interest from her aerie overlooking Washington Square.

She often was nicest before a scolding, so his hand trembled as he closed the door behind him. "Hope I'm not bothering you," he said tentatively.

"No, but you look as if something's troubling you, Nathanial."

"I have a confession to make and fear you'll get angry. Perhaps you should prepare yourself."

"What is it this time?"

He took a deep breath. "I intend to marry again, Mother."

Amalia Barrington was brilliant at maintaining outward calm, but she turned red, then patted her breast daintily. "But you're not divorced yet."

"I'll wait, of course."

The dowager stiffened her spine as she prepared to take the blow. "Who is she?"

"Clarissa Rowland."

Again, Amalia Barrington's carefully constructed facade cracked. She managed to say, "But she's engaged to one of your best friends!"

"I hope he doesn't challenge me to a duel, because I don't want to kill him."

"You're not on the frontier now, my son. I doubt that Mr. Soames will challenge you to anything." She paused for a few moments, her brow wrinkled in thought, then she remembered who Clarissa Rowland was. "But you hardly know her."

"I know her well enough, and she plays the piano wonderfully."

"This isn't someone whom you've met in a frontier saloon. Her family has known ours for more than a hundred years. I and your no-good father would be very angry if you were to ruin her life, Nathanial."

"I don't think you understand, Mother. I love this woman. Why would I ruin her?"

"You've loved so many women, you are no longer a reliable witness, my son." She touched her hand to his cheek. "Promise that you won't break her heart."

"You have my oath. We're a perfect couple because she's a natural performer and I'm a natural spectator. What a joy it'll be to come home after a long scout and listen to Mozart expertly played."

"There's going to be a scandal, I'm afraid."

"Why do you worry about what others think?"

"Because sometimes others are right. Have you ever stopped to consider that your behavior is outrageous?"

"What's outrageous about getting married? I'll have a talk with Ronald, and if he doesn't shoot me in the back I'm sure everything will be fine."

"For how long?" asked his mother.

"You have no confidence in me, as if I'm an utter blackguard."

"Correct," replied his mother.

Ronald Soames liked to spend a few hours each evening at his club, where he drank whiskey, read newspapers, and related tales of lawyer glory with friends. Then he'd go home to his brick house between Gramercy Park and Fifth Avenue, one of the nicer neighborhoods in the city.

My life will change drastically after I'm married, he reflected. I won't be able to come here after work and read the *Tribune*. The lead story was a report that Russians had evacuated Moldavia and Walachia, while Austria massed troops in Galicia and Transylvania. A major battle was looming for the key city of Sebastopol, with hundreds of thousands of men and five armies involved, trying to hack each other to ribbons.

Soames was a dyed-in-the-wool New Yorker, so events in far-off lands took on a certain fantastical aspect. Military experts said that France, England, and Austria would experience no difficulty defeating doddering Russia, and the victors would expand into central Asia. How can America keep up if we don't increase our markets too? wondered Soames.

While analyzing the news, he heard the approach of one of the servants. "Sir, a lady asked me to give this to you."

It was an envelope carrying Clarissa's perfume. Probably a love poem or some other endearing message, he speculated, although she'd never sent love poems or endearing messages in the past. He tore it open and read:

Dear Ronald,
   I am waiting outside in a carriage, and have something important to tell you. It can't wait.
Clarissa

What's this? Soames asked himself. His tactics had been to exert no demands upon Clarissa, for it was a marriage of convenience, his lustful urges satisfied by her requirement to marry well. Yet Soames genuinely cared for Clarissa and believed she genuinely cared for him.

He descended stone steps in front of the club, noticing her waving from a carriage at the curb. "What's wrong?" he asked as he climbed opposite her.

She was calm, dressed in black, her blond curls furling beneath a black bonnet. "Thank you for coming, Ronald," she said in a steady voice.

"Has someone died?" he inquired wryly.

She was still as stone. "I am afraid I have very surprising news for you. Perhaps you'd better prepare yourself."

He examined her face, determining that she was controlling powerful emotions. "Whatever it is, it can't be *that* serious."

"I apologize from the bottom of my heart, but I have decided to break our engagement." She opened her hand and held out the engagement ring.

A lawyer must be prepared for anything, but Soames hadn't expected such a barrage. "But . . . but . . ." he sputtered.

"I will always admire you," she stated matter-of-factly. "We've had beautiful times together, and I'm flattered that such an accomplished gentleman could care for a fool such as I, but I've decided that I don't love you completely."

Soames realized with dismay that her lovely body would never belong to him. Remorse and sadness dropped onto him like a load of rotting oysters. "Don't you think it's a little late to come to that determination?" he asked through a throat constricted by inner pain.

"Better now than after we're married."

He looked at the ring. "Keep it to remember me by."

She wasn't interested in remembrances, but replied, "I shall cherish it always. Every time I look at it, I'll think of you."

He glanced at her. "Is there another man?"

"I'm afraid there is."

For the first time, Soames felt anger. "Who is he?"

"I don't want you to do anything ridiculous, like challenge him to a duel."

"What kind of barbarian do you think I am?"

"It's not something we planned. It just sort of happened, like destiny."

"Who is he?"

"A friend of yours, I'm sorry to say."

"Anybody who'd steal you is no friend of mine. Name the scum."

"Nathanial Barrington," she said in a low voice.

Soames's lungs emptied of air. "And to think I arranged his divorce! Clarissa, I'm not the finest human being who ever walked the earth, but Nathanial Barrington has had love affairs with so many women you couldn't fit them in Castle Garden. Until recently, he was seeing an actress who'd slept with just about everyone."

"Including you?"

Soames turned a sickly purple. "What will you do when he leaves you, as he inevitably will?"

"He won't."

"You're more immature than I realized," replied Soames icily.

Then, as he was about to leave the coach, he realized that he'd just insulted the wife-to-be of a client. Whoa, he said to himself. He smiled, leaned back into the carriage, and said, "Forgive me, my dear Clarissa. My feelings have been injured, but on reflection, I think you and Nathanial might have a very successful marriage. Perhaps you'll make a decent man out of him, which is what I'd hoped you do for me, actually."

She pointed her finger at him. "I don't want any funny business from you, Ronald. You'd better not hold up the divorce."

"But, my dear Clarissa—aren't you aware that the sooner the divorce is final, the sooner I'll be paid?"

Sergeant Berwick had learned his most important military lesson during his first enlistment. *Don't volunteer for anything.* Therefore, he thought it odd that he was becoming embroiled in the life of Private Doakes.

The sergeant entered the Silver Palace Saloon, and the three stripes on his arm cleared a path to the bar. "I want to speak with Cole Bannon," he said.

"In back," replied the man in the apron.

Sergeant Berwick shoved his way toward the corridor as a few drunkards pushed back. He passed a prostitute who stuck out her tongue at him. "What's yer hurry, First Sergeant?"

"Got to talk with Cole Bannon."

She blew him a kiss as he continued toward the corridor, then knocked on a door. "Come in."

The Texas Ranger sat behind his desk, on which stood a bottle and a glass half full of whiskey. Cole was bleary-eyed, face puffy. "What can I do for you?"

"It's about Doakes. The more I'm with him, the stranger he gits. Can't look you in the eye, has no friends, and when he's not workin', he's just wanderin' around, a funny look on his face. I don't know if he's yer man, but he sure is a little loco in the coco, if you knows what I mean."

Bannon took another sip. "He's more than loco, because innocent bystanders don't peep into people's windows. Regardless of what the judge said, I saw him with my own eyes. I'm convinced he's the killer."

There was a knock on the door. "I thought you'd be alone," said Maria Dolores.

"I was just leaving," replied Sergeant Berwick, grabbing his hat.

Maria Dolores stepped to the side as Sergeant Berwick clomped out of the office. Then she sat on the chair, leaned toward Cole Bannon, and said, "Where have you been?"

He shrugged. "Busy."

"When you lie, you show disrespect. Perhaps we should stop pretending that we are having a love affair."

"Maybe you're right."

Maria Dolores never realized he'd give up so easily. She felt faint, but instead raised herself to her full height. With great majesty she walked out of the office, but this time he didn't follow her. In the dark corridor outside, she waited a few moments. She didn't hear him coming so she continued, unsure of herself, wanting to cry.

In the main saloon, lonely men stared at her hungrily. She knew she could have any of them, but for how long? At least prostitutes get paid for what they do, she thought ruefully as she headed for the door. What a fool I was to trust men, who don't even trust each other.

Chapter Seventeen

Business-suited men carried satchels across Pearl Street as Nathanial paused beside the doorway of a six-story brick building. The neighborhood surrounding him financed enterprises across America, with he himself a beneficiary. He climbed the stairs to the offices of Soames and Soames. The clerk recognized him immediately. "Right this way, sir."

The clerk opened a door, Soames looked up with bloodshot eyes, the faint odor of alcohol exuding from his person, and he forced a smile. "What can I do for you today," he said in a shaky voice.

Nathanial walked up to him, placed his hand on his shoulder, and said, "I'm sorry."

"I haven't heard about your divorce yet, and was planning to mail a letter of inquiry this very day."

"Ronald, I said I'm sorry."

The lawyer's mask crumbled. "I accept your apology, of course. Clarissa prefers you and there's nothing I can do about it." He opened a drawer of his desk. "Care for a drink?"

"Don't mind if I do."

Soames poured two glasses, each took deep swigs. Nathanial wondered if Soames maintained a pistol in one of his drawers. The dragoon watched the lawyer's hands carefully as alcohol performed its medicinal task of calming two men in tense confrontation.

"She certainly is a pretty girl," sighed Soames. "I can understand why you couldn't resist."

"It wasn't like that at all. It was more like . . ."

"Destiny?" offered Soames, a mocking tone in his voice.

"It may sound like a cliché, but yes, it did seem like destiny."

"You can't fool me—it's lust pure and simple, but don't get me wrong—I've never been opposed to lust pure and simple. In fact, I've always considered it the most wonderful thing in the world, something we should all aspire to. I felt that way about Clarissa, but evidently she didn't share my ardor. I'm merely a lawyer, whereas you're her knight in shining armor. When Venus fell in love, did she not choose Mars?"

"Clarissa is the girl I've always searched for but never found. I don't know what she sees in me, but I don't give a damn. All that matters is she loves me."

Soames smiled sourly. "You're a charming fellow. I suppose you can have whatever you want."

"If that's so, why am I a lieutenant after nine years in the Army!"

"Because you're a man of impulse. Come to think of it, Clarissa will make the ideal officer's wife because she's really a clever little vixen beneath her fine cosmopolitan manners. I wonder what she'll be in ten years?"

"Where she's going," replied Nathanial, "she may not be alive in ten years. I feel terrible about what I've done to you, but . . ."

Soames raised his hand. "Please spare me this

cheap sentimentality, because we both know there is no honor among men where women are concerned. In a small corner of my heart, I shall hate you until the day I die, but there's no reason to let these relatively insignificant matters interfere with our professional relationship. You can rest assured that I shall continue to manage your legal affairs with my usual punctilious attention to detail, and now, if you'll excuse me, I'd like to be alone."

Maria Dolores decided the time had come to look through her father's belongings. She'd been too upset and busy to confront his memory, but now needed to connect with something, anything, even his clothes.

She saw them hanging in his closet as he'd left them, neat, plain suits in dark solid colors; he'd never appreciated finery or ostentation. Diego Carbajal had been a reader of books, an amateur philosopher or theologian who in another era might've become a rabbi.

The Catholic Church would receive his Jewish clothes, except one dark gray wool sweater with brown leather buttons. She intended to keep his collection of books, because nothing reminded her of her father as much as books.

Displayed prominently in the middle of his desk was his Bible. She opened it absentmindedly, noting he'd underlined certain passages.

My God, my God, why has thou forsaken me? Why are thou so far from helping me, and from the words of my longing?

Maria Dolores felt remote from God, although she'd gone to Mass every day prior to marriage. She remembered happiness during her first year with Nathanial, but then he spent increasingly long periods away from home, and finally was transferred to Fort Union. It was around that time that he'd confessed his offhand romance with the Apache squaw.

It had been the most sickening, painful blow of Maria Dolores's life. Many times she'd thought of shooting him. She flipped a few pages and was astonished to see underlined:

> But whoso committeth adultery lacketh understanding; he that doeth it destroyeth his own soul. A wound and dishonour shall he get; and his reproach shall not be wiped away.

It was as if God were speaking to her; she felt a chill in her bones. These were the words her father had lived by, realized Dolores. How different was he from Nathanial, a complete sensualist. I thought I loved Nathanial, then thought I loved Cole Bannon. But what is Love? She recalled the answer in I Corinthians 13, to which she turned. To her surprise, her Jewish father had underlined:

> Love beareth all things
> believeth all things
> hopeth all things
> endureth all things

I married a morally weak man and Cole was no better, concluded Maria Dolores. What does it say about me, for I pursued them, knowing full well they were liars.

She didn't miss Cole terribly, but her special wrath was reserved for Nathanial. Cole merely had been a fling, but Nathanial continued to stomp his cavalry boots through her Roman Catholic soul. I'm sure he's romancing another woman even as I sit here, she thought. He's selfish, utterly lost, or perhaps in love with love itself. Whoever his next wife is, she has my unqualified sympathy.

"Where are you going, dear?" asked Myra Rowland as her daughter headed for the front door.

"For a walk, Mother."

"Are you meeting *him*?"

"Yes."

"Don't you think you should introduce him to us, before you are seen alone with him."

"How can I introduce him to you if he's still married to someone else?"

"Perhaps you should wait until after the divorce before spending so much time with him."

"Susan B. Anthony says that women should break out of these outmoded notions of so-called 'proper' behavior."

"Susan B. Anthony never had a daughter, or even a husband. I would hardly call her an expert on the matter."

"Elizabeth Cady Stanton is married, has five children, and she says the same thing."

Her mother couldn't think of a rejoinder, so Clarissa kissed her cheek and was out the door. She wore a white summer dress with little blue flowers embroidered into the fabric, but no hat or parasol.

Her mother watched her cross Gramercy Park, eager to meet her man. I've never seen her so happy, her mother thought.

Guards were posted at all exits of the stable, plus at the front gate of Fort Marcy. It was night and Fletcher Doakes couldn't figure how to desert the Army. Seven dollars and change sat in his pocket, enough for a trip to the hog pens, but he didn't dare kill whores with the ranger and Sergeant Berwick asking the wrong questions.

On San Francisco Street, Doakes took note of horses tied to rails in front of saloons and cantinas. What if I simply climbed on one and rode out of town? he conjectured, glancing surreptitiously about him. Be just my luck that the cowboy who owns the horse will shoot me for a thief. And even if I got away, Apaches would slit my throat before I traveled a mile. Will I have to spend five years in this god-damned sorry excuse for a town? He stepped into an alley to be alone with his thoughts, but four privates were playing a game of dice. "Care to join in?" asked one of them.

"No, thank you," replied polite Private Doakes, the stranger among them. He walked deeper into the alley, passing a trooper lying on his back, a bottle in his hand, passed out cold.

Doakes peered across the backyard, spotting three whores in another alley. They smoked cigarettes and chatted in that loose suggestive manner reminiscent of his mother. Rage bubbled like poisonous potions in Doakes's heart as he reached for the length of twine that wasn't there. No longer did he carry it due to fear of arrest.

He narrowed his eyes at the three whores, wondering which to take with his bare hands. The need came on him like a tidal wave, and he was about to step across the backyard when something grabbed him by the throat! He let out a scream, as his eyes bulged at an iron gun barrel staring at him.

It was grasped tightly in the hand of Cole Bannon. "Looking for something?" asked the Texas Ranger. "Maybe you and your crooked lawyer fooled the judge, but you haven't fooled me. I ought to kill you right now."

"I didn't do nothin'," replied Doakes, teeth chattering. "You've got the wrong man."

Bannon's trigger knuckle went white, Doakes opened his lips to scream, and Cole Bannon rammed the barrel into his mouth, bruising lips and gums. In one-sixteenth of an inch, the trigger would fire, putting a hole in Doakes's skull. The image was so horrific, Doakes fainted dead away.

The killer lay on the ground in the shape of an S. Cole Bannon crouched over him, aiming his gun at Doakes's head, but Cole was a Texas Ranger sworn to uphold the law. He'd do the world a favor if he killed Doakes, but a shadow of doubt crossed his mind. I have no hard evidence and no jury will ever convict him. Do I have the right to take the law into my hands?

Doakes stirred on the ground, moaning softly as blood covered his mouth. Cole snarled, "I'm going to catch you someday, you piece of shit. Just when you think you're safe, you'll look over your shoulder and there I'll be."

In the darkness, Doakes's bloody lips made him look like a painted prostitute in army uniform.

"You're persecuting an innocent man," he tried to say.

Bannon couldn't control himself anymore. He drew back his gun and smacked it across Doakes's face. The killer rolled over, his cheek torn open by the blow. Bannon watched him whimpering, then holstered his gun and walked casually out of the alley.

The People monitored activity in their homeland through a network of carefully placed spies. One of these was Loco, a warrior of the Mimbreno clan. He lay on a ledge of the Sierra de la Madera Mountains and peered into the town of Janos, where a wagon train was being unloaded.

Loco had followed the wagons from southern Mexico, wondering what was contained in long boxes and tall barrels. Now he saw them lowered to the ground by soldiers. One took a tool and pried open the top of a box. A musket was lifted out, bringing a smile to Loco's deeply tanned face. Evidently the wagon was delivering weapons and ammunition to army posts.

Loco was accompanied by the apprentice warrior known as Antelope Boy, a grandson of Mangas Coloradas. "Ride back to our camp and tell the chief what is here," ordered Loco.

Antelope Boy wore his leather apprentice cap, and carried his Killer of Enemies Bandolier diagonally across his chest. Without a word, he crept back to his horse and began the long ride back to the Chiricahua Mountains.

Loco returned his eyes to the boxes of rifles. When they are ours, we shall wage more effective war. Why is it that the White Eyes and the Mexicans always have the best weapons?

He recalled the ancient legend about Child of Water and Killer of Enemies, sons of White Painted Woman, mother of the universe. One day Yusn lay a bow and arrow in front of them, and a rifle. "Choose," he said. Killer of Enemies snatched the rifle, so Child of Water was left with the bow and arrow. Killer of Enemies became father of the White Eyes, and Child of Water begat the People. According to the wisdom of the People, that was why the White Eyes possessed the best weapons.

A war dance was held two nights later in the Chiricahua Mountains. All the warriors gathered around a fire flickering on an open place within sight of the camp. Miguel Narbona was too old and weak to address them, so Cochise spoke in his stead.

Cochise had sharp eyes and a bare chest striated with muscles. His hair was tied in back, and the long bottoms of his breechclout were tucked into his belt. He raised his hand and intoned, "A wagon train of muskets is traveling through Chihuahua. It is supplying the forts, where more Mexican soldiers have been coming from the south. They intend to make big war against us, but we need those muskets for ourselves. I will go after them with Victorio, Delgadito, and Nana. Who is with us?"

A line of musicians pounded drums as Cochise, Victorio, Delgadito, and Nana stepped into the middle of the circle. They bowed to the four directions, then danced around the fire four times. Cochise and Delgadito took the northern position while Victorio and Nana stationed themselves to the south. In teams of two, the four prominent warriors danced toward each other, changed sides, turned, then returned to their original positions.

The four subchiefs sang of courageous war deeds as drummers beat their skins frantically and women made eerie ululating sounds. Warriors fired rifles into the air, and others danced as if engaged in hand-to-hand combat with enemies.

More warriors joined the original four as drums echoed more loudly. The warriors leapt through the air, thrust lances through imaginary enemies, or beat them to death with their bare hands. Some of the warriors carried cartridges in their fingers and mouths, others brandished knives. "Wah, wah, wah," they murmured. It was considered dangerous for warriors to shout before going on a raid, but women and children were exempted from the prohibition.

Cochise vaulted into the air, performed a somersault, and landed on his feet. Spinning, he saw young Geronimo, the brave Bedonko warrior. "You—Geronimo!" sang Cochise. "What will you do?"

Geronimo darted past the dancers, slashing his knife through the air as if disemboweling Mexican soldiers. Cochise hopped on one foot, then the other as he turned to Juh of the Nednai. "You—Juh!" called Cochise. "What will you do?"

Juh charged across the open space, bashing Mexican soldiers with his war club. Warriors danced themselves into war frenzy, and then Nana spotted Jocita, the warrior woman. "You—Jocita! What will you do?" She raised her bow and let fly an arrow at bats circling above the campfire, happily eating insects. One fell to the ground, an arrow through his heart.

"Wah! Wah! Wah!" sang the warrior woman as she shook her hips in the middle of the circle. Cochise called on new warriors to demonstrate their prowess as the ground became covered with dancing warriors, each stroking and strengthening the other's resolve. Oh, Yusn, please crown our efforts with victory.

At the edge of the dance, little Running Deer made threatening gestures with his hands, nearly falling onto his rear end, but managed to remain afoot as he pretended to be a warrior. The power of the people energized his growing bones, and he yearned for the day when he too could kill the *Nakai-yes* and the *Pindah-lickoyee*.

On their way back to Gramercy Park that night, Nathanial and Clarissa stopped at the new Academy of Music under construction at Fourteenth Street and Washington Irving Place. Covered with scaffolding, it appeared foreboding in the gaslight.

"There won't be any symphony orchestras on the frontier, I'm afraid," cautioned Nathanial. "Can you be happy without the culture that is so much a part of your life?"

"As long as I have a piano, I shall have Beethoven, Bach, and Mozart."

They continued uptown, passing two- and three-story brownstone homes with shuttered parlors. Trees lined the street, and in the glow of gaslight, it appeared an enchanted pathway. Nathanial felt Clarissa's young body against his side, and no one was looking. In the shadow of an elm tree, he bent and kissed her cheek.

She didn't push him away, so boldly he embraced her. She sighed in his ear, clasping him tightly. "I've had such fun tonight," she said. "I didn't know I could dance the polka."

"We'll have many good times together, Clarissa—I just know it."

"I can't wait until we're married."

"Neither can I."

"But we must."

They'd agreed not to make love before they were married, so restrained themselves somewhat as they continued to embrace in the shadows.

Next morning, Lieutenant Manuel Benitez raised himself in his saddle because he couldn't see his right flank guard. The terrain was uneven and the guard had dropped out of sight, hidden by foliage and rock outcroppings.

Lieutenant Benitez wore a thick black mustache and a green standard issue officer's cap with the eagle of Mexico in front. He wanted to call a halt and search the surrounding territory, but he'd cover less than a mile a day if he stopped whenever he felt uneasy.

His cargo of munitions was precious to Apaches, and he was surprised they hadn't attacked before. *Perhaps they are afraid, now that so many soldiers are in northern Mexico,* he guessed.

Lieutenant Benitez noticed that his left flank guard was out of sight as well, and was tempted to order his men to take up defensive positions. He turned around to inspect them, and they were the usual sullen lot who'd rather ride to the nearest town, with wine, guitars, and pretty senoritas.

"Sergeant Concho—have you seen the flank guards?"

"I was just wonderin' what happened to 'em myself, sir."

"Order the men to . . ."

Lieutenant Benitez never completed the sentence.

Dead Mexican soldiers covered the landscape, their animals had been taken prisoner, and now the warriors of the People were attending to their commissary.

They swarmed over wagons, tearing covers off crates, unloading new grease-packed muskets of antiquated design, but the warriors thought they were powerful medicine. Cochise sniffed a musket, then wiped grease away with his thumb. He drew back the hammer, pulled the trigger, and grease spattered. With a happy shout, he raised the rifle in the air.

The warriors sang songs of triumph, and among them was Victorio opening a crate of cartridges, even more valuable than guns. He held one in his fingers, admiring the round lead head and paper jacket filled with gunpowder. Such wondrous things do these people make, thought Victorio. But they are land thieves.

Other warriors removed gold rings from lifeless fingers, took shirts, pants, boots, and hats. Delgadito had selected a jacket with shiny yellow buttons, former property of the *Nakai-yes* war chief who lay on his back, an arrow through his heart. It was a fine trophy of war, a garment Delgadito would wear with pride, for it had been his arrow that had brought the *Nakai-yes* war chief down.

Something shiny caught the eyes of Jocita, the

warrior woman. It was a cross made of yellow metal around the neck of a soldier, and she thought it would look fine on her son. She advanced closer and pulled the cross away.

It was suspended from a gold chain, and showed the figure of a miniature man lying on the cross, apparently asleep. Then she noticed he was fastened by his hands and feet. She turned the cross around, and on the back was stamped:

TERRA CATACUMBA ROMA

She had no idea what it meant. At the figure's feet, there was an odd circle in which something indistinguishable was displayed. She thought it the work of evil sorcerers, but the amulet was so beautiful and mysterious she couldn't resist, dropping it into the deerskin pouch suspended from her belt.

Nearby, Nana wasn't searching for trinkets. His eyes were fixed on the pistol lying in the hand of a mutilated sergeant. He picked it up gingerly, afraid it would go off in his hands. It was cocked and loaded, so gently his thumb eased the hammer forward. He looked at the weapon as an extension of his arm. In close fighting, he wouldn't have to rely on his knife anymore.

On the other side of the killing ground, Geronimo's nose wrinkled in puzzlement as he held up a strange object that made a constant ticking sound. Is it alive or a machine? he wondered. What kind of enemies would build such a thing? And what is its purpose? The talisman had a round white face and appeared to be laughing at him. Geronimo laughed back, then dropped the shiny object into his saddle-bags.

Nathanial sat in the dining room of the Saint Nicholas Hotel, feasting on broiled Long Island lobster. It was his first evening alone since he'd become engaged to Clarissa, and he felt as if half of his very own being were missing.

The dining room was filled with patrons, waiters wore white jackets, the dessert tray covered with cakes, pies, puddings, and exotic cream-filled pastries, but he considered Clarissa the most delicious meal in the world.

Yet he'd thought the same about Maria Dolores, and feared one day his beautiful young maiden would leave him, as did his Mexican wife. If Clarissa gave up Soames for me, maybe she'll give me up for another.

Doubt came over him. What if Clarissa should become a harpy and nag? But surely we love each other, and our love will conquer all difficulties, although I thought the same when I married Maria Dolores. What if I get tired of Clarissa after a few years?

A bellboy entered the dining room, then headed straight for Nathanial. "A message for you, sir."

Nathanial opened the envelope with a salad knife. The letterhead was from the law office of Soames and Soames, and the message read:

Dear Nathanial,
    I've received the requisite documents from your former wife's lawyer. Congratulations—you're a di-

vorced man. I hope you won't forget to invite your
devoted lawyer to the wedding.

Ronald Soames
Counselor at Law

Chapter Eighteen

On September 16, 1854, Nathanial Barrington married Clarissa Rowland at Trinity Church before a congregation that included family, dignitaries, politicians, army officers, and even the retired Colonel Barrington was in attendance, having ridden from Washington, D.C., on a train. He sat dutifully beside his legal wife, although everyone knew he was residing in Washington, D.C., with an octoroon.

Reginald van Zweinen was best man, and Clarissa's younger sister Marion was maid of honor. Nathanial was attired in a new blue army uniform, while Clarissa wore a long white gown and veil. A choir performed selections from Bach and Handel, and the service was conducted by the Reverend William Berrian, rector of Trinity Church.

"I pronounce you man and wife."

The bride and groom walked arm in arm down the aisle, flowers and rice fell upon them, and Nathanial recalled his marriage in Santa Fe, with a few friends in attendance at the small abode church, and Apaches raiding the countryside.

The wedding procession rode in carriages to the Saint Nicholas Hotel, where a fifteen-piece orchestra was waiting in the grand ballroom, playing

Beethoven's *Eroica* Symphony. With Clarissa on his arm, the Napoleon of Broadway shook hands with friends, people he'd never seen before, vague uncles, remote cousins, souls he'd known in the first grade, classmates from West Point, women he'd seduced, other women who'd successfully resisted his advances, and his Uncle Jasper wearing a big red carnation in his lapel, his white false teeth gleaming in gaslight streaming down from four chandeliers. Nathanial wondered if he was asleep on the New Mexican desert, having the grandest dream of his life.

Reginald van Zweinen brought glasses of champagne and proposed a toast to the newlyweds, then wedding guests made way as Reginald led the magic couple to the floor. The band played and the newlyweds waltzed to enthusiastic applause. Waiters rolled wagons covered with beef, turkey, and lamb into the ballroom while Nathanial and his bride twirled gracefully in the gaslight.

Nathanial Barrington had killed Apaches and Mexicans, and had gazed into their eyes as they'd gone down. Yet despite the travails and disappointments of military service, he felt sanctified in a strange new way. He looked into the eyes of his beloved, and said, "It's getting off to a great start, wouldn't you say?"

"The best is yet to come," she replied as they glided smoothly across the floor.

The bridal suite consisted of six large rooms on the top floor of the hotel, with a view of Trinity Church, the Battery, and the juncture of the Hudson and East rivers sparkling in moonlight.

The bride and groom finally were alone, the consecrated longed-for time had arrived, all doors securely locked, and a bottle of champagne stood askew like a drunken soldier in a bucket of ice. Nathanial and Clarissa were legally married in the eyes of God and man, with all barriers gone.

They didn't have much to say because they'd been talking constantly nearly every evening since they'd met. They knew each other's opinions, moods, quirks, and tendencies, except one.

His practiced hand worked down her spine, unfastening the buttons of her gown, then his naughty fingers came to rest on the bare flesh of her back as she held his face and kissed his lips.

She wasn't afraid, he wasn't awkward, and she was becoming rather wanton now that no restrictions remained. Her dress fell off and he took a step backward to admire her clad only in chemise and longcloth drawers.

He raised the chemise over her head, revealing pert breasts he'd glimpsed briefly before, but now were his possessions for life according to Reverend Berrian. Then he pulled down her drawers, leaving her naked before him.

An artery pounded his throat and he felt the urge to throw her onto the bed, but she stepped forward and unbuttoned his tunic. Next was his shirt, then she boldly unfastened his pants. The garments dropped to the floor.

Naked, he lifted her in his arms and said, "Do you remember the night when I held you like this, and was going to throw you into Cortlandt Lake?"

"Instead you kissed me."

He repeated the performance, then laid her on the

bed. They embraced naked for the first time, their tongues touched, and hands explored new and interesting flesh. It was the intimacy they'd been longing for, and they indulged their passion with increasing audacity, while on Broadway, weary wedding guests were piling into a row of waiting coaches.

The lovers forgot their wedding guests as they feasted upon each other's bodies. Whenever Clarissa hesitated to perform a new and delightful act, Nathanial gently encouraged her to proceed. It was all she had hoped her wedding might be, while her patient professor, the former whorehouse connoisseur, achieved new heights of ecstasy in her silken arms.

Several hours later, Nathanial opened his eyes in semidarkness. It was midmorning, blue velvet drapes covered the windows, and carriages rumbling on Broadway could be heard through open windows. He felt his little wife sleeping beside him.

He hugged her more tightly and touched his lips to the top of her head. Some uncharitable men might say she was skinny, mousy, or too goody-good, but he considered her a work of art with her spare but aesthetically perfect body. She had just enough of everything, in his opinion.

He couldn't help recalling other women in his life, even as he held his lovely new wife in his arms. How similar they were in the toils of passion, as if their personalities vanished, leaving behind only the elemental growling woman.

When it came to passion, he'd never known anything quite like the Apache woman. Occasionally, at odd moments, she came to mind like an apparition.

Her savage grace, not to mention her powerful but feminine muscles, had driven him berserk. I wonder what she's doing right now, he mused as his latest wife whispered something unintelligible in the darkness.

I just got married but I'm thinking about another woman, thought Nathanial with a smile. He touched his lips to Clarissa's golden hair, inhaling its flowerlike fragrance. From this day onward, I am your property.

The People frowned upon solitary spirit guests, such as those of Plains and other Indians. They believed solutions and answers could be provided best within the context of family, clan, and tribe.

Twenty-eight-year-old Geronimo was an aberration in this regard, but he was a di-yin medicine man in addition to being a warrior, and often liked to go off by himself, probing questions that perplexed him. Where did the sun go at night, and what is meant by the markings of the moon? Geronimo believed every living or inanimate thing held power, secrets, and meanings.

If there had been no *Nakai-yes* and *Pindah-lickoyee*, Geronimo would not have become a warrior. His strongest inclination was to the depths, but then his family had been murdered by Mexicans, so he'd taken the warrior trail.

During his youth, prior to his first marriage, he'd gone on a pilgrimage with other medicine men, in search of power. They'd traveled to distant lands, meeting Crow, Comanche, and Sioux, learning new customs and methods of attaining power, and nearly getting killed a few times.

One practice had been taught Geronimo by Happy Elk of the Osage People. It was a plant called peyotl that the initiate chewed and swallowed. Geronimo had learned where to find the plant, how to harvest and prepare it, and how it should be ingested.

He'd placed a few dried chips of sacramental vegetative matter into his mouth at dawn, and now could see faint orange pulsations on the horizon, a new day dawning in the Dragoon Mountains. Rock formations like gray blood sausages arose around him as he sat on a rock plateau, gazing at vistas of valleys, plains, mountains, and meandering streams.

He felt as if someone were pumping fresh blood into his head as he watched strange multicolored images in the skies. He thought they were mountain spirits gesturing to him, trying to teach him esoteric truths.

He wanted them to help him understand his enemies, so he picked up the shiny yellow object and held it close to his ear. It still was ticking. He tapped it curiously, fingered the little wheel on top, made it click back and forth. What is this thing? wondered Geronimo in the delirium of peyotl.

It troubled him to know that White Eyes possessed power utterly incomprehensible to him. Was there a demon inside, working at a tiny contraption? Geronimo shook the watch, but the tick continued strongly. Perhaps the little demon is tied in place, surmised Geronimo.

The more it ticked, the more he wondered what would happen if he broke it open. Possibly it would explode like a shell from the cannon of the bluecoat soldiers. Maybe the demon would grab him by the throat.

Geronimo lay the ticker on the ground, picked up a rock, then dropped it. The crystal shattered. He found an opening in the case, inserted the blade of his knife and twisted.

There were little wheels of shiny metal. Geronimo marveled at fingers that could craft such objects, or perhaps they were evoked by sorcerers. He dropped the watch and took a step backward. A feeling of dread came over him as he caught a vision of himself as an old man planting corn in a faraway land. That will never happen to me, he swore as he kicked the watch off the ledge.

He heard sounds of the thing falling down the mountain, its wheels and springs bursting into the air. Then the ticking stopped at last, and the holy mountain became tranquil once more.

Fletcher Doakes turned on his cot, itching and scratching. No matter where he moved, he couldn't sleep. He wanted to run naked through the barracks, screeching at the top of his lungs, lopping off heads with a sabre.

He felt as if he were dying of an insidious disease. No matter where he lay, he felt uncomfortable. Hornets and snakes crawled over him and something bored into his left shinbone.

Finally he crawled out of his cot, put on his uniform, and tiptoed out the door. The cool night tweaked his nose as he gazed longingly at the stable. He couldn't think clearly, as if waterfalls were flooding his mind.

He needed solace desperately, but no one would

place her arm over his shoulders. He remembered how he'd cried as a child while his mother ignored him, too busy reading newspapers, applying cosmetics, or going and coming with men. Fletcher hated them all, but he'd especially despised his mother. The other children had made fun of him at school, calling the sensitive boy *son of a whore*. He held his hands over his ears, to block their voices.

A guard stood at the proscenium door to the stable, his rifle slung over his shoulder. "Can't sleep?" he asked.

"Thought I'd lie down in the loft. You know how it is sometimes."

"A few of the boys git to a-snorin'," replied the guard, "it sounds like lumberjacks sawin' down trees."

The clerk smiled as he entered the stable, but continued to scratch when out of sight. It felt as if a worm wriggled in his ear. He found an empty stall, climbed inside, stuck out his tongue, and dug his fingernails into his skull, drawing tiny dots of blood. The straw on the bottom of the stable looked like rising flames, and he wondered if the stable was on fire.

Why couldn't I have been born a horse? he wondered. He gazed at the gray mare in the next stall, who examined him warily. "I won't hurt you, girl," said Fletcher softly. "You're too beautiful to kill, and I know you're a good mother because it's your instinct. The trouble with people is we think too much."

The horse looked at him curiously as Fletcher heard the crackle of straw behind him. He turned and saw a figure approaching in the darkness. "Who goes there!" he demanded, reaching for his pistol.

A familiar face loomed out of the shadows. "It's just Sergeant Berwick. I was on my way to the latrine and thought I saw you wandering about. Are you all right, Doakes?" In the dim light, with his shirt half unbuttoned, Berwick looked like one of Doakes's mother's lovers in the morning, trying to be polite.

"I ain't feeling so good, Sarge."

"You'll feel better if you unburden your heart, my boy." Sergeant Berwick climbed into the stall, then placed his hand on Doakes's shoulder and said softly, "I'm your friend. You can trust me."

"I do trust you, Sergeant," said Doakes as he lowered his hand toward the knife on his belt. "What do you want to know?"

Berwick peered into his eyes. "What's bothering you?"

"I'm a murderer, Sergeant. Didn't you know?"

Berwick smiled. "Yes, I did. It's because you're sick in the mind, isn't it?"

"I hear voices that tell me to kill."

"You should listen to those that tell you to be good."

An unholy light burned in Doakes's eyes. "But I'm only happy when I kill, Sergeant. Some people die of disease, others of old age, and a few die of me. I am the scourge of God." He casually rested his hand on the knife. "Have we ever met before?"

"Who do you think I am?"

"Didn't you sleep with my mother last night?"

"I never knew your mother. You're really quite confused, aren't you?"

"Yes," replied Doakes as he plunged the knife toward Berwick's gut.

Berwick raised his arm to protect himself while opening his mouth to scream. But he was taken by surprise, Doakes changed direction and slashed his throat. No sound issued from the sergeant save one last gasp.

"Fool," whispered Doakes as Sergeant Berwick collapsed onto the floor. "You thought you could outsmart me?" Doakes kicked the corpse. "At least I won't have to worry about your damned snooping anymore."

Doakes felt dizzy as the mare looked at him reproachfully. "I couldn't help it," said Doakes. "It was him or me."

Suddenly Doakes realized the enormity of his deed, and broke into a cold sweat. He'd need a horse and saddle, and was in the stable where those things were kept. The guards had not been roused from their usual torpor. Perhaps I can get away with another murder, thought Doakes.

He saddled the mare and slipped on the bridle. I may be shot in the back, but it's my only chance. He climbed into the saddle and held the reins. "If you get me out of this mess," he told the horse, "I'll turn you loose, all right?"

It's a deal, the horse seemed to be saying.

Doakes rammed his heels into the horse's ribs. She leapt forward and galloped past rows of stalls as captive horses cheered her on, or at least that's how it seemed to Doakes. The guard was standing at the entrance, rifle in hand. "What the hell's goin' on thar!" he bellowed.

Doakes fired his service revolver at the guard, the

startled soldier leapt out of the way, and the mare charged past him, galloped across the parade ground, and headed for the main gate. "Halt—who goes there!" yelled two guards.

Doakes's response was two quick shots from his pistol. The soldiers dropped to their bellies and managed to trigger a few wild ones, then frantically rolled out of the way. Doakes passed through the gate, nearly falling off the horse's back.

The guards shouted the alarm as Doakes turned the first corner, hugging the horse's throat with his arms, heading for the open range.

The bartender was a tall broad-shouldered man with a long swooping mustache. He wiped his hands on a towel as he approached the table where Cole Bannon sat with an old newspaper and a mug of beer. "I just heard somethin' you might be interested in," said the bartender. "Remember that sergeant you was talkin' with t'other night, name of Berwick?"

"What about him?" asked Cole, raising his eyes.

"Some soldier killed him, then stole an army horse."

"What was the soldier's name?"

"I don't remember."

Cole gulped down the rest of his beer, put on his hat, and was out the door. He walked swiftly toward Fort Marcy, suspecting that Doakes had struck again. He climbed the stairs to the command post headquarters and found it full of officers and sergeants. He removed his Texas Ranger tin badge from his shirt pocket and showed it to a captain.

"Sergeant Berwick was helping with one of my cases. I heard he was killed tonight."

"That's right," replied Captain Milligan. "He's in the hospital if you want to see his corpse."

"Who did it?"

"A recruit named Fletcher Doakes. We've got two detachments looking for him and expect to bring him in soon."

The stolen mare galloped across a rock-strewn plateau as Fletcher Doakes looked at his back trail. He couldn't see far, but knew he was leaving an easy trail. Somehow he had to reach Mexico before the Army caught him. Facing forward in the saddle, he whipped the reins against the haunch of his horse and jabbed his spurs hard into her belly. "Faster," he told her.

"You said you'd set me free," she seemed to be saying.

"Later."

He kicked her again, then noticed she was slowing. It occurred to him that perhaps he'd pushed her too hard. "What's wrong with you?" he asked.

A glazed expression was in her eyes as she slogged to a stop, her great sides heaving. Blood dripped from her withers, where he'd spurred her. "We can take a rest," said Doakes, trying to be friendly. "I'll give you water from my canteen, all right?"

He raised his leg to climb out of the saddle, when he realized she was going down. He jumped clear, then turned and saw her land on her side, where she quivered and twitched. He was stranded on the desert with no canteen, horse, or compass. The beast stopped moving, her tongue hanging out.

Doakes realized it would be harder for the cavalry to track him on foot. In the morning he'd climb to a high place and look for patches of green, where there'd be water. Perhaps I can waylay a hapless traveler, he thought optimistically, withdrawing his knife, still stained with Sergeant Berwick's blood. Doakes cut out the horse's loin, then wrapped the bloody flesh around his neck. "Bye bye," he said to the dead animal as he began his long trek to Mexico.

In the morning, Maria Dolores read to her children in the parlor. She'd chosen the story of Joseph and his coat of many colors. It illustrated a point that she wanted them to learn, that rivalry among family members was wrong.

There was a knock on the door, which was opened by one of her maids. "Senor Bannon wants to see you," she said.

Maria Dolores was annoyed, because she didn't want him coming to her home. "Read to the children while I speak with him."

Maria Dolores made her way to the vestibule. Cole stood in the doorway, hat in hand, while behind him a saddle horse and packhorse were tied to the rail.

"I've come to say good-bye," he said awkwardly. "I arrived in Santa Fe looking for a certain murderer, and he left town a few hours ago. I'm sorry, but . . ."

"There is no need to explain."

"Maybe we'll get together down the trail."

They touched lips coolly, then gazed into each other's eyes, recalling burning nights in his hotel room. Then he turned and walked toward his horses, as she realized he was the second man who'd left her out of so-called "duty."

He climbed onto his horse and rode out of her

life, his packhorse trailing behind him. They love you madly and promise anything, reflected Maria Dolores, until they find something more important to do.

At sunset, Jocita and Running Deer sat on a level bed of leaves high in the Chiricahua Mountains. They could see distant peaks, immense valleys, rolling mountains, and the red glimmer of the setting sun on the surface of a creek.

"I have something for you, my son," said Jocita. She reached into her leather pouch, withdrew the gold cross and chain, and held it before his eyes.

"What is it, Mother?"

"It is an amulet of great power."

"It looks like a man who is asleep. What power is that?"

"He is having great dreams."

The boy stared at the man on the cross. There was something interesting about him. "Who is he?"

She dropped the necklace around his neck. "He is God of the White Eyes and the Mexicans. When you discover his secret, you will accomplish great deeds."

His mother and father always spoke of great deeds, yet he was a little boy unskilled in the ways of the world. Please help me, god of the cross, he prayed as the symbol branded his malleable soul.

Chapter Nineteen

For their honeymoon, Nathanial and Clarissa Barrington sailed across the Atlantic Ocean on the clipper ship *Flying Cloud*. They landed in Southampton, rode a train to London, checked into a hotel, and proceeded to venture forth to museums, concert halls, theaters, and restaurants.

Newspapers were filled with the Crimean War, and soldiers in the multivaried uniforms of the Crown could be seen everywhere, plus flags and patriotic signs. The newlyweds visited Shakespeare's grave in Stratford-upon-Avon, watched the changing of the guard at Buckingham Palace, and in late September removed to Paris, another city at war. It wasn't unusual to see troops marching on the Champs D'Elysees, and what if the Tsar decided to spend the winter at Versailles? But Nathanial and Clarissa felt remote from the turmoil as they dined one evening at a café on the Boulevard Malesherbes.

"Isn't there someplace we can go where they're not having a war?" asked Clarissa.

He brought her hand to his lips. "We're off to Venice."

The next day they rode a train to Dijon, sitting opposite each other. Nathanial observed her fine profile as she gazed out the window at picturesque country farms. These are the happiest days of my life, he told himself.

They arrived in Venice and rented the top floor of a small hotel off the Grand Canal, often remaining in bed all day as the world passed in the murky waters below. From their pillows, they could see over the rooftops of Venice to the glittering Adriatic Sea.

They rented a gondola, and Apaches were far from their minds as they floated down the Grand Canal, a mandolin player strumming the rhythms of Umbria, and the gondolier warbling an out-of-tune chorus of an apparently different song.

In weeks to come, the Indian fighter and his pianist bride spent many hours aboard gondolas, accompanied by bottles of wine, loaves of bread, and fontina, provolone, and Gorgonzola cheeses.

One night, the rooms at the Doge's Palace were brightly lit as Nathanial and Clarissa drifted past on their gondola. It was the Festival of All Souls, when everyone wore colorful costumes. Clarissa was dressed as a Gypsy dancer, while Nathanial had on the red-and-white stripes of a clown. They drank wine as crowds danced gaily and cannon fired at the fort that defended Venice from the sea.

Nathanial leaned toward Clarissa and kissed her ear. "If we're as rich as everybody says, why don't we stay in Venice for the rest of our lives?"

One bright November afternoon on the Journado del Muertos, the army scout Thaddeus Singleton spotted a figure that looked like a man on the trail ahead. Singleton had known something was waiting for him, for he'd seen buzzards circling since early morning. The scout rode ahead to investigate, and it was indeed an emaciated bearded traveler in raggedy clothes, barefoot, filthy, barely moving, mumbling about his mother. The rest of the detachment arrived, commanded by recently commissioned Second Lieutenant Arnold Haskell.

"He's alive," said Singleton, "but not by much."

Private Johnson was a medical orderly, and the first thing he did was search for wounds. There were none, but the stranger appeared nearly starved. "Who are you?" asked Johnson.

A strangled wheeze emitted from the stranger's throat. Johnson cradled the hapless traveler in his arms and gave him water from his canteen. "What are you doing here?"

The man whispered something that sounded like, "The Apaches."

"Give him something to eat," said Lieutenant Haskell. "Looks like he was on a wagon train and Indians got them."

Fletcher Doakes was able to swallow a bit of biscuit soaked in coffee. He'd lost track of time.

"What's your name?" asked the orderly.

Doakes managed to shake his head slightly.

The orderly looked at his commanding officer. "I think his mind's gone, sir."

"Load him onto the wagon and let's get a move on. I'd want to be in Fort Craig by sundown."

In January of 1855, Captain Richard Stoddert "Baldy" Ewell sat on his horse in the Pecos country of west Texas and watched a Mescalero Apache encampment of eighty teepees go up in smoke.

The newly expanded U.S. Army was finally getting

serious about Apaches, and in the Ninth Department, it had been a difficult winter campaign, but Captain Ewell had just delivered the death blow to the Mescalero resistance. Surviving warriors fled on foot into the mountains, women and children wailed over the dead as the tribe's economic base burned before their eyes. The victorious dragoons felt exhilarated, for no training can prepare a man for shooting another at point-blank range.

Captain Ewell was a Virginian and a graduate of West Point, class of 1840. He knew that the majority of warriors had escaped, but the destruction of a village would send an important message to the Mescaleros. The dragoons also had captured a large herd of horses, mules, and stolen sheep.

Captain Ewell wasn't a lover of war or an ogre in a blue-and-gold army uniform. His job was to defend American settlers, and he never doubted the correctness of that policy. Next time the Mescaleros decide to steal sheep or ambush stray American detachments, they'll give it a second thought, he calculated. If they don't stop their damned raiding, I'll burn the whole damned Apache nation to the ground.

The Journada del Muertos, the Santa Fe Trail, and the Gila Trail were highways through New Mexico Territory, but there also existed other less used paths and trails. Here and there, on those barely marked ways, the weary traveler might find a small general store and saloon with a makeshift bar, a few tables, and shelves suspending an odd collection of merchandise, depending on what the owner had been able to acquire.

One general store sat in the Pinos Altos Mountains, where occasionally a pack train of miners passed by, or a few lost wandering vaqueros. They permitted the owner, Pedro Martinez, to eke out a meager existence.

He was sixty-seven years old, with a thick head of white hair and a long, white beard. His old wife helped him run the place, and they spent long hours together, going about their respective chores. Apaches never bothered them, because Pedro merely bought their stolen goods and sold them back whatever they wanted, including guns and ammunition. Throughout the bloodshed and betrayals of the Apache Wars, certain Apaches and Mexicans went on with business as usual.

One night in February, as Pedro was about to blow out the candle on the bar, he heard a hoofbeat outside. He glanced at his wife in alarm, because both knew the frontier was full of thieves, murderers, and cutthroats. His wife carried a Colt .44 beneath her serape, and he maintained a shotgun behind the bar.

A horse snorted outside, then the door opened. A stranger of medium height, wearing a brown cowhide jacket and a black wide-brimmed hat, entered the general store, his hand near his holster. He glanced around, then relaxed and sauntered to the bar. "Bed for the night?"

"That is what we are here for, senor. You look like you need a drink." Pedro poured a half glass of whiskey. The stranger took an enormous gulp, then sat heavily at the table.

"I hope you've got feed for my horse."

"The best oats, sir. Do you need tobacco?"

"Don't mind if I do."

The storekeeper placed a white cotton bag filled

with two ounces of tobacco on the table. "Are you a miner?"

"No—a Texas Ranger." Cole Bannon displayed the tin badge affixed to his shirt. "I'm looking for a man named Fletcher Doakes, although I suspect he's changed his handle by now. He's about five feet ten, got a face like a rat, and acts kind of strange, as if somebody dropped a can of worms down his back. Ever see anything like that?"

Pedro looked at his wife. "There are many men who fit that description, senor."

"Have you heard anything about murdered women?"

"It is only my wife and me here, senor. I will take care of your horse and she will prepare your bed."

Maybe the Apaches got him, Cole figured as he relaxed in the cozy saloon. Or maybe I'll ride into some little settlement one of these days, and they'll tell me about murdered women. I'm the only one who can stop Fletcher Doakes, but next time I won't lock him in jail. Cole drew his Colt and aimed at a knot of wood on the wall. Next time I'll take care of him myself.

Chapter Twenty

Jefferson Davis's reorganization of the Army became official on March 3, 1855. The new First and Second Cavalry Regiments were authorized, along with a new regiment of mounted riflemen, plus three more regiments of infantry. The Secretary of War's efforts to designate all mounted units as cavalry failed due to resistance from the First and Second Dragoons, who held fast to their traditions, achievements, and sacrifices.

Also effective that day, the musketoon was scheduled for replacement by new rifles utilizing the Minie ball principle. Invented by a French infantry captain, the Minie ball was a lead plug that expanded upon detonation, filling the grooves in the bore, greatly improving accuracy. Units would be issued the new muzzle-loader in .58 caliber as fast as they could be manufactured, while old musketoons would be rebored for the new projectile. In addition, new Sharp's breechloading rifles were issued to selected units for testing in the field.

On April 20th, 1855, Jefferson Davis's own Second Cavalry Regiment was commissioned at the army barracks in Louisville, Kentucky. Officers and men in newly designed uniforms sat on their mounts and presented arms as the gold-and-black regimental colors were run up the flagpole.

All was silent except the breeze over parade ground grass, the slap of the flagpole rope, and the occasional thud of a hoof. Every officer and soldier in the ranks knew it was a hallowed moment, and each had been especially selected.

Colonel Albert Sidney Johnston of Texas, commander of the Second Cavalry, was absent on that auspicious day, pulling court martial duty at Fort Leavenworth, but instead his executive officer led the inauguration ceremony, sitting upon his white stallion, holding his sword hilt before his eyes.

He was Lieutenant Colonel Robert E. Lee, Mexican War hero from Virginia. Other Southern officers present for duty that morning included Captain Earl Van Doren, Captain Kirby Smith, Lieutenant John Hood, and Major William Hardee, author of the Army's manual on cavalry tactics.

Their uniforms had been designed by Jefferson Davis himself, consisting of close-fitting blue jackets, yellow braid, silk sashes, and stiff black hats decorated with ostrich feathers sticking out of the hatbands, their left brims fastened to crowns with gleaming gold eagle insignia.

They also wore highly polished brass shoulder shields to turn sabre strokes of the enemy, and all were armed with the latest Colt .36 caliber pistols. In addition, enlisted men carried across their pommels experimental models of the new Sharps breechloading carbine. Their horses cost one hundred fifty dollars apiece, twice what the Army usually paid for

mounts. Their orders were proceed to Texas and sub-
due the Comanches.

And thus was the nucleus of the new Southern
Army born.

On June 7, 1855, the Mescalero Apaches and
some Gila Apache tribes signed a peace treaty with
Dr. Steck at Fort Thorn. The doctor was painfully
aware that Mangas Coloradas wasn't a party to the
agreement, because the old chief staunchly refused
to cede any Mimbreno land to the U. S. government.

Following the signing ceremony, Dr. Steck gave
presents to the defeated Mescaleros. The ex-
physician felt like an accomplice to a crime, but
General Garland's tactics had achieved results deci-
sively and quickly.

The proud Mescaleros were a conquered people
like their brothers and sisters, the Jicarillas. With
great shame the warriors accepted bags of beans
given them by sarcastic soldiers. Dr. Steck knew it
wouldn't be long before General Garland took the
field against the western Apaches, and that would be
the end of Apaches in America.

Dr. Steck wished he could heal pain in the hearts
of the Mescaleros, but defeat was bitter to proud
warriors. There has to be a better way, the doctor
told himself as he returned to his office after the ceremony. It's a dirty job that I've got, but better than
shooting poor, ignorant savages, like the soldiers.

Maybe something hopeful will come out of this
shameful day, he thought. Mangas Coloradas might
come to his senses when he hears about the destruction of the Mescaleros.

* * *

One morning the nearly decrepit Miguel Narbona and the aging Mangas Coloradas went off by themselves and held council. They selected a rock plateau atop a tall mountain covered with spruce and pine. Incredible distances spread before them, expanding the walls of their minds. They sat cross-legged on the ground, laid out the food they'd brought, and ate nuts, jerked venison, and dried mescal, at ease with grand vistas surrounding them.

After the meal, they passed the pipe back and forth. The horizon took on a golden hue, the blue sky pulsated, and two old chiefs viewed each other as young warriors again, covered with war paint.

In truth, Miguel Narbona was ancient and gnarled, but his eyes glowed like amethysts as he broached the subject that had brought them together. "Are we next?" he asked.

Mangas Coloradas nodded tragically. "First they destroyed the Jicarillas, now the Mescaleros. But they will not destroy the Chiricahuas and Mimbrenos."

"But your holy mountains are now occupied by the White Eyes."

"Perhaps, if I sign a paper, I can gain time."

Miguel Narbona's wrinkled eyes grew wet with tears. "The era of the People is ending, I fear."

Mangas Coloradas held the older chief's shoulder steady. "No—the People are like the mountains themselves, who remain unto eternity. A terrible holocaust is coming, but you and I will not be here to see it, my warrior brother. It is Cochise, Victorio, Juh, Loco, Chatto, Nana, and Geronimo the Bedonko—they are the ones who shall meet the challenges in times to come."

Miguel Narbona looked both ways, as if someone else might hear. Then he turned to Mangas Coloradas and said, "They are young warriors, and their blood may be too hot for the tribulations of the future."

The great chief Mangas Coloradas replied, "They are exactly the ones whom the People shall require, to show the White Eyes we are not weaklings. Perhaps Yusn has ordained the ultimate defeat of the People, but the deeds of the warriors I named shall be written in blood, and their names shall never be forgotten."

In the small bustling settlement next to Fort Craig, an adobe church and convent had been dedicated to Saint Cecilia. It was here that the survivor of the massacre was nursed back to health.

The patient no longer called himself Fletcher Doakes, and his story of the massacre had been pure fabrication. He lay on clean white sheets in a tiny cell, similar to the ones occupied by nuns. The pious women brought delicious meals, prayed over him four times a day, treated his wounds and believed he was a merchant.

He now called himself Norbert Denigran, because the name had a certain flair that he admired. The convent was far from Fort Macy, but next to an army camp, of all places.

The reborn Norbert Denigran was happy to be alive. After the horse meat had been consumed, he'd lived on any hapless creature that came his way, regardless of how many legs or wings it possessed. When at death's door, he'd finally stumbled upon a trail. Now he was fellowshipping with pious nuns.

One was Sister Teresa, sixteen, with bright rosy cheeks and a slight form beneath her pale blue habit. She carried his breakfast tray into the room and said, "You look wonderful today, Senor Denigran. May I feed you?"

"Can feed myself," he wheezed, his hand trembling as he raised the fork.

She smiled beatifically and held her hands together.

"Are you praying?" he asked weakly.

"Yes, for you."

Had he possessed strength, he would've laughed in her face. But instead he said, "Pray for someone more needy than I, perhaps a sick child, or a mother."

"You are a good man, Senor Denigran," she replied. "When first they brought you here, you looked like Christ. Your experience in the desert has brought you closer to Him, I think."

She smiled beatifically, and he wondered how she'd look with a rope around her throat, her tongue distended, and her eyes popping out of her head.

Miguelito stood in the doorway. "There is a drifter who wants to be a guard."

"What does he look like?" asked Maria Dolores.

A hand appeared, pushing Miguelito away. Then a gigantic cowboy or bullwhacker strolled confidently into her office. "If you want to know what the hell I look like, why don't you use your own two eyes?"

Never had she seen such a chest, not even with her former husband. This brute's biceps bulged at his shirtsleeves. "You're the biggest fellow I've ever seen," she said in genuine awe.

He stood before her desk, a knife sticking out of each boot, a pistol slung low and tied down. He had the face of a bulldog. "Name's McCabe. Mind if I sit?" Without waiting for an answer, he dropped to the chair in front of her.

"What can I do for you?" she asked politely, not wanting to rile such a man.

"I'm lookin' fer a job and I'll don't care what it is."

"I could use a guard, but not a hired killer."

"It's a deal." One moment he lay back in the chair, a grin on his face, and then in a blur he whacked out his Colt, pointing it at her head. "I know what you want, Mrs. Barrington. I'm not afraid of a goddamn thing 'cept gettin' old."

"At the rate you're going, I doubt you have anything to worry about. You're hired."

He winked confidently. "I don't want to be rude, but I heard you live alone." He leaned closer and shrugged. "Don't you ever get lonely?"

"What an odd question."

He angled his head toward the sofa. "Why don't you and me . . ."

She stared at him. "Just like that?"

"Why the hell not?"

"We don't even know each other!"

He grinned. "It's the best way to find out!"

"Mr. McCabe—let's understand each other. You're my employee, not my lover."

He peered confidently into her eyes. "We'll see about that."

Chapter Twenty-one

On September 9th, 1855, the Russian Army evacuated Sebastopol, after seven months of siege, battle, starvation, and shelling. In October a Freesoil Constitutional Convention was held in Topeka, Kansas, to elect a new antislavery government. The population of the disputed territory was estimated at eighty-five hundred, of which two hundred forty-two were slaves, and peace farther away than ever.

These events seemed distant to Nathanial and Clarissa, who were spending the autumn in Rome, following summer on the beaches of Sicily. They visited the usual Roman fountains, museums, and churches, and even attended a Mass in Saint Peter's Square presided over by Pope Pious the Ninth, known among the people as "Pio Nono."

It was in Rome that mail caught up with the honeymooners. One large envelope had come from Nathanial's mother, and inside was another envelope from the War Department.

Dear Lieutenant Barrington,
    How long do you intend to remain on sick leave?

"What are you going to do?" asked Clarissa.

They sat in a café near the Coliseum. "I don't know," he replied, "but to tell you the truth, I'm getting tired of ruins."

She gazed at him in surprise. "I was just thinking— isn't it wonderful to be from a country that's growing every day, instead of always looking backwards?"

"History teaches many valid lessons, say the philosophers."

"I don't care about philosophers. I want to *do* something."

"We could go out West and build our own ranch," suggested Nathanial off the top of his head. "We've seen beautiful European cities, but there's nothing quite like a New Mexico sunset."

"What about the Army?"

"I'll resign my commission."

"Who'll defend our ranch against the Apaches?"

The fatal flaw in his grand design caused the ranch to crumble in his mind. It always came down to Apaches. "To tell you the truth," he said, "I always liked the idea of you and me in the frontier Army. At least it's not boring."

"A person can see so many museums," she replied, "and after a while it's a blur. Surely I was meant for more than traveling from city to city in a quest for God knows what. I've even been neglecting my piano. We've had a magnificent honeymoon, Nathanial, and I'll never forget our Italian hours, but maybe it's time we went home."

McCabe stood in the doorway, thumbs hooked in his belt, chewing a match. "You wanted to see me, ma'am?"

"Please escort me to the bank," replied Maria Dolores as she slung the satchel full of money over her shoulder.

"I'll do anything you want, Mrs. Barrington." He looked her up and down. "Anything."

"McCabe—I'm getting tired of your innuendos."

He appeared genuinely puzzled. "My what?"

He was an ignorant uneducated beast with a powerful physical presence, and sometimes she felt like giving herself to him, although she knew that heartbreak or murder would result from a liaison with such a man. He'd been toying with her during the past weeks, and she could almost feel those bulging muscles across the room. "I mean the remarks you make about doing anything I want."

"Just tryin' to be a good employee, ma'am." He examined her breasts, then her lower limbs.

"That's it," she said angrily. "You're fired."

"What'd I do wrong?" he asked, a mock expression of hurt on his face.

"You're leering at me."

"What's wrong with that?"

"Get out of here!"

He leaned his head to one side. "What if I don't wanna?"

"I'll call the sheriff."

One moment McCabe stood in front of her desk, thumbs hooked in his belt, and next moment, his Colt was aiming at her. "What's he gonna do to me? I'll shoot the son of a bitch where he stands."

She gazed coldly at the gun. "Are you planning to kill me?"

"I'm just sayin' that I'm the best man in Santa Fe

to protect you on the way to the bank. You need me, Mrs. Barrington. Only you don't know it."

"I need a guard, not a man who insults and threatens me."

He dropped the gun into his holster. "I was tryin' to make it easy for you, but all right—I'll play it your way. When you change your mind, I'll make you get down on your knees and beg for it. Are you ready to go to the bank?"

"I'm wondering who'll protect me from you?"

"That's the funny part, Mrs. Barrington. Nobody can protect you from me, and I can do anything to you that I want. But don't worry none. I never kill the people I like."

Nathanial and Clarissa arrived in New York City in time for Christmas, 1855, and after the New Year, Nathanial traveled alone to Washington, D.C., to discuss his career with his father. Shortly thereafter the War Department issued orders that Lieutenant Nathanial, U.S. Dragoons, should proceed without delay to Fort Craig, New Mexico Territory, and report to the commanding officer.

Nathanial and Clarissa shopped for frontier wear, and Nathanial bought his little wife her first gun, a Colt .36 Navy Model with ivory grips. They found time for a trip up the Hudson to West Point, where he showed her the barracks in which his mind had been formed, and tried to explain his commitment to the Army, although he didn't understand it himself.

Then it was back to New York, where Nathanial purchased the two finest pianos he could find, and shipped them to New Mexico on two different days.

If the Indians captured one, perhaps the other would get through. He also purchased a new dining room table, matching chairs, a bed and mattress, sending them by train on a third day.

Jeffrey was planning to enter West Point that fall, as Tobey continued his efforts to become a lawyer. Otis and Belinda had married during Nathanial's honeymoon, and Belinda's son now lived with them on Washington Square. Named Johnny after his father, the boy appeared overwhelmed by the move from the slave quarters. As expected, the elder Davidsons were happy to get rid of him.

Nathanial said good-bye to one and all, tears were shed, and many hands shaken heartily, and one snowy winter day the no-longer-newlyweds departed New York City via ferry, caught a train in Jersey City, and as the locomotive gathered speed in the white-blanketed New Jersey countryside, Clarissa said excitedly, "It's going to be wonderful fun—I just know it."

They slept several nights on the train, but to Nathanial's surprise she never complained. Their diet was bread, chunks of cheese, and the occasional slice of smoked meat. Toilet facilities were not what one found in the Saint Nicholas Hotel, but she made the necessary adjustments.

As days passed, Nathanial realized he'd married a woman who thought she could manage any situation and therefore did. Her curious mind constantly ingested new information, and she was so thoroughly alive he often admired her.

Train tracks came to an end in Pennsylvania, they boarded a stagecoach and rode west with four other passengers: a lawyer, a hardware salesmen, the agent for a New York bank, and a ruffian in worn clothes.

They opened the shutters for fresh air during the day, but it became quite chilly in the carriage. Clarissa had brought sweaters and a blanket, so she was toasty warm as she held her husband's arm and gazed at naked trees in snow-covered valleys.

They spent occasional nights on the floor of stage-coach stops, some with leaks in the roofs. Periodically they slept in beds with other people, the men in one and women in the other.

Nathanial studied his wife carefully, wondering when she'd beg to return to New York. But she was a doughty little soldier, wouldn't let anything stop her, not even the occasional louse or primitive toilet facilities.

They made it to the great Mother Mississippi, where they exchanged the smelly stagecoach for the *Natchez,* a double paddle wheeler headed for New Orleans. Nathanial bribed their way into a cabin with white painted walls, where they bathed, bar-bered, changed into evening clothes, and repaired to the lounge, where they dined on shrimp creole-style, with rice, fried okra, and pots of buttered peas.

After dinner, Nathanial lost two hundred dollars to a kindly old man whom he suspected of being a cardsharp. Then the West Pointer threw down his last hand with disgust, strolled with his wife to the veranda surrounding the *Natchez,* and watched the crescent moon floating above the smokestack.

"I must say—you're holding up very well, my dear," he said, pecking her cheek.

"Isn't it strange that I've seen the Thames, the Seine, and the Rhine, but this is the first time I'm seeing the Mississippi? We have so much wealth in America—we've barely begun to explore it."

"Things get pretty wild once you're on the other side of the river," he cautioned her. "The only thing frontier people respect, be they white or Indian, is main force. So be on your guard, and if I ever tell you to get away from me, I expect you to move quickly."

"What for?" she asked, mystified by his rough new tone.

"Sometimes I require freedom of movement. Don't feel insulted, but do as I say. Do you understand?"

"You're the man who knows the territory," she replied.

Clarissa has no vanity, realized Nathanial. She knows she's good at the piano, and that gives her confidence in all situations. Also, she was raised the old-fashioned way. She knows what's important and that enables her to adapt quickly.

"Nathanial," she mused, "sometimes when you look at me that way, I wonder what you see?"

"The woman who owns me lock, stock, and barrel."

She wrinkled her funny pointed nose. "But I don't want a slave."

"The longer I know you, the more captivated I become. We'll have fun in the Army, I think."

They kissed beside the polished brass rail as the moon cut a dimpled silver swathe down the Mississippi, leading them to New Orleans.

In January 1856, Governor Lee Meriwether of New Mexico Territory submitted his Indian report for the previous year. He estimated 700 to 750 Mes-

calero Apaches, eight hundred to eight hundred fifty
Mimbrenos, five hundred to six hundred Mogollons,
three thousand to four thousand Coyoteros, seven
hundred to eight hundred Garroteros, and eight hundred to nine hundred Tontos. His grand total was approximately seventy-five hundred Apaches, of whom
sixteen hundred were warriors.

The warrior woman awoke suddenly in the middle
of the night. She was covered with perspiration,
chest heaving, mouth dry. She'd been dreaming of a
bloody battle in which she'd been shot by the bluecoat soldiers of the *Pindah-lickoyee*.

She tried to catch her breath in the darkness.
She'd dreamed that a slug of lead slammed into her
chest, knocking her to the ground. She saw herself
lying there, bleeding to death, then awakened suddenly.

The dream had been so vivid, she thought it por-
tentous. She'd been taught since birth that pain
and death were inevitable for warriors, and now
the mountain spirits had sent their warning. She
would be killed in battle soon, and had to prepare
herself.

Running Deer slept on the other side of the wickiup. She readjusted his blanket, then kissed his forehead. *Juh will raise him when I am gone, but who
will love him as I?*

The Mother Superior looked up from her desk as
the man in the black suit stood before her. "You
wanted to see me?" he asked gently.

"Have a seat, Mr. Denigran."

He sat in the chair, folded his hands in his lap,

and appeared properly humble, yet there was something uncertain about him. The Mother Superior was fifty-four years old and thought she understood the depths of the human soul. "You're well enough to leave the convent, Mr. Denigran. What did you plan to do?"

"I reckon I'll look for a job in this here town."

"What kind of work can you do?"

Denigran smiled. "Clerical or farm work. I'll even sweep floors and clean cuspidors."

"You've had an education, haven't you?"

"Eight years, ma'am."

"How'd you like to be a teacher? We have an opening in our school."

"But I've never been a teacher before."

"If you can read and write, that's enough. It's the little ones that you'll teach. Four, five, six years old."

"Like cherubs."

She smiled. "Exactly."

"It's sounds like a job where a man could do some good," said Denigran with a straight face. "I love children."

"You won't have any religious instruction. That's the province of the sisters. I think you'll set a good example for our children, Mr. Denigran. What do you say?"

It was Saturday night in Albuquerque as Cole Bannon strode through the saloon district. Hitching rails were packed with horses, and Cole wondered if one belonged to Fletcher Doakes.

He dismounted, then led his horse into the narrow space between an Appaloosa and a pinto gelding. He threw the reins over the rail, climbed onto the planked sidewalk, and ahead was a cantina with a sign above the door: EL ZAPATO VIEJO.

Cole looked over his shoulder, because he never could be sure when a criminal from his past might shoot a hunk of lead into his ear. Then he opened the door and stepped out of the backlight, his hand near his Colt .44.

The cantina was filled with Mexicans, Americans, Indians, and mixtures thereof, both sexes. Small rough-hewn tables crowded the floor, the bar in back. Cole scanned faces, but didn't see anyone resembling Fletcher Doakes. He spotted an empty table and made his way toward it, passing a stout middle-aged prostitute smoking a cigarette. "May I join you?" she asked.

"Sure."

They sat at the table, their knees nearly touched. She had blue pouches beneath her eyes and deep lines around her mouth. "You look like you've just arrived," she said. "Maybe you'd better lie down."

"I ain't tired," he replied. Reaching into his shirt pocket, he withdrew his tin badge. "I'm looking for a man named Fletcher Doakes. Ever hear of him?"

"Mister, I hear so many names, I can't remember 'em all. What's he done."

"Killed some prostitutes."

"What's he look like?"

"About five ten, on the slim side, black hair, face like a rat."

"I'll keep my eyes open fer him. How'd you like to have some fun?"

"Not in the mood."

She touched him in a sensitive place, then rubbed gently. "How about now?"

Cole Bannon had been on the trail eleven days. "Let's go."

A stagecoach wheel had been removed, and in the blacksmith shop the proprietor banged it with his hammer. It was morning and the long-bearded stagecoach driver looked on unhappily, because the dispatcher would bawl him out for running into the tree.

The stagecoach stop was two ramshackle structures on one side of the trail somewhere in central Texas. Most passengers sat in the combination general store, restaurant, and saloon, complaining about the delay, while being waited on by the proprietor's wife and children.

Shots could be heard behind the sorry excuse for a building as Nathanial patiently showed Clarissa how to use her Colt. "Draw, thumb back the hammer, and fire in one smooth motion," he told her as he positioned her arm. "Accuracy is more important than speed. Raise the barrel up your opponent's body and squeeze the trigger. It's better to shoot low than high."

He smiled as Clarissa spread her legs, hunched like a desperado, and pulled the Colt out of her holster. Her little pink tongue stuck out the corner of her mouth as she aimed with both hands and pulled the trigger. It blasted, but she was growing used to the horrific noise and kick. Cans and bottles were lined on a plank of wood, and occasionally she'd hit one, perhaps by mistake.

Nathanial enjoyed his job as professor of the

shooting arts, because it provided opportunities to touch his wife during his efforts to improve her aim. Quite often he found himself undressing her with his eyes. He gave thanks to the powers that had caused her to become his bedmate.

Her confidence with the weapon was growing. "It's one thing to aim at objects that aren't shooting back," she told him, "but I wonder if I could really kill someone."

"If you ever feel threatened, just follow my instructions and shoot the son of a bitch down. Don't even think about it."

Covered with perspiration, Maria Dolores awakened in the middle of the night. She'd been dreaming about performing erotic acts with McCabe, and her breath came in gasps.

What's wrong with me? she asked herself. There is virtually no difference between McCabe and a gorilla. Yet she found herself longing for him, although he appeared incapable of understanding her mind.

But I need somebody to understand my body, she reminded herself, and thought he was just what she needed. In her rational mind, she knew she should stay away from McCabe, but her hunger got the best of her.

Why not? she teased herself. This time I won't fool myself into thinking it's love. I'll just take it for what it is and not expect more. But wait a minute, Maria Dolores. Do you really want the love of a brute?

She thought for a few minutes, then whispered into the night, "Yes."

But he had stopped flirting with her, as she'd requested. If she wanted to sleep with him, she'd have to initiate the activity. I could never proposition him, she thought. It would be too humiliating, wouldn't it? I'm not that desperate . . . yet.

Chapter Twenty-two

In the season of Little Eagles, a council was held in the Mimbreno camp. Warriors and subchiefs sat in a large circle, and pipes were passed among them as again they debated the future of the People. Some Chiricahuas attended the meeting, among them Chief Miguel Narbona and Cochise. They listened carefully as Chief Mangas Coloradas spoke.

"Cochise and the Chiricahuas are generous brothers," declared the Mimbreno chief. "But I hear the blood of ancestors calling me back to our sacred homeland. To settle my heart, I must return and meet with my brother, Cuchillo Negro. If I see with my own eyes that he is content with the White Eyes, perhaps I can learn something. And if the White Eyes have betrayed him, we can bring him back with us. If any warrior and his family wishes to accompany me, that will make us stronger. I warn you that many White Eyes are in the homeland, and if any warrior did not wish to come, I respect him. It will be a hazardous journey but soon we shall know the truth."

Most of the older warriors didn't want to return to the Mimbres Mountains, because they preferred to avoid bluecoat soldiers. Therefore, it was only the wildest and most daring warriors who agreed to escort the great chief Mangas Coloradas on his historic return to the homeland.

On the appointed day, he rode at the head of the column as it made its way through the Dos Cabezas Mountains. Behind him came Victorio, Delgadito, Juh, and Geronimo, among other fighters, with their wives and children.

They comprised about fifty souls, and among them was Jocita the warrior woman and her son riding the same horse. She wanted Running Deer to see the land of his birth, because who could say when the next opportunity would come. Jocita wasn't optimistic about the White Eyes, and suspected the Mimbrenos might be exiled forever.

She wondered if her dream would be fulfilled during the pilgrimage, but feared weakness more. She could stay safe in her wickiup, but the only way to defeat fear was to ignore it, she'd learned. With her son rocking back and forth in the saddle before her, the warrior woman returned to the holy land of her birth.

The stagecoach stopped before the command post headquarters at Fort Craig, New Mexico Territory. Clarissa stared out the window at scattered adobe buildings alongside the Rio Grande. She'd thought forts had high walls to keep out Apaches, but not Fort Craig.

A soldier helped her to the ground. Fort Craig looked bleak and barren, at the edge of a marsh surrounded by mountains. "I hope you're not too disappointed," said Nathanial, noticing dismay on her face.

"No—it's lovely," she replied unconvincingly.

"Let's tell the sergeant major we're here."

They climbed the front steps and entered the orderly room, where a bald sergeant major with a black mustache sat among his clerks. "I'm Nathanial Barrington, and this is my wife, Clarissa."

The sergeant major gave her hand a firm shake. "Welcome to Fort Craig, ma'am. I'll have someone show you your quarters, and Colonel Chandler will speak with the lieutenant directly."

"We'll wait outside," said Nathanial.

He escorted her to the porch. She stood at the rail and looked at mountains that made the Catskills look like foothills.

"You can always catch the next stagecoach east," he suggested.

"If other army wives get along here, so can I. We've had enough paradise, and it's time to get to work on your captain's bars."

Amazing, thought Nathanial. I have a wife who'll help accomplish my goals, instead of dragging me down. Why, this could be the beginning of a whole new life for me.

Her new home was a solid but plain adobe hut with two rooms, one the bedroom, the other a combination kitchen, dining room, parlor, and vestibule. It would occupy a corner of her father's home on Gramercy Park, and it boasted an outhouse in back.

On the bright side, it was scrupulously clean, soldiers having painted and plastered. The furniture was old but in good repair, and the bed sagged in the middle. Now she understood why Nathanial had bought a new mattress in New York. She searched for a place to put her piano after it arrived.

Someone knocked on the door. Clarissa opened it happily, expecting her husband, but instead a tall woman with salt-and-pepper hair stood in front of her. "How do you do," she said with a smile. "I'm Libby Chandler. Welcome to Fort Craig."

Colonel Chandler's wife, realized Clarissa. My commanding officer. The New Yorker straightened her spine and introduced herself, then said, "I think this home will do nicely."

"You're new to the Army, I understand."

"Yes, but my husband has served in New Mexico for nearly ten years."

Libby Chandler smiled. "I've been in the Army nearly twenty years, and sometimes I think I was born in the supply room and issued to my husband. We hope you'll be comfortable here, and if you have any problems, feel free to come directly to me. I don't mean to meddle in your marriage, but we can't have scandals among officers' wives. Do you understand?"

"You'll get no scandals from Nathanial and me, I assure you. May I ask a question?" Clarissa leaned forward and looked the colonel's wife in the eye. "Can you tell me, woman to woman, just how dangerous it is?"

"Exceedingly dangerous—make no mistake about that. The Apaches seldom attack army forts, but might sneak in at night and steal a few things, or worse. So be on your guard. Do you have a pistol?"

"Yes, and my husband taught me to use it." Clarissa reached beneath the folds of her coat and pulled out her Colt. "He says I'm a very good shot."

The colonel's wife narrowed her eyes. "Do you think you could kill somebody?"

"No question about it."

"You're from New York City, I'm told. Well, I'm from Atlanta. We're probably the only city girls at Fort Union, so I'm sure we'll have a lot to talk about. You must come over for supper after you're settled."

The door closed behind the colonel's wife as a faint smirk came over Clarissa's face. Men appeared to rule the world, but were maneuvered by wives, she knew. If Libby Chandler likes me, Nathanial will get his captain's bars, she reasoned. His problem is he didn't marry me ten years earlier.

Brevet Lieutenant Colonel Daniel T. Chandler sat behind his desk, appraising the tall, husky officer standing at attention before him. The officer had just reported, and Colonel Chandler noted his well-tailored but dusty uniform, blond beard, and perfect West Point posture.

"Have a seat, Lieutenant," said Chandler, West Point class of 1825. "I've examined your records and noted that you're an experienced company commander, so I'm giving you Company I. It's comprised mostly of men fresh from the recruit depots back east, they haven't received any training to speak of, and it's up to you to whip them into shape. You've been gone from New Mexico for a while, so let me bring you up to date. The western Apaches have been peaceful lately, but it's only a matter of time before they commit another outrage. It is my belief that they won't accept peace until we inflict a severe defeat upon them. As you know, the Congress has authorized us more men and equipment, so we've got to show results. Some people think western Apaches are invincible, but I'm confident we can handle them just as we've handled the others. I am also of the opinion that we shouldn't let them get away with a damned thing, so be prepared to move out on not much notice."

Nathanial entered his new orderly room, where a sad-eyed clerk looked up from the morning report. When he saw silver bars on Nathanial's shoulder straps, the clerk jumped to attention. "Corporal Dunlop reporting, sir!"

"I'm Lieutenant Barrington, your new commanding officer. Where's Lieutenant Haskell?"

"In his office, sir."

The door was marked COMMANDING OFFICER. Nathanial turned the knob and saw a second lieutenant sitting behind the desk. "I'm Lieutenant Barrington."

Haskell arose and saluted. "I'll clear my belongings out in a minute," he said. "Boy, am I glad to see you."

"What's wrong?"

"The men are a stubborn, quarrelsome lot, and it's difficult to make them obey. I'm just out of the Virginia Military Institute, sir, and nobody ever told me I'd have soldiers like these."

"I'll address them at the evening formation, and then we'll get to work. If they don't follow orders properly, we'll see how they like the stockade."

"The stockade is full, sir. The colonel wants company officers to discipline men themselves."

"In that case we might have to shoot a few."

Haskell blinked. He was a man of medium height

with a close-trimmed brown mustache. "Did you say *shoot* a few, Lieutenant Barrington."

"That's what I said."

Someone knocked on the door as Clarissa instinctively reached for her gun. "Who's there?"

"My name is Rosita."

Clarissa opened the door, revealing a Mexican woman in her forties. "I was wondering if you need a maid, senora."

"I certainly do," replied Clarissa. "Can you cook?"

"*Sí*, senora, in the Americano style. I used to work for the family who lived here before—Mrs. Chandler told me to see you." She held up a gunnysack. "I have brought supper."

"Who lived here before?"

Rosita became serious. "Captain Simmons and his wife. He was . . . killed . . . by the Apache, and his wife has gone back East with the children."

A chill came over Clarissa. "What were the Simmons like?"

"Decent people. The lieutenant drank a bit."

Clarissa recalled scars on her husband's body, and maybe he wouldn't be so lucky next time. A terrible foreboding came over her, she shivered, and now understood what Nathanial had been trying to say. New Mexico Territory wasn't like Venice or the Hudson Highlands, where personal safety was taken for granted. She lowered her hand and wrapped her pianist fingers around the handle of her Colt. She was in the Army too, with all the dangers of men and special vulnerabilities of women.

* * *

Nathanial walked through the stable, displeased to note dirty stalls. The horses appeared restless and unkempt as they looked at him with hopeful eyes. "Who's in charge here!" he demanded.

There were bustling sounds, Nathanial yanked his Colt, then perplexed faces appeared over the top of a stall. "I am," said a feisty-looking sergeant with a red beard.

"Why are the stables dirty?"

"Don't worry, sir. We'll get to them."

"When you're finished with your poker game?"

The sergeant winked. "It was dice, to tell you the truth."

"What's your name?"

"McMahon, sir."

"You have just become Private McMahon. Who's the next ranking man?"

A corporal with a brown beard stepped forward. "Corporal Norris reporting sir."

"You're in charge of this detail, and I expect these stables to be clean when I come back."

Norris appeared shocked. "All of them?"

"You have just been relieved of command. Can anyone tell me where the shovels are?"

"Over there," said a private, pointing.

"Each man take a shovel and start cleaning those stalls."

The men looked at him as though he were mad. "But we ain't finished our game," said one of them.

"The Army isn't a gambling casino. What's your name?"

"Winthrop."

"Don't you say, sir?"

"What for?"

"How'd you like to spend the night in the stockade, Private Winthrop?"

"How'd you like to go fuck yourself, sir?"

Nathanial brought one up from the floor, connecting with the side of the soldier's face. The force of the blow sent Winthrop hurtling against the wall, which he slid down and then became motionless on a pile of horse manure.

"Who's next?" asked Nathanial.

The soldiers slunk toward the shovels. Nathanial ran after them and kicked one in the buttocks. "Stand straight!"

Private Richardson turned around. "Sir, perhaps you've forgotten that it's a court-martial offense for an officer to strike an enlisted man."

"I'm the law in this stable and I'll kill you before I tolerate insubordination."

Richardson smiled as he glanced at his friends. "He'll *kill* me?"

Nathanial drew his Colt and aimed at the space between the soldier's eyes. "Without hesitation."

Nathanial's knuckles went white around the grips, prompting Richardson to hold out his hands. "All right—all right!"

"Get to work! I shall return in an hour to inspect the stable, and I will not tolerate back talk on this post. Any questions?"

Nathanial holstered his gun, walked three steps to the back of the stable, then drew the weapon again and spun around suddenly, taking them by surprise. "If any of you sorry excuses for soldiers think you might want to bushwhack me some dark night, be advised that I enjoy a little sport now and then. Get to work or I'll stuff those dice down your throats!"

Nathanial walked out the back door of the stable as the fragrance of the sage hit him in the face. *This isn't going to be easy, but I'm not letting a bunch of raggedy-ass recruits defy me.* He walked deeper into the wilderness, and for some unknown reason, the warrior woman came to mind. They'd stripped in terrain very similar to where he was standing, and proceeded to go insane with each other's bodies.

Nathanial loved Clarissa deeply, passionately, and lustfully, but the warrior woman would always be part of him, he knew. He gazed into the chaparral as he listened to her voice calling to him through whistling spines of cacti. *Come to me, my White Eyes darling. Where have you gone, my love?*

Nathanial arrived home after sundown, then Clarissa led him to a table illuminated by a single candle. "I've hired a maid and she's made supper. It's still warm."

Nathanial glanced around in surprise. The home seemed picturesque, with colorful Indian blankets covering the walls. Clarissa lifted the cover from the pot, revealing chunks of beef swimming in beans and potatoes.

"Are you hungry?" she asked.

He swept her up in her arms. "I think it's time we christened the bed."

He blew out the candle, plunging the home into darkness. Then he carried his wife to the bedroom, kicked open the door, and lay her down. "I love your moods," she whispered. "I never know what to expect."

He didn't reply as he unbuttoned her bodice. *There's nothing like the sight of this woman's body to* bring me back to reality, he told himself. I can manage anything as long as I have my little wife to comfort me.

McCabe sat at a table in the Silver Palace, nursing a glass of whiskey and smoking a fat cigarette. Two bullwhackers were arguing at the bar while five Santa Fe gentleman played poker at a round table. Outside of a few other random drinkers, there wasn't much activity at two o'clock on a Wednesday morning.

The usual troop of prostitutes was present, and McCabe knew he could have any of them. For a reason not clear to him, women had been attracted to him all his life, even nice women who should know better. He seemed to exude something, but didn't care either way.

Life, death, and love didn't impress him, after the blood and guts of the Mexican War. Another veteran of that tumultuous conflict, he had learned that people were worse than animals. Sometimes McCabe even hated himself.

But he wasn't totally numb and nearly dropped his cigarette when he saw the boss lady walk into the saloon, wearing a black shawl over her head. She glanced from side to side, then headed in his direction. Wa'al, I'll be a son of a bitch, thought McCabe.

She appeared troubled and half asleep as she sat opposite him. She had difficulty looking him in the eye, so instead directed her gaze at the open collar of his shirt. "I have been thinking about you," she said, and then paused, to gather her courage. "You're always talking about doing those things to me. Well, I've decided to take you up on it."

He leaned back lazily on his chair. "What if I changed my mind?"

Maria Dolores's eyes blazed with anger. "You have been flirting ever since I set eyes on you," she said icily, "and now that I have embarrassed myself, you change your mind?"

"I didn't say I'd changed my mind. But don't ever take me for granted, lady. Because I don't owe you a damn thing."

"I did not mean to offend you," she replied, "although you offend me every day with your insolent manner."

"I wanted to know if you were just another bitch, or a real woman. You've got guts, boss lady—I'll say that for you. Let's go."

She didn't like being seen with him, but was tired of worrying about what others thought of her. She felt safe walking down Burro Alley with such a man, although she was surrounded by rough-looking outlaws carrying guns and knives. McCabe would even tower over Nathanial.

Finally they arrived at his hotel, a large adobe hut in poor repair. He held her hand as he led her down a dark hall, unlocked a door, and lit a candle. It was a small room in need of cleaning, and his bed hadn't been made. The mixed odors of whiskey and stale tobacco were heavy in the air, although the window was half open.

He undressed without even kissing her, and it was so squalid she felt like fleeing, but it also appeared intensely erotic to a passionate but proper lady. He was even more enormous without his clothes, and covered with hair.

"Get your clothes off," he growled. "What are you waiting for?"

The sound of his voice sent a tremor through her. They'd never even kissed, but she found herself unbuttoning her bodice as he crawled onto the bed and lay on his back. Then he pulled the cork on a bottle of whiskey on the dresser and took a swig.

Maria Dolores felt as if she were losing her mind as she peeled away her blouse. She saw him gazing calmly at her breasts and knew he cared for her in his own twisted way, just as she cared for him. She realized that he was practically a stranger as she stepped out of her skirt. Naked, she crawled into bed with him.

"Whiskey?" he asked.

"No thank you."

"Bet you're surprised to be here, right?"

"You probably don't believe me, but I usually don't do this sort of thing."

"You're right—I don't believe you—but so what?"

One moment he was lying on his back, totally relaxed, and then he was all over her, kissing, groping, clutching and overwhelming. Never had she been taken with such force, and the very newness of the experience thrilled her. She dug her fingernails into his shoulders and kissed his lips wildly as he pressed her against the mattress. "It's always the 'ladies' what show me the best time," he murmured, wrestling her into submission.

Chapter Twenty-three

Geronimo raised his head above a clump of bayberry bushes. Twigs were stuck into his headband, smeared dirt blending his face with the surroundings. He counted approximately three hundred sheep, fifty head of cattle, and twenty-odd horses heading east with a crew of eight vaqueros.

Geronimo studied the heavily armed vaqueros, but they didn't impress him. Moreover, they were trespassing on the homeland and whatever they owned was fair game for the rightful owners. Geronimo saw no peace with the *Nakai-yes* and the *Pindah-lickoyee*. His faction believed in unrelenting warfare against invaders, not watching seeds grow.

He made the sound of a whippoorwill, then retreated to the horses. His warriors joined him, their faces painted with stripes of ocher across their noses, and carrying Killer of Enemies Bandoliers over hardy chests. Among them were Juh, Chatto, Loco, Nana the medicine man, and Jocita the warrior woman in a deerskin shirt worked with pale blue beads.

It was a tribute to Geronimo's growing skills that so many distinguished warriors had chosen to follow the Bedonko on his first raid as war chief. Each knew his or her assignment, there was no need for orders. They climbed into their saddles, kicked the flanks of their horses, and worked the animals into a full gallop.

The horses accelerated across the desert, dodging cactus plants as tall as a man, or leaping over hedges of chaparral. Like a brown tornado, they burst onto the plain where sheep and cattle were trudging along.

The People sang war songs and brandished pistols as they charged the vaqueros, who took one look and sped in the opposite direction. Meanwhile, the sheep stampeded toward the west while the cattle headed north.

The warriors split up and easily gathered the animals, then herded them with captured wagons. No one had been killed or wounded during the transfer of property. "While we're back in the homeland, we might as well do a little business, eh Juh?" asked Geronimo as they headed for the main Mimbreno column.

"It was wrong to give up this land so easily," replied the Nednai chief. "Now we are back and our enemies had better beware."

That evening, Nathanial and Clarissa sat to supper with the colonel and his wife.

The main course was the usual beef and whatever vegetables could be found, prepared by the Chandlers' Mexican maid, who happened to be the sister of Clarissa's maid.

"According to your records, you've been on sick leave for over a year," said Colonel Chandler to Nathanial. "I trust you've recovered from your wounds?"

"Once in a while I feel a twinge, but otherwise I'm fine."

"I heard a report that you beat up a couple of enlisted men the other day."

"They were insubordinate, sir."

Clarissa appeared surprised. "You beat up a couple of enlisted men, Nathanial? Why didn't you mention it to me?"

"I didn't think you'd be interested, dear." Then he turned back to the colonel. "Once discipline starts breaking down, a military unit is no longer effective."

"That's why I tossed the report into the dustbin. I have too few experienced officers and sergeants trying to control hordes of civilians in uniform, most of whom are wanted for crimes in the East."

"I've always believed that the best way to train soldiers is take them on a campaign. They'll learn the importance of discipline and training quickly, I assure you."

The colonel smiled. "What if we run into Apaches before the lessons are learned?"

"War is the best classroom of all, sir."

Meanwhile, at the other end of the table, Mrs. Chandler was carrying on a different conversation with Clarissa. "The worst problem we wives have is laziness," confessed Libby Chandler. "We all have maids and if we're not careful we can become quite useless."

"I'll be fine once my pianos arrive," replied Clarissa. "Nathanial has bought two for me, and they're on their way even as we speak."

"Do you play both at the same time?" asked Mrs. Chandler, mystified.

"Nathanial thought if one was captured by the Indians, maybe the other would get through. If they both arrive, I guess we'll give one to the men's recreation room."

Mrs. Chandler realized that money was no object to the lieutenant and his young wife, and they came from a higher class than she. "I've always wanted to play the piano," she said. "Is it difficult to learn?"

"I'd be happy to give you lessons, if you like."

On the other side of the table, Colonel Chandler asked, "What did you do on your sick leave, Lieutenant?"

"I went on my honeymoon, sir. We traveled in England, France, and Italy."

These are not poor people, mused Colonel Chandler, independent of his wife. He must have influential friends in the War Department to get that much time off. "Tell me something, Lieutenant Barrington. I can't help being curious about you, because you're an experienced frontier officer and you've served with distinction in the Mexican War. Why aren't you a captain?"

Nathanial shrugged with embarrassment. "After West Point, I started drinking rather heavily, I'm afraid, and then got into a few fights with other officers. But that was a long time ago and I hardly ever drink anymore. Clarissa has made a man out of me."

Colonel Chandler gazed down the table at the vivacious blonde speaking with his wife. "Isn't it strange, the effect they have on us? A bad one can ruin a man, and a good one can make him . . ." The post commander searched for the perfect word, but it eluded him.

"A colonel," suggested Nathanial with a smile.

"I've just had an idea, Lieutenant Barrington. Instead of commanding Company I, why don't you join my staff? I could use an experienced officer to help me run this post, and it's time you exercised command at higher levels. You do a good job—I'll recommend you for captain. What do you say?"

Mangas Coloradas was troubled when he stopped for supper that night. He hadn't planned on traveling with stolen sheep and cattle, and hadn't even been consulted about the raid. He feared what bluecoat soldiers would do if they saw stolen property grazing near his camp.

After the meal, as he was preparing to go to sleep, Geronimo and Juh visited his fire to pay their respects. "We have found very fine horses," said Geronimo. "You are welcome to your pick, great chief."

Mangas Coloradas looked at them coldly. "You have endangered the People with your rash act."

"The People need to eat," replied Geronimo. "And our enemies should pay for use of our land."

"Tell that to the bluecoat soldiers when they ask where you acquired the animals."

"Bluecoat soldiers travel in small detachments. I do not think they will bother us."

"What if they do?"

Geronimo deferred to his cousin Juh.

"We shall destroy them," said Juh.

At three o'clock in the morning, a lone vaquero was spotted riding hard toward Fort Craig. He waved his sombrero frantically as he bore down on the two guards at the gate. "I have a message for the *com-mandante!*" he screamed.

The guards waved him onward as the vaquero galloped toward the command post headquarters. Two more guards were waiting at the door, they stepped aside, and the Charge of Quarters arose sleepily from his cot, his service revolver in hand.

"Senor," reported the vaquero, "a herd of sheep, cattle, and horses have been stolen about two days east of here. I was there and counted thirty-six Apaches, although there may have been more." The Mexican banged his fist on the desk. "The Army is supposed to protect the citizens of this territory. My employer, Don Emilio Torrezon, is proprietor of much land and livestock. He wants to know: what are you going to do about it?"

Nathanial and Clarissa lay naked and asleep in each other's arms when there was a knock on the door. Nathanial reached for the Colt in the holster hanging from the bedpost. "Sounds like trouble." He put on his maroon silk robe, purchased at a shop not far from the Doge's Palace in Venice, then opened the door.

It was the charge of quarters. "The colonel wants all officers to report to his office at once, sir. There's been an Apache attack, and he'll explain everything after you get there."

Nathanial donned his shirt and tied on his holster. He was half asleep, regretting leaving his naked wife beneath the covers.

"I'll be back as soon as I can," he told her. "Keep your gun close by." He kissed her lips, squeezed her left breast, and was out the door.

He adjusted his campaign hat on his head as he crossed the parade ground. The post was coming to life, candles flickered in the barracks and a detail was being marched to the stable. He arrived at the command post headquarters, where a few officers had gathered, notepads on their knees. Nathanial barely knew any of them, but they appeared the usual mixed lot of competent officers and time servers. The door opened and Colonel Chandler entered the room, whereupon the officers snapped to attention.

"At ease," said the colonel as he stood before a map of the Ninth Department tacked to the wall. "I've known the Apaches would commit a robbery before long, and it looks like they've finally done it. The brazen bastards have stolen approximately three hundred sheep, fifty cattle, and twenty horses from a ranch in this vicinity"—he touched his finger to the map—"but I'm afraid they've made a serious error. Such a herd will slow down even Apaches, while we employ four of the best trackers in the territory. We're going to take the stolen property back and if the Apaches resist, they shall be chastised."

There was a knock on the door, it was flung open, and standing before the colonel was the Indian commissioner, Dr. Michael Steck, who happened to be visiting Fort Craig. "What's this I hear about a campaign against Apaches?"

Colonel Chandler straightened his spine and looked down at the shorter man. "Apaches have stolen a large herd of livestock and the Army is going after them."

Dr. Steck was unshaven and hastily dressed. He held out his hands and said, "But I'm trying to make peace—a very sensitive process. A military campaign will scare away peaceful Apaches."

"One good scare is worth a hundred peace treaties, I've always believed."

"In that case—I'll go with you. Someone must safeguard the interests of the Apaches."

Colonel Chandler caught hold of himself, because he couldn't lose his temper with a civilian official. "You may accompany us if you wish, but I shall place you under arrest if you interfere with my command. We're departing Fort Craig at sunup, Dr. Steck. Prepare yourself for an arduous campaign."

In the moonlight, Juh walked among stolen horses. He still was furious following his discussion with Mangas Coloradas. *I am a chief in my own right. How dare he criticize me?*

Juh could see no point in making accommodations with enemies. He was bred from the Nednai People, most extreme of all Apaches. *Mangas Coloradas is old*, decided Juh, *and old men like to lie around, smoke their pipes, and recall the days when they were fearsome warriors. I would rather die on this very night than become a doddering old fool.*

He heard a footfall behind him and spun around with knife in hand. But it was only his cousin, Geronimo the Bedonko. "Jocita would like to speak with you," he said.

Juh turned his gaze to her wickiup. "I wonder what she wants."

Geronimo smiled. "How do you manage so many wives?"

"You have it backwards, my cousin. They manage me."

Juh walked to Jocita's wickiup, hoping to receive her favors. She was moody and he never knew when she'd insult him. But a chief is entitled to sons.

He arrived at her wickiup and spoke her name. She crawled out, a red bandanna wrapped around her jet black hair. "I want to talk with you," she said. "Alone."

They strolled along the edge of the campsite, and Juh noticed that Jocita seemed agitated. "What is wrong?" he asked.

She peered deeply into his eyes. "If something happens to me—promise that you'll care for Running Deer."

"He is my son—do you think I would abandon him? But what makes you think something will happen?"

"I dreamed I would die in battle, Juh."

He offered no clever retort, for dreams were how the mountain spirits spoke to people. "You should not have come on this journey."

"A warrior does not hide from death."

He grabbed her arm. "Listen to me, my love. If there's trouble, stay close. I shall defend you personally."

"No one can deny the mountain spirits. Promise me that you will not punish Running Deer because of my evil deeds."

"You do not trust me?"

"How can I trust you after you have betrayed me so many times? You must give me your word, Juh."

"I give you my word sealed in blood," replied Juh as he whipped out his knife. In a flash, he cut his arm. "Now do you believe me?"

She watched blood stream down his arm. "Yes."

* * *

It was two in the morning when McCabe entered the stable, carrying a saddle over his shoulder. He found his gray stallion, threw the blanket onto its back, then dropped on the saddle.

A young Mexican man walked toward him, carrying a lantern. "Going somewhere, senor?"

"Movin' on," replied McCabe curtly. He reached into his pocket and removed coins. "That should take care of you."

The stableman counted the coins. "It is always best to get an early start, eh, senor? But do not worry. I will not say that I saw you."

"Say what you want," replied McCabe. "I don't give a damn either way."

McCabe tied on his bedroll as the stableman retreated. Then McCabe climbed into the saddle and rode out of the stable. Giant constellations swirled in the sky as he steered his horse toward the open range. It wasn't long before Santa Fe's lights receded behind him.

McCabe hadn't said good-bye, nor had he left a note. He'd been disappearing from one town after another since the war ended, in an aimless quest for meaning and truth in a world gone mad. The last thing he needed was getting tied to a woman, because that would be the end of him.

His crude demeanor was his protection against the cruelties he inevitably encountered, and he feared once he started getting soft and gooey over a woman, that would make him less combative. It was only a matter of time before he'd bring Maria Dolores flowers or sing love songs beneath her window.

McCabe spat into the dirt as his horse carried him

away from her. Despite his menacing and mocking exterior, McCabe was a terrified man. He wasn't afraid of physical pain, but despised gentleness in himself. In a cruel world, he had to be crueler in order to survive.

Unfortunately, the Mexican woman had warmed the ashes in his heart. McCabe loved to sleep with her and had come to feel dependent upon her. No matter where he went, he always was falling for women. They tempted him to settle down and raise a family, but how could he bring babes into a hideous world?

He'd sleep with his scratchy woolen blanket on the cold hard ground for the foreseeable future, instead of warm and wonderful Maria Dolores. His meat would be semicooked over an open fire, provided it didn't rain, instead of grilled to perfection in the comfort of the Silver Palace Saloon. The future didn't appear attractive to McCabe as his horse plodded into the night.

McCabe refused to let anyone take advantage of him, yet was bereft inside. Maria Dolores had made him feel happy and needed, even offering to introduce him to her children. He felt at war with himself, but the more he thought about Maria Dolores, the less attractive his scratchy old blanket seemed. "Oh, what the hell," he said aloud as he pulled the reins of his horse. Then he turned the animal and headed back to Santa Fe.

Chapter Twenty-four

The band played "The Girl I Left Behind Me," as half asleep and unruly dragoons followed officers and sergeants to the main gate of Fort Craig. Nathanial could hear their groans and complaints all the way at the head of the column, where he rode alongside Colonel Chandler.

Wives and children congregated near the gate, waving goodbye to their men. Nathanial sat taller in his saddle as he spotted his little wife in the crowd. He raised his arm and threw her a regulation West Point salute. "I love you," he formed with his lips, and then she broke free from the others, ran to his side, and clasped his hand.

"Forgive me, Nathanial, but I had to touch you."

"I'll be back soon," he reassured her. "We probably won't see Apaches. Don't go anywhere without your gun, all right?"

He leaned over and kissed Clarissa, nearly falling out of his saddle. Behind him, he heard cheers from the men. He righted himself as she stepped back. Their eyes met, and for the first time it occurred to Nathanial that he might never see her again. He blew her a kiss, and for a moment considered resigning his commission on the spot, but turned front, settled into the saddle, and rode toward his next rendezvous with destiny.

Cole Bannon watched from his horse as the Army left Fort Craig. He'd been on the trail five days, sleeping during daylight, traveling by night. His tin badge remained in his shirt pocket as he followed the trail of Fletcher Doakes.

He'd stopped at every town, settlement, and ranch that he saw, inquiring about Doakes. The more he thought about it, the more he believed Doakes wasn't in New Mexico anymore, or maybe the Apaches had gotten him. Perhaps I'm chasing a mirage, reflected Cole as he stopped in front of a cantina, climbed down from the saddle, and threw his reins over the rail.

The cantina was nearly empty at that early hour, except for a Mexican working the bar. He took one look at the dusty bearded traveler and poured a shot of mescal. Cole took it in his hand and tossed half the liquid down his throat. It sizzled his innards, steamed his brain, and when the cantina returned, he reached into his shirt pocket and took out his badge. "Any whores been killed around here lately?"

The bartender blinked. "As a matter of fact, one was strangled by some son of a bitch about a week ago."

Two days later, Mangas Coloradas rode through Cuchillo Negro's camp, horrified by wickiups in poor repair, warriors lying about in drunken stupors, their arms around snoring wives, as skinny naked children scurried about like sad-eyed imps. Never had the great chief imagined it would be so bad. He stopped

his horse before the wickiup of Cuchillo Negro, noticing the garbage-strewn ground.

Cuchillo Negro stepped out of his wickiup, just
awakened from deep slumber although it was nearly
noon. From atop his saddle, Mangas Coloradas
turned down the corners of his mouth. "I do not like
what I see here, brother."

"We have had bad times," explained Cuchillo Negro. "The White Father in the East does not listen to
Dr. Steck."

Mangas Coloradas spat at the ground. "That is
what I think of the White Father in the East. You
must come away from here, Cuchillo Negro. Otherwise you shall surely die."

"You do not understand, my brother. Huge numbers of bluecoat soldiers have come to the homeland.
Resistance will lead to bloodshed."

"Let it spill," replied Mangas Coloradas. "A warrior
lives a sacred life and dies a sacred death." He
pointed at mountains in the distance. "We will camp
there for the night, then continue our journey. You
may join us if you wish. How many times must the
White Eyes cheat you before you learn your lesson?"

Cuchillo Negro compared his warriors with Juh,
Geronimo, Chatto, and Loco; the answer was clear.
"How pitiful we must appear," he replied. "I shall go
with you, Mangas Coloradas. Once more you have
shown me the true path."

That evening, Norbert Denigran, formerly Fetcher
Doakes, walked humbly down a corridor of the convent, his hands clasped as if in prayer, a beatific
smile on his face. It was after Vespers, all offices

darkened except for the one where the Mother Superior worked late.

Her door open, he peered inside. A chubby elderly woman in a black habit was bent over her desk. What a business this church is, thought Denigran. They work their fingers to the bone and make the Pope richer.

She glanced up and appeared startled to see him there. "Is it you, Mr. Denigran?"

"Indeed it is," he replied, slithering into her office. "I wondered if I might have a word with you, Mother Superior?"

She laid down her pen. "Please don't feel rushed. I'm interested in what you have to say, Mr. Denigran."

Denigran's ferretlike eyes spotted the cast-iron safe in the corner. Now he knew where the money was, and next step was to lay his hands on it. "I thought I should thank you, Mother Superior, for all you've done for me. I was a vagabond on the face on the earth, then you took me in."

"You've been a great help to us here," she replied.

"I don't think the children like me much. They think I'm odd. Do you think I'm odd, Mother Superior?"

"We're all odd in our own way, I suppose. God made each of us for His own special purpose."

It took all Denigran's willpower to prevent himself from laughing. "I wonder what my purpose is?"

"Pray on it, Mr. Denigran."

Bells rang, announcing Compline. The schoolmaster followed the Mother Superior down the corridor, and he thought of jumping her from behind, slitting her throat, and ravishing her upon the cold stone floor. She comes this way every night, he deduced as they arrived at the chapel. One night I'll be waiting, to give her the best theology lesson of her life.

Clarissa felt nauseous, her joints hurt, and she had a headache. Her mother was far away and her husband had ridden off on a campaign from which he might never return.

When not sick, she was hungry. Often she sat in her parlor and looked out the window, an open book on her lap. She'd never been so alone. Sometimes she suspected she might lose her mind in the vast emptiness of the frontier.

She wondered what had driven Nathanial to return to New Mexico, land of nothing at all. She could tolerate Fort Craig if she had music, but neither of her pianos had arrived. She felt cut off from the wellsprings of creativity, and there wasn't a damned thing she could do about it.

She heard footsteps and turned to see her maid. "Senora, you look so sad. Is there anything I can do?"

"Not unless you can find me a piano. I have been a musician all my life and miss making music."

Rosita rolled her eyes. "I love music too, senora. It is food for the soul, no? There are no pianos here that I know of, but perhaps you should play the guitar."

Clarissa pondered what her maid had suggested. "Actually that's a very good suggestion. It's one of the world's oldest and finest instruments. Where can I buy one?"

"I will take you to Senor Sanchez. He is a very great musician, and he makes guitars. Besides, it is good for a pregnant woman to take walks, no?"

* * *

"Zachary, this is a friend of mine, Mr. Francis McCabe."

They stood in the parlor of Maria Dolores's home, and little Zachary looked glumly at the intruder. "How do you do, sir."

Maria Dolores continued introductions, although she hadn't liked the icicles in her son's voice. "Francis, this is my daughter, Carmen."

The little girl refused to talk to McCabe, who thought they were surly goblins. "Howdy," he said, trying to be friendly.

McCabe was dressed in his usual saloon outfit, having taken a few drinks before the visit. Zachary and little Carmen could see that their mother liked him. Finally Zachary turned to her and announced, "Just because he's a friend of yours, that doesn't mean he's a friend of mine." Without another word, the boy walked away.

"Me neither," said little Carmen, holding her little nose in the air as she followed her brother out the room.

McCabe reached into his back pocket and pulled out his flask. "I don't think they like me."

"They miss their father, although he was never home when they were little."

McCabe took a swig from his flask, then asked, "Whatever happened to him?"

"He just arrived at Fort Craig, according to a letter he sent me, and has not seen his children for two years."

McCabe looked at her sideways as an ash from his cigar fell to the rug. "You still in love with him?"

"Not in the least."

"What if I didn't believe you?"

"You can go to hell."

He smiled. "I'd rather go to the hotel."

"We're supposed to have dinner with my children, remember?"

"I ain't sittin' at a table with them two pups. They'd probably put a gnat in my mashed potatoes. After you're finished, I'll be waitin' at the hotel."

She smiled a secret smile as she stood at the window, watching him swagger down the street. He provides what I need and perhaps I shouldn't expect more, she reflected. Then she continued to the dining room, where her children already were seated. She took her place at the head of the table as the maid ladled soup into bowls.

"You were rude, Zachary," she said.

Zachary grumbled, "I don't want to see him anymore."

"I shall bring anyone here that I like," she replied.

Zachary jumped to his feet and pounded his fist on the table. "No you shall not, because this is my *father*'s house!"

She looked the little boy in the eye. "It is *my* house, and if you don't sit down, I shall slap you."

"I hate you!" he screamed as he leapt toward her, flailing his little fists.

She grabbed his wrists in one hand, the seat of his pants in the other, then hoisted him like a bag of beans and carried him to his room. He twisted and fought but she was much stronger than he. Finally she dropped him on his bed.

"Behave yourself," she said, a tremor in her voice. "You are making me very angry."

He pointed at her, tears running down his cheeks.

"It's your fault that my father doesn't live here anymore!"

With a sigh, she sat on Zachary's bed. In a way,
he's right, she admitted. She felt guilty and defeated
as she collapsed onto her back and moaned softly.

"Are you all right, Mother?" he asked, a frightened
tone in his voice.

"Just tired, Zachary."

He kissed her cheek. "I'm sorry, Mother."

"No, I'm the one who's sorry. I'll never bring Mr.
McCabe here again. Come back to the table."

She took his hand and together they descended
the stairs. It's not their fault that they love their father, thought Maria Dolores. It troubled her to know
that Nathanial's presence, through his children, still
dominated her home.

Chapter Twenty-five

On April 15, 1856, chief of scouts Thaddeus Single-ton found Cuchillo Negro's abandoned village. "The stolen sheep and cattle grazed there," he explained to Colonel Chandler, pointing to a grassy plain. "Then Cuchillo Negro and his people left with the thieves in that direction."

The colonel and his staff were on horseback, gathered around Singleton, with Dr. Steck among them. "It's hardly surprising," said the doctor, "that Cuchillo Negro ran from a military force of this size. I believe you've scared him, Colonel Chandler, with this ludicrous expedition."

Colonel Chandler lit his last thin black cheroot. "Ludicrous?" he asked, raising his eyebrows. "On the contrary, we represent a very credible threat to the Apaches. They probably aren't moving quickly so we should catch them before long. Singleton, ride ahead and find out where they are."

"Now just a minute!" protested Dr. Steck. "These Indians are under my protection!"

"Go ahead and protect them," replied Colonel Chandler, still smiling. "You may even warn them we're coming, but if they refuse to give up what they've stolen, they shall be forced at the points of guns. In the meanwhile, I advise you to keep out of the line of fire. 'Twould be a tragedy if you were killed by a stray bullet."

"Or an aimed one," replied Dr. Steck.

"Mangas Coloradas, I must speak with you."

The People were riding into the foothills of the sacred Mimbres Mountains, where slopes of cactus and scrub brush made way for coniferous trees. Mangas Coloradas and Victorio rode at the head of the long spread-out caravan, and Juh had just joined them, accompanied by Geronimo and Loco, three of the most warlike firebrands.

"What is it, Juh?" asked Mangas Coloradas.

"We are vulnerable because so many sick people are slowing us down. I think we should give Cuchillo Negro a few head of cattle, then send him and his cowards back to the Chiricahua Mountains on their own."

Mangas Coloradas raised his eyebrows at Juh. "We were slowed by the sheep and cattle you stole, but I could not make you give them up. Are sheep more important that our unfortunate brothers?"

"They are traitors," replied Juh, "and they are endangering our march."

"Your theft of those animals is the worse crime, because the bluecoat soldiers may be looking for them."

"I am not afraid of bluecoat soldiers," replied Juh.

Colonel Chandler, riding at the head of the army column, shielded his eyes with his hand. It appeared that his scouts were galloping toward him. "Evidently they've found something," he said with satisfaction.

Tension had been building since they'd found the trail of stolen animals. Their wagons and heavy equipment had been left behind and they were gaining steadily on the Apache raiders.

Colonel Chandler appeared excited to Nathanial, not a good sign. Nathanial's mode of deportment under fire was General Zachary Taylor, under whom he'd served in the Mexican War. Old Rough and Ready had been tranquil during the most uncertain moments of battle, and that's why the men had confidence in him.

The scouts galloped closer, pulled back their reins, and came to a stop in front of Colonel Chandler. Singleton made an awkward military salute. "Sir, the Apaches have the animals with 'em and are about an hour ahead of us."

"Sergeant Ames, please tell the company commanders that I wish to speak with them. The men can take a break."

Colonel Chandler raised his hand, the blue column ground to a halt, and Nathanial climbed down from his new horse, a black stallion whom he'd named Duke V, in honor of his other army horses. Nathanial drank water from his canteen, then poured some into his hat and let Duke V wet his lips.

Dr. Steck rode toward Colonel Chandler and looked down at him from his perch atop the saddle. "What are you going to do?"

"Stay out of my way," replied Colonel Chandler. "I have no time for civilian folderol, if you don't mind."

"Are you planning to attack without warning?"

"If you ask one more question, I shall order you bound and gagged."

Dr. Steck watched grimly as officers coalesced around their commanding officer. "The Apaches are dead ahead," the colonel told them. "If we pick up the pace, we should engage them before the sun goes down. Tell the men to check their weapons and get ready for action. As soon as I see the Apaches, I shall order the attack. When you hear the bugle, move your men out quickly."

Lieutenant Haskell raised his hand. "What about women and children, sir?"

"An Apache woman can kill you as quickly as any warrior, and even the children are deadly with bows and arrows. Once we close with the enemy, the men will know what to do."

The company commanders returned to their units, where dragoons were tightening cinches beneath the saddles of their horses. Nathanial examined his Colt .44 as he recalled the canals of Venice. Why'd I come back here? he asked himself.

"Call the men to horse!" said the colonel.

The orders were passed along, and a clamor could be heard as the men climbed into their saddles. Nathanial took his position in front with Colonel Chandler and the other staff officers. No bugles were blown, because they didn't want to alert the Apaches. Colonel Chandler urged his horse to proceed along the trail of stolen sheep, the detachment followed, and Nathanial found himself advancing toward another battlefield.

He couldn't help remembering Embudo Canyon, where his friend Johnny Davidson had died in his arms. That bloody moment came back with full ferocity as Nathanial sat straighter in his saddle, his lips set in a thin line. The time has come to pay back you Apache bastards, he thought.

"Such beautiful fingers," said Sanchez the guitar maker, sitting in his adobe home. He held up Clarissa's hand and examined them closely. "You were born to play the guitar, senora."

"I can imitate what you do, Mr. Sanchez, but perhaps a person who isn't Spanish could never play the guitar well."

"Playing the guitar is not dependent upon where you were born," replied the teacher. "Ultimately, it is a matter of love."

It was growing late, and Clarissa knew she should go home, but home was an empty adobe hut, whereas old Sanchez was music. She leaned back in her chair and listened to him strum the melodies of Andalusia, letting the chords sink into her tissues.

Sanchez was seventy-three, a wrinkled and unshaven guitar maker who carried the faint trace of stale mescal about his gray beard, but she imagined him as a carefree young vaquero riding his horse down the main street of a Mexican town, playing his guitar as senoritas watched breathlessly from the sidewalks, fluttering their fans and trying to catch his attention. Yes, agreed Clarissa as she touched her fingers lightly to the edge of the vibrating guitar. It is a matter of love.

After supper, Norbert Denigran often took a walk through the small settlement beside Fort Craig. Ecclesiastical platitudes and pointless rituals were a lump of coal in his throat, and he needed to refresh himself.

The settlement existed mainly to service the fort with supplies, entertainment, and prostitutes. It reminded him of a smaller Santa Fe, and often he was tempted to have a few drinks at a cantina, but a respected schoolmaster could never be seen in such places.

A wagon rolled down the middle of the street, loaded with bags of flour. Few soldiers could be seen, since most had left on the expedition to the Mimbres Mountains. The usual conglomerations of merchants, bullwhackers, vaqueros, and drifters strolled down the dirt sidewalks.

Denigran came to the alley where he'd killed the most recent whore. The ground was bare where she'd lain after he'd strangled her. The fiend smiled as he remembered tightening and loosening the tension, toying with the last moments of her life.

His smile vanished when he saw a familiar figure enter the alley from the opposite end. It's the Texas Ranger! Denigran was tempted to run for his life, but instead recalled that he'd shaved his beard, and he wasn't in uniform. He turned away from the alley as his heart pounded violently in his chest.

He's still after me, realized Denigran as he circled back to the convent. He felt the noose tightening around his throat, as during his last days in Santa Fe. I've got to steal some money and get the hell out of here.

The People smelled danger as they stopped for the night near a stream bordered by willows. The stolen sheep and cattle were settled on a grassy plain, under the watchful eyes of warriors, while women gathered wood for fires and other warriors butchered a horse. Guards were posted and even the children were vigilant.

The warrior woman whirled a stick between her hands as curls of smoke arose from dried grass. She blew gently on the sparks, and soon a tiny tongue of flame appeared. She piled on twigs as the fire crackled.

Her son held his crucifix to the light, cooing to it, trying to evoke its power, when something appeared in the corner of the warrior woman's sharp eyes. It was a warrior riding hard toward the encampment, shouting at the top of his lungs, "Many bluecoat soldiers coming!"

The camp sprang to life, and everyone turned to Mangas Coloradas for leadership. He reached for his stolen musket, rammed a cartridge in the barrel, and cocked the hammer.

His warriors followed his example as the rider charged toward the fire of Mangas Coloradas. "They are right behind me!" he said, pointing at a cloud of dust gathering ominously on distant desert wastes. "Many more bluecoats than we!"

Again, all eyes turned to the great chief Mangas Coloradas. He'd been a fighting chief most of his life, made cold calculations, and knew they could give up the sheep and cattle, but not Cuchillo Negro and the nearly starved Mimbrenos. "I will talk with them," said the chief. "We will strike a bargain."

Juh looked at him in astonishment. "They are coming to make war, and if we do not leave this place, they will kill us all!"

"You may leave if you like, young Juh, but I am staying with my brother Cuchillo Negro and his people. If I give back the animals that you have stolen, there will be no difficulty."

Juh stuttered when he became excited. "Th-there will b-be a massacre here, and it will b-be on your hands!"

"No, it will be on your hands, because you stole those animals."

"Your opinion hasn't affected your appetite for fresh meat, great chief. You have partaken nightly, as I recall."

Victorio strode between them, holding his right arm in the air. "We have no time for recrimination. Those who want to run away should do so, and the rest will make our stand right here."

At that moment somebody shouted, "Here they come!"

The First Dragoons were at full gallop, pistols in the hands of soldiers, guidon flags fluttering in the breeze, and the bugler was blowing the signal to attack. Most of the men had never trained for an all-out hellbent-for-leather cavalry charge, and they were formed in three ragged lines, with stragglers to the rear, and a few men had fallen off their horses, because they'd never ridden at a gallop in their lives.

Some had never fired more than a few cartridges out of their pistols, and others were having impromptu bowel movements. The roughest and meanest of the lot raced in front of the others, brandishing pistols and hollering insults at Apaches fleeing in all directions.

Nathanial's horse galloped to the right of Colonel Chandler, the breeze plastering back the front brim of his hat. Nathanial held his pistol in his right hand as he looked back at the men. The formation was falling apart, and the commanding officer was becoming isolated from his men, although he didn't seem to notice. Colonel Chandler was focused entirely on the enemy as he aimed his pistol straight ahead. "At them!" he screamed. "Don't let any get away!"

The warrior woman glanced at charging bluecoat soldiers as she carried Running Deer to a thick clump of chaparral. "Now is the time to practice what I have taught you, my warrior son," she said. "The enemy will be here soon and you must be still."

She kissed him one last time, then pushed him beneath the leaves, covered him with clumps of dead branches, and said, "Don't move."

She took a step backward to satisfy herself that he couldn't be seen, then uttered a prayer to Yusn as she strung the first arrow into her bow.

Through dust, smoke, and screams, Nathanial saw a warrior perched on one knee, aiming a musket at him. The West Pointer fired wildly to upset the warrior's aim, but the warrior was rock solid as he pulled the trigger. The musket blasted a slug of lead at Nathanial, who heard it whistle past his ear. He held the Apache in his sights and triggered again.

The Apache was hurled backward by the force of the projectile, and Nathanial murmured, "That's for Lieutenant John Davidson, you son of a bitch!" All the emotion and madness of that day in Embudo Canyon came back to Nathanial, only now *he* was on the offensive.

The momentum of his horse carried him deeper

into the Apache encampment. He saw their scattered fires and pathetic possessions but his heart was unmoved. He aimed at an Apache warrior fleeing, squeezed his trigger, and brought him down. Then he aimed at another Apache, but missed.

Dragoons rampaged across the campsite, shooting at everything that moved. Nathanial surveyed the terrain, and it appeared that most of the Apaches had fled, but one group was making a stand in the chaparral to the right.

And then Nathanial saw something that stopped him cold. Through the melee he spotted a tall Apache waving a white square of cloth. Many years had passed, but Nathanial would never forget that face as long as he lived. It's Mangas Coloradas!

The aging chief Mangas Coloradas was searching for the bluecoat officer in charge, so that he could smoke with him. A bullet had pierced his wrist in the early moments of the encounter, but he paid no attention to the pain. "We come in peace!" he told them. "We want to be friends!"

Lieutenant Haskell spotted the old warrior, but had no idea who he was. It was Haskell's first battle and he'd yet to kill an Indian. He jerked his reins in the direction of the tall Apache, kicked the flanks of his horse, and charged. His pistol was cocked as he aimed down the barrel. "You're one dead Injun," muttered Haskell as he squeezed the trigger.

His pistol was a sixteenth of an inch from firing when an arrow pierced his chest. He stared at it in horror, and his expression never changed as he fell off his horse, bounced on the ground, and lay still.

Victorio ran toward Haskell's horse and leapt into

the saddle. Chief Mangas Coloradas appeared befuddled as Victorio bore down on him, leaned to the side, and swept him away in his strong right arm.

"What are you doing!" cried Mangas Coloradas, struggling to get loose. "I must stop them!"

"Not today, my chief," replied gallant Victorio as his horse fled into the thickest chaparral.

A group of warriors hadn't been able to reach their horses and were conducting a fighting retreat on foot. They fired arrows at the horses of inexperienced bluecoat soldiers, a tactic that was slowing them down.

Juh rode onto the desperate scene, bleeding from a bullet through his left calf. He spotted the warrior woman dodging among cactus, then urged his horse closer toward her. "Take my hand!" he hollered. "I shall carry you away."

"No! Save your son!" she screamed.

Juh knew that Running Deer wasn't his true son, but could not deny him before Jocita. "Where are you, little warrior!" he bellowed.

The boy crawled out of his hiding place and held out his arms. Juh whipped the flanks of his horse as the animal galloped toward Jocita's half-breed child. Juh leaned to the side, grabbed the boy about the waist, scooped him up, then aimed his horse toward the highest mountains he could see.

Nathanial rounded up a dozen troopers and led them to where the Apaches were making their stand. "Follow me, men, we've got them where we want them now!"

He aimed his pistol forward as Duke V plunged

into tangled vines, cholla, and prickly pear cactus. The officer fired at a brown Apache body darting behind a yucca plant, the Apache fell backward, then Nathanial shot at another, missed, and thumbed back his hammer when suddenly a warrior rose behind a hackberry bush and fired an arrow at Nathanial's horse. The Apache ducked as Nathanial felt his horse going down.

It wasn't the first time Nathanial had a horse shot out from underneath him. He held tightly to his gun as he tumbled through the air, another arrow whizzed past, then his shoulder hit the ground, he rolled, came to a stop, and fired a quick shot into the bush where his Apache assailant had hidden.

He heard a cry that sent a chill to his marrow. It's impossible, he thought, but he'd never forget that voice. No, he thought as he charged toward the bush. It can't be.

An Apache who looked frighteningly familiar lay facedown in a pool of blood, and Nathanial thought he was losing his mind. The tumult of battle came to his ears as he rolled the Apache onto her back.

It was the warrior woman, his bullet having struck beneath her left breast. Nathanial's eyes widened with consternation when he realized that he'd killed her! He stared at her in shame, remembering their night of passionate love. Her eyes opened to slits, she regarded him for a few moments, then whispered in her language, "You."

He didn't understand, but clearly she'd recognized him as he'd recognized her. A dribble of blood appeared at the corner of her mouth, she appeared to be dying, tears filled Nathanial's eyes as he realized the enormity of his deed.

He felt as if a cannonball had hit him in the head, and even as she lay there trying to speak, he knew he'd never stopped loving her, and always yearned to see her again. Even in Paris, Rome, and London, in the arms of his beautiful young wife, he'd never forgotten the warrior woman.

He heard a horse approaching, a dragoon mount whose owner had been killed. Nathanial grabbed the reins, and as the horse tried to escape, Nathanial punched him in the mouth. "Stand!" he hollered.

The horse obeyed as Nathanial lay the limp warrior woman over the saddle. Then he climbed onto the space behind her, the battlefield covered with smoke, shouts, cries for help, confusion. She was his prisoner of war, but they'd throw her in jail or before a firing squad, because she was Apache.

He gazed at the dying woman who personified the land that he loved so profoundly. He should return with her to friendly lines, but something told him *go the other way.* Ultimately, he couldn't bear to see the warrior woman hauled before enemies who'd mock her fighting pride, and if that wasn't enough, he'd made love with her on the most bizarre night of his life.

There was only one path to take, and he knew it was fraught with peril. A little voice in his ear told him he might be killed, but he had to save his warrior love. What the hell, he thought defiantly as he steered his reins in the direction of the Apache retreat. I'll say I got lost.

He kicked his spurs into the horse, who followed his command with a mighty leap. The warrior woman's blood dripped on brown desert leaves and her arms flopped crazily as Nathanial pushed the horse into a gallop. The smoky battlefield darkened as they rode deeper into the wilderness, then a shot was fired somewhere behind them, and a bullet slammed into Nathanial's back. He was rocked in the saddle, nearly fainted from pain, but struggled to hold on to the warrior woman as they disappeared together into the twilight.

Clarissa felt uneasy as she rode back to Camp Craig that night. She'd remained with Senor Sanchez longer than she'd intended, so captivated had she been by the lessons.

"There are many bad men in this settlement," he warned her as they approached the church. "We must never practice this late again, but I could not help myself. It is a pleasure to have a student who learns so quickly."

"It is only because you are such a wonderful teacher, Senor Sanchez."

He placed his hand on her shoulder and squeezed in a fatherly way. She couldn't help thinking of her own father, the stockbroker. He'd devoted his life to money, while Senor Sanchez had consecrated his to music. Who is the peasant and who is civilized? she wondered.

Inside the church, the Mother Superior looked up from her desk. "Is it you, Mr. Denigran?"

He walked into the office, carrying a gunnysack in his left hand, pleased to note that she was alone. "I wanted to ask you a question about God, Mother Superior. How can we believe in Him, since there's so much suffering in the world?"

"But it's people who usually cause suffering, not God."

A strange new note came into his voice. "Do you know what suffering is, Mother Superior? I mean, do you *really* know?"

"I've worked among sick and dying people all my life, and have been ill myself. We all have our crosses to bear, and we must bear them gracefully."

In a flash, his knife was out, pressed to her throat before she could scream. "Don't move, Mother Superior. Or I'll take your head off and use it for a football. We'll see how well you manage suffering as you open the safe. Now get moving!"

He pressed the knife into the folds of fat beneath her chin, a thin red line appeared, the Mother Superior's hand trembled as she unbuttoned the top of her habit and pulled out a key on a leather thong. "If you needed money, I would have given it to you," she replied in a choked voice.

"All you gave me was a job teaching your mealy-mouthed children for a pittance. Move, because I don't have much time."

Side by side they made their way to the safe, and he never relaxed the blade pressure on her throat. He could see her exposed white undergarment, which excited him. She knelt in front of the safe, turned the key, opened the door. "Take it all," she said in a quavering voice.

"Are you afraid, Mother Superior?" he asked.

"Yes," she replied, her breath coming in gasps.

"Where is your God now?"

"Everywhere."

"Do you know how beautiful you are, and how much I love you?"

"If you love me, you must let me free!"

"You don't understand, Mother Superior. Death is the only freedom we have."

His wrist made a sudden motion, then she dropped to the floor. He wanted to roll her onto her back and pick up her dress, but had to get out of there. He stuffed his gunnysack with money when he heard a scream behind him.

He turned, and it was dear little Sister Teresa standing in the doorway, holding her hands to her face and giving the alarm. He chased her down the corridor, but she was a strong-limbed young woman shouting at the top of her lungs. "The Mother Superior has been murdered by Mr. Denigran, and he is in the building right now! Lock yourself in your rooms."

Denigran opened the first door and found himself in the chapel. It was silent, Christ on the cross illuminated by a ray of moonlight streaming through the windows. Denigran ran to the front door, then drew his Colt. He opened the door and a smile wreathed his rodent face as he saw two riders heading toward the church.

He ran at the riders, aiming his gun at them as Sister Teresa's voice pierced the night. "There he goes—the murderer!"

The rider on the left was a white-bearded old man. He reached for his gun, but Denigran was coming fast, aiming straight at him. Denigran's gun barked once, the old man leaned to the side, the murderer dragged him out of the saddle, then mounted up and turned his pistol on the young blond woman with whom the old man had been riding.

His hammer snapped forward at the same moment the spooked horse tried to dance away from his master lying on the ground. The bullet fired harmlessly into the air as Denigran kicked his heels into the flanks of the stolen horse.

The animal balked at carrying off the murderer of his old friend, and he fought the reins as Clarissa came to her senses. Everything seemed to be moving more slowly than normal, and she felt light-headed as she reached beneath her black leather jacket and whipped out the Colt Navy that her husband had given her.

"He's a murderer!" shouted the nun in the window of the convent.

The culprit looked like Satan in a dark suit as he worked to control the panicked horse. Clarissa thumbed back her hammer and squeezed the trigger.

The cartridge exploded, then Norbert Denigran felt his innards rip apart. A howl burst from his mouth, the second bullet smacked him in the chest and knocked him out of the saddle. He opened his eyes and saw a beautiful blond woman above him, aiming at his nose.

"Are you going to . . . spank me again, Mother?" he asked dreamily as black curtains descended around him. "Why don't . . . you ever reward me . . . for the good things . . . I do?"

Clarissa saw him go limp on the ground, but kept her pistol aimed at him anyway. She wondered if she was having a nightmare, because it was so different from her cosmopolitan New York life. Armed townspeople came running, nuns spilled out of the convent, and a crowd formed around Clarissa and the dead man. "Who was he?" asked the sheriff.

"A teacher in the school," explained Sister Teresa. "I saw him kill the Mother Superior and take money in the safe."

A citizen picked up the gunnysack full of coins. Another citizen pointed at the murderer's bloody hand. "How could anyone kill a nun?"

A tall man with a Colt in one hand and a tin badge in another strolled onto the scene. "I'm a Texas Ranger," he said. "Name's Cole Bannon. I've been hunting this man a long time—he's killed over a dozen women. Who stopped him?"

"She did," said the sheriff.

The Texas Ranger turned to a small ordinary-looking blond woman who looked like she'd faint at the first sign of danger. She was pale as new washed wool, but she'd closed the case that had occupied his life for the past three years. Cole Bannon took off his hat and smiled. "Good shootin', ma'am."

The lone lobo licked his chops as he crept closer to two figures sprawled on the ground. The female two-legged lay on her back, the male two-legged on his stomach, both covered with delicious blood. They'd fallen off their horse, who stood nearby, gazing warily at the lobo, who growled. You try to stop me, big fellow, I'll chew your hamstrings out from beneath you.

The lobo knew he was fast, smart, hungry. It would take more than a clumsy horse to stop him. He decided the female would have more tender meat, so he approached her warily. She breathed just barely, and the lobo thought he was safe. Her left breast appeared tempting. He opened his jaws, moonlight glinted on his fangs, and he prepared to take a healthy bite.

He spotted a faint flash in the corner of his eye, then an arrow pierced both his lungs, shooting out the other side of his body. The lobo's jaws closed on thin air as he collapsed to the ground.

Stars glittered above, a faint breeze was on the sage, and a hawk screamed in a dark corner of night. The horse continued to munch grass, not as dumb as he looked. A head appeared, wearing a bandanna. Then another warrior popped up. The peaceful scene transmogrified into seven warriors arising from the foliage. Chatto kneeled beside Jocita and raised her eyelid with his thumb. It showed white. Meanwhile Nana pressed his ear to her chest. "She is alive."

Loco turned at the bluecoat officer. "In the press of battle, I saw him ride off with her. He tried to save her life, but evidently he has been shot."

"In the back," said Victorio, standing nearby. "He was running away from his people, to us. Perhaps he was lost. I do not know if Nana can save them, for these are very deep wounds."

Chapter Twenty-six

Clarissa sat in the parlor, picking her Spanish guitar. Neither of her pianos had arrived, but her skill with five shimmering strings increased every day. She'd even taught herself to strum melodies from Mozart, Bach, and Handel, lost in music as she waited for Nathanial and the others to return.

Sometimes she performed impromptu concerts for lonely wives of other officers, and often took meals with them, trying to raise each other's morale. Clarissa had gained a certain notoriety at Fort Craig, because she'd killed an outlaw that even the Texas Ranger hadn't been able to catch. She'd never forget the moment she'd pulled the trigger, and every day thanked God for the presence of mind that told her to shoot the son of a bitch down.

She worked a few hours every day as volunteer in the post hospital, but her main interest was music. She tried not to deliberate about the dangers and hardships faced by soldiers, otherwise she'd lay on the sofa and worry about Nathanial all day long.

Her ears were unusually sensitive, due to her years of studying music. One afternoon, as she plucked one of Senor Sanchez's old fandango tunes, and fondly remembered the brave guitar-mater, she heard shouting on the parade ground. She arose from her chair as Rosita entered the living room. "The soldiers have returned!" she announced gaily.

Clarissa hung her guitar from its peg on the wall, then stood before the mirror and looked at herself. No longer was she a pale and wispy New York debutante, for her cheeks were deeply tanned and a new frontier vitality could be seen in her manner.

The parade ground filled with wives, children, and the soldiers who'd stayed behind. Colonel Chandler rode through the main gate, followed by his staff officers, guidon flags fluttering in the breeze as ragged dusty men proceeded to the command post headquarters.

Clarissa ran toward them, holding the front of her long flowing Mexican skirt. She didn't see Nathanial among the staff officers, and assumed he was farther back in the formation.

Then she noticed a curious event. Colonel Chandler pulled the reins of his horse to the right and appeared to be heading directly toward her. An icy hand gripped her heart; she stopped in her tracks. Oh my God—no, she said to herself.

The post spun like a carousel as the colonel drew closer. Everyone watched the fair-haired young pregnant woman clasp her hands together and look up at the commanding officer, a hopeful expression on her face. They saw the colonel's lips move as he conveyed the awful message. "I'm sorry, Mrs. Barrington, but your husband has been killed by Apaches. Evidently they've taken his . . . body . . . away."

Fort Craig was rent by a heartfelt scream, then the young bride's legs gave out beneath her and she went crashing to the ground.

* * *

On a warm summer afternoon, while working at her desk, there was a knock on Maria Dolores's door. It was Miquelito. "A soldier wants to see you, senora. Says his name is Duffy."

Maria Dolores remembered her former husband's first sergeant and wondered how much he wanted to borrow. "Send him in."

A red-bearded soldier appeared in her doorway, Jeff Davis hat in hand. "Howdy," he said.

"Come in, Sergeant Duffy," she replied warmly. "It's so good to see you again, but you look sad. Is anything wrong?"

"There's somethin' you should know, ma'am," he replied haltedly. "The lieutenant has been . . . killed by the Apaches."

The pen fell from Maria Dolores's hand. "How'd it happen?"

"The way I heered it, the lieutenant got into the middle of a fight with Apaches and they shot him." Sergeant Duffy shook his head as a tear rolled down his cheek. "That's the way the lieutenant was—God help anybody who got in his way."

Maria Dolores didn't know what to say as she stared at the Irishman. "Thank you," she replied at last. "Please have as many drinks as you want at the bar."

"A few men from the old company are with me . . ."

"Free drinks for them too," she told him.

The door closed, then Maria Dolores burst into tears. She took a handkerchief from her sleeve and mopped her eyes, wondering why she felt so terribly sad. She and Nathanial had been apart over two years, but once they'd been happy together. I knew this would happen someday, she told herself. He had the body of man but the mind of a child. What shall I tell Zachary and Carmen? Maria Dolores pondered it for a few moments, then decided to tell them nothing. I'll wait until they're older, she decided. They haven't seen him for so long—what does it matter?

In August of 1856, the plebe class stood at attention on West Point's parade ground. Their first official formation, they wore new blue-and-gray uniforms, with white shako hats in the style of Prussian hussars.

The superintendent of West Point, Major Richard Delafield, class of 1818, addressed them from the podium. "You have been selected to attend the finest military academy in the world!" he declared, then proceeded to enumerate their duties and obligations, the glories of the U. S. Army, the great victories won against her enemies, and deeds of valor performed by men who'd once stood upon that very grassy plain. "You are the future of America! The fate of the nation rests in your hands!"

In the fifth rank of B Company stood eighteen-year-old Jeffrey Barrington, whom his classmates had nicknamed Buck. He wasn't certain of the position of attention, but it was only his third day at the Point.

The commandant droned onward about honor, duty, and country as Buck recalled his departed brother Nathanial standing on that very field long ago, listening to a similar speech. Nathanial had given his life to the Army, and now was assumed dead, his body never identified. Apparently the Apaches had mutilated him beyond recognition. Buck's mother had virtually locked herself in her bedroom since the death notice had arrived.

The stars and stripes snapped in the breeze blowing up the Hudson, and in the distance Buck Barrington could see the brick barracks where he'd spend the next four years. Stern discipline lay ahead, but there was no alternative for the eldest living Barrington son.

Nathanial had been the hero of Buck's life, although Buck only saw his brother on rare occasions during the past sixteen years. Nathanial was everything that Buck had wanted to become.

The band began to play as guidons shot into the air. "For-ward march!" shouted the cadet captain.

The cadets stepped out smartly and began their journey to the reviewing stand. No parents were there, no distinguished visitors, only the officers and teachers who'd mold Buck's mind in years to come. He felt their sharp eyes upon him as his company strutted down the runway in front of the stand.

"Present arms!"

Buck raised his arm in salute along with other hopeful cadets. He saw Old Glory fluttering in the breeze, and pudgy Major Delafield at the podium. The music swelled while the Hudson highlands were covered with green leaves.

I'll get through this damned West Point somehow, Buck swore as he marched. And when it's over, I'll put in for New Mexico Territory. Those damned Apache bastards had better watch out for me when I arrive in their so-called homeland. The blood of my brother shall be avenged, so help me God!

* * *

Nathanial opened his eyes, and his first thought was: I've gone to hell. His surroundings appeared murky and indistinct, he lay in wrenching pain, while his hands and feet were numb. He felt on the verge of fainting, when golden effulgence appeared in the vicinity of his feet.

He breathed shallowly as throbbing torture threatened to overwhelm him. He lay in a crude shelter of branches, leaves, scraps of leather, and other primitive materials. There was an inverted V opening in front, and a small boy stood there, examining him thoughtfully.

The boy was aureoled by sunlight, a cross shone brightly upon his chest, and he had strange light hair. Nathanial became aware of voices speaking in Apache language, hoofbeats of a horse passing nearby, sounds of a campsite. Golden cords seemed to draw him closer to the boy, who looked like an Apache angel. Nathanial tried to extend his hand, but agony drowned him, his eyes closed and he sank backward into a coma.

In autumn of 1856, the Pierce Administration was coming to an end, the President having been denied a second term by the Democratic Party Convention. At the War Department, Jefferson Davis was finishing his duties. They consisted mostly of administrative odds and ends, and he could leave the work for the next Secretary of War, but the West Pointer took his obligations seriously.

He sat at the desk and worked his way down a pile of documents, secure in the knowledge that soon he'd be back in Mississippi, running for the U.S.

Senate. The Democrats had overwhelmingly endorsed his candidacy and he was considered a sure winner against the more moderate Jacob Thompson.

He looked forward to his old senatorial platform, with the eyes of the nation upon him. He keenly believed that America was facing the greatest crisis in its history, as the Kansas-Nebraska crisis continued to worsen. In May, a proslavery army from Missouri had attacked the antislavery town of Lawrence, ransacking the offices of the *Herald of Freedom* antislavery newspaper, destroying the printing presses, then burning down Governor Charles Robinson's house and barn.

Also in May, Senator Charles Sumner of Massachusetts had been assaulted physically by Congressman Preston Brooks of South Carolina on the floor of the U.S. Senate. With a gutta-percha cane, Brooks had beaten Sumner senseless, and Sumner had not yet recovered, while the Congress refused to censure Brooks for his bloody deed.

In Jefferson Davis's opinion, the nation was a tinderbox ready to explode. James Buchanan, former senator from Pennsylvania and current ambassador to England, had been awarded the Democratic nomination for President, defeating Senator Stephen Douglas of Illinois after seventeen contentious ballots in Cincinnati.

Jefferson Davis saw in Buchanan another party hack who lacked the will to truly lead the nation. It's time we had another soldier like Zachary Taylor in the White House, figured the former commander of the Mississippi Rifles. Where can we find a president who can make unpopular decisions and stick to them?

The newly formed Republican Party had nominated a military man, the former Colonel John C. Fremont, known popularly as the Great Pathfinder, but Jeff Davis doubted there were enough Republicans to defeat the unified Democratic South together with the antiabolitionist middle-of-the-road North. Jeff Davis believed the next four years would decide the future of America, and if the North tried to force its military will on the South, the hero of Buena Vista would not hesitate to take the field once more.

His final batch of documents concerned a controversy that had arisen in New Mexico Territory. It appeared that Colonel Chandler of Fort Craig had attacked an Apache camp in the Mimbres Mountains, but a protest had been lodged by the local Indian Commissioner, Dr. Michael Steck. According to Steck, it was a wanton attack on a peaceful camp, but Colonel Chandler had insisted that stolen livestock were in possession of the Apaches.

Former Colonel Jefferson Davis believed in backing his men to the hilt. He wrote at the bottom of Chandler's report: "I concur with the decisions of the commanding officer."

Jefferson Davis lay down his pen and raised his eyes. No newspaper reporters or historians saw him gaze at the American flag hanging on the wall. He'd followed those stars and stripes into the hell of Buena Vista, Monterry, and the heights of La Teneria, but he feared terrible times ahead for the nation. He tossed Dr. Steck's protest into the wastebasket, then put on his hat and departed the office.

Officers and clerks were waiting in the corridor to bid farewell to the great man. He shook every hand, even engaging in light banter with his underlings, a rare occasion for the aristocratic officer of the old school. His left eye was clouded by thin yellow mucous, but his right lens showed strange refracted images of the same officers in torn uniforms, covered with blood, limping in defeat from incredible battlefields.

A carriage was waiting in front of the War Department, where an honor guard saluted the famous American hero. Jeff Davis climbed into his coach, then matched black horses pulled him across Lafayette Square. He passed the White House, where his friend Frank Pierce was ending his failed administration. A man's got to be crazy to take that job, thought Jefferson Davis as he rode up Pennsylvania Avenue. He closed his eyes and again caught a vision of massed cannon firing, with verdant meadows carpeted with corpses.

Another face hovered above Nathanial. It was Nana the medicine man, whom the officer had met at the Santa Rita Copper Mines during the summer of 1851.

"I am going to roll you over," said Nana in Spanish. "It will hurt."

Nathanial thought he was being ripped in two, he lost consciousness intermittently, and when his mind cleared he lay on his stomach, Nana peeling something wet off his back. "You have been in the other world for a long time, Sunny Hair," Nana told him. "That was a very brave act you committed, but perhaps you are loco as I have always believed. Did you know that you have saved the life of Chief Juh's wife? You are going to be with us for many moons, I am sorry to say, but we will take good care of you. You will learn what it is to be an Apache and perhaps never return home again."

"Extremely doubtful," Nathanial wanted to reply, but the exertion was too great, tenebrous shrouds fell over him, and once more he was swallowed by the endless Apache night.

**Don't miss the
previous books from
Frank Burleson
in
*The Apache Wars Saga***

DESERT HAWKS

Three-Sided Struggle

The year was 1846—and the great American Southwest was the prize in an epic conflict. The U.S.
Army and the army of Mexico met in a battle that
would shape the course of history, while the legend-
ary Apache warrior chief Mangus Coloradas looked
on, determined to defend his ancestral lands and
age-old tribal traditions against either of the invaders or both. On this bloody battlefield, young Lieutenant Nathanial Barrington faced his first great test
of manhood . . . as he began a career that would
take him to the heart of the conflict sweeping over
the West from Texas to New Mexico . . . and plunge
him into passions that would force him to choose
between two very different frontier beauties. This
enthralling first novel of *The Apache Wars Saga* trilogy captures the drama and real history of a struggle
in which no side wanted to surrender . . . in a series
alive with all the excitement and adventures of
brave men and women—white and Native American—who decided the future of America.

WAR EAGLES

Fields of Battle

In the North, a lanky lawyer named Abraham Lincoln was recovering from a brutal political setback. In the South, eloquent U.S. Senator Jefferson Davis was risking all in a race for governor of his native Mississippi. And far to the Southwest, the future of the frontier was being decided as the U.S. Army, under Colonel Bull Moose Sumner, faced the growing alliance of Native Americans led by the great Mangus Coloradas and determined to defend their ancestral lands.

For First Lieutenant Nathanial Barrington it was his first test as a professional soldier following orders he distrusted in an undeclared war without conscience or quarter—and his test as a man when he met the Apache woman warrior Jocita in a night lit by passion that would yield to a day of dark decision . . . *War Eagles* is the tremendous second novel of the authentic *Apache Wars* epic trilogy that began with *Desert Hawks*.